THE WILD CARD

THE WILD CARD

RENÉE

THE CUBA
PRESS

Cover design by Sarah Bolland.
Cover images by Felix Wolf and SuperHerftigGeneral/Pixabay.
Typesetting and book design by Sarah Bolland and Paul Stewart.
Edited by Mary McCallum.
Production assistance by Steffi Dryden.

A catalogue record for this book is available from
the National Library of New Zealand.

ISBN 978-1-98-859503-0

Printed in Aotearoa New Zealand by Ligare.

THE CUBA PRESS
Box 9321 Wellington 6141
Aotearoa New Zealand

To Christopher, David & Timothy,
with love.

Every chapter begins with a quote from Oscar Wilde's play
The Importance of Being Earnest.
Excerpts are taken from the Project Gutenberg eBook #844 (2006),
transcribed from the 1915 Methuen & Co Ltd edition by David Price.
www.gutenberg.org

1

'To lose one parent, Mr Worthing, may be regarded as a misfortune; to lose both looks like carelessness.'

It was pure impulse. She was fizzing like a well-shaken bottle of Coke with the top still on. She needed to think about the notebook. About those card players. About Betty. About justice. A few spits of chilly rain, but she thought of Kate and decided to risk it.

Promise me you'll find your parents.

Seven o'clock wasn't late but on this mid-May evening it was dark. Not black-dark yet, that was an hour away. The rain hadn't made up its mind. Clouds like grey gauze curtains were draped over everything. Good thing she wasn't planning on a long stay. A quick recce, that was all.

She moved swiftly but carefully, wanted this over as soon as possible, but the driveway was rough – breaks in the tarseal, lots of little bits of shingle, traps for an unwary foot to slip on. The raggedy untidy mess of mānuka, koromiko, harakeke and a thousand weeds that occupied the land around the house made awkward ghostly shapes in the dim light. The grounds of the Home had had the minimum amount of upkeep and it showed.

She could smell mint.

There hadn't been a vegetable garden here for thirty years. Must be wild mint in the paddock over the stream at the back of the property. Mint loved water; even the promise of it was enough to make it send out a perfume. When she made her own garden she would grow mint in pots. Only a foolish gardener would plant mint in the garden.

Mint was a great coloniser, brought here by other great colonisers.

Crushed beer cans, cigarette butts, paper coffee cups and plastic tops were scattered along the sides of the driveway like someone had indulged in a tantrum. A few parties perhaps? They'd have been fairly safe from irritated neighbours if they could hack the weather. Only rough grass paddocks either side and at the back, and over the stream, mainly macrocarpa, blackberries and rabbits. People in the houses further along probably only heard a faint noise, and if they had the radio or TV on, not even that. Must have been a bit wet though. Perhaps on the wet nights the people looking for a party sheltered in the old sheds around the back.

The last time she'd been on this driveway she was seven, and so terrified that she'd wet her pants as she ran. Now, thirty years later, she was more concerned about getting in and out without being seen.

She felt as scratchy as a pot-scrubber and very nervous about Bracknell. Don't think about it, she told herself. She'd been mad to agree to do it, she was too young, wrong skin colour, but too late now.

Opening night tomorrow. Friday. Hester always did Friday opening nights.

She stopped and stared at the old house. It looked like one good push would send it sliding in a heap down the slope.

Where would be the easiest place to break in?

Window or door?

The door would be better. Long sash windows were notoriously easy to jiggle but you ran the risk of breaking the glass. Although did that matter if the building was going to be pulled down anyway? No doubt the law wouldn't see it that way. She'd be in and out reasonably quickly, whichever way she chose.

She should really have gone to see Meg rather than coming here. She'd go and see her on her way to work tomorrow, organise sleeping there for the weekend – much better than coming up from Wellington with the play on. It would be a lot easier if Meg answered her damn phone but she didn't, so no good whining. Kate's mother marched to a different drum and that was the end of it.

The weekend was a ticker-tape going round and round in Ruby's head. She'd get the first night of the play over, sleep in Saturday, check out Meg's briar patch in the afternoon and organise how to turn it back into a rose garden, then there was the second night of *Earnest*, maybe a little sleep-in at Meg's on Sunday? Come back here in the afternoon with Kristina. Ruby didn't want to break in on her own and Kristina was the only person she wanted along for that ride. That it would be a waste of time was irrelevant. She had to take a proper look before she could tick it off.

The bushes were dripping from that earlier shower so she kept to the middle of the path, which was a steep haul on this last curve up to the old two-storey building that was rotting to the ground. Another smell. Lavender. Probably dentata. Used to be the most popular and still her favourite. When she was finished fixing up Meg's garden everything growing there would be scented, she decided. She'd clear anything else away and replace them with perfumed plants, bushes or climbers.

The driveway was really steep. No worries. She could catch her breath on the flat area at the back. In her head she knew this old house and grounds so well, but tonight in the dim light it looked different. Not so big but still a bit scary. Just don't lean on it, she told herself.

Then again, local organisations had been using it for meetings until six months ago so it couldn't be too bad. Maybe the cheap room hire made it attractive whatever the state of disrepair?

Ruby stopped by the path over the large culvert, ignored the stream glaring palely through the gloom and stared at the back of the house. The door on the side opened into a room that used to be the laundry, and the door in the middle opened onto a passage that led to the main corridor, passing the kitchen on the way. There was a rickety fire-escape ladder from the top floor to the lower one. It stopped a good human-length from the ground so you'd have to let yourself fall the last metre or so. God help you if you had a broken leg or were old and frail.

Well. This wasn't too bad. No ghosts of Matron or the balaclava man. No drowned Betty lying on the path. Why had she built up such a fear of the place? It was nothing but a sad old house that had outlived its time. It wasn't responsible for what human beings had done inside its walls. She took hold of the windowframe and shook it. The house grumbled in protest. The window was secured by little levers each side – not really burglar-proof. If she slid her knife up the side, where age had warped the wood, it shouldn't be too difficult. The old back door was a bit creaky but held firm. Same thing. If she pushed the knife between the lock and the frame surely it would give enough to force the tongue?

She leaned on the door and the house moaned like a ghost was walking the old passage. Human footsteps? Ruby listened intently.

Shivery possibilities trembled in the air.

Okay. Time to go. She'd come back.

She turned and stared at the shed. The door hung open a little bit so she pushed it, clicked on her phone torch and had a look inside. A mess of cans and bottles, some Kentucky Fried packets, Big Mac burger bags, even a used condom. Yucko. Must have been really drunk or really desperate.

Ruby started down the other side. Her arm caught the end of a wet branch and water splashed her jeans. Cold needle tips on warm skin. This light had exactly the right feel for a Swedish noir movie. The dark shapes of the bushes and trees, misty air and the sound of water dripping. Any minute someone called Arne would step out of the bushes, throw away his cigarette and say in a thick accent, 'Okay, Ruby, time to talk.'

The lower she went, the more she became aware of the change in light. It hadn't exactly been well lit further up but down here it was really dark. The clinging moisture embraced her in its damp grey arms, made her want to be home, warm and alone, sipping a glass of red, listening to one of those old songs that Kate had liked and she liked too. Sam Cooke, she thought, 'A Change is Gonna Come'.

Change has already come and I hate it.

One of the bushes moved.

She stopped thinking, breathed quickly, heart beating like a snare-drum tattoo. An illusion caused by the wind? Hardly. This was a breeze by Porohiwi standards.

First rule. *Don't muck around.*

She swerved away, and now it was definite. The shadow moved too. *Shit.*

She was three quarters of the way down the slope. Too late to go back. What to do? *Take cover? Take off? Take them on?* The old mantra.

Not much choice.

She felt in her pocket, yes, okay, phone. Turned. Took up the stance. The shadow moved faster now, unworried about noise as it crashed through the bushes. *Fuck.*

He came out of the dark, a running black ghost. Black balaclava, black trousers, black top. He was not quite as tall as Ruby but bigger. She yelled and kicked out.

Got the top of his leg which must have hurt but not as much as if she'd connected with his balls.

Momentum carried him on, anger helped. She ducked but he was too quick. A closed heavy fist thudded on her cheek, another sharp slap around her left eye, blood slid down her face and throat. He hit her on the arm and she staggered.

Her heart was pounding, serious pain a second or two away. Don't fall, she told herself, *don't fall*, but when he hit her again she fell. Her face hit the ground. As she skewed around she yelled again.

Make as much noise as you can.

She kept yelling, grabbed at a bush and hung on.

Then voices from the street. Someone laughed.

She screamed. A moan was all that came out.

He grabbed at her jeans, found the phone, got it out, threw it. Felt in the other pocket. Car key. Threw it.

A final kick and he was gone.

And so was she.

2

'Dearest Gwendolen, there is no reason why I should make a secret of it to you. Our little county newspaper is sure to chronicle the fact next week.'

Ruby came to. Brown eyes looked straight up into blue.

'Holy fuck,' she said, and shut them again.

'Nothing wrong with her memory,' said Oscar.

Rain started falling, big cold drops made sharp by the wind. She shivered.

'Ruby, it's me and Oscar,' said Kristina. 'We were having a meeting. That emergency locator thing went off – it worked perfectly. Position followed immediately. Bax should get a gold star for setting it up.'

Kristina talked quickly like she was trying to assure Ruby that Oscar's presence was simply chance. Ruby supposed she and her ex had to meet sometime now he was back, but why today?

She opened her eyes again. Kristina was kneeling beside her.

'Can you move?'

'Of course I can move,' said Ruby.

But it wasn't quite as easy as she'd thought. Her body always did what she asked of it but now it had gone on strike. Every muscle was screaming *nah nah, fuck off, forget it*. She stung and ached all over, her face was on fire, one eye closed. She thought if anyone laid a finger on her she'd deck them. *Just get me up before I cark from the cold.*

Hands were feeling her legs and arms, her body.

'No broken bones,' said Oscar. Water dripped from his hair. Rain

12

always made those blond curls extra curly, thought Ruby.

'Ruby?' said Kristina.

Focus, Ruby told herself, focus.

'Came out of the bushes,' she said. 'All in black. Balaclava. Male. Saw hands. Pākehā. Can we go? I'm freezing.'

'We'll call the cops.'

'No,' said Ruby, making up her mind instantly. 'I just need a hand up, that's all.'

There was silence. She knew what was happening. Kristina and Oscar were looking at each other, deliberating over whether they could persuade her to let them ring the cops.

'What if he attacks other women?' said Oscar.

'It was random. He only did it because I saw him move.' Her voice sounded strange. Hollow. Gritty. Like it was coming out of a concrete mixer.

'And the balaclava? The black gear?'

'For god's sake,' Ruby said. 'It's raining, I'm freezing – can we just go? Old house for sale. Everyone knows it's going to be pulled down. Bet lots have looked around.'

'You could have asked Door for the key.' Oscar's brother had been christened Handel but renamed Door by the kids at Porohiwi Playcentre, and it had stuck. Fifteen years ago he'd said to his brother, *A Māori girl from nowhere? You crazy?*

Sure, he'd apologised but she hadn't forgotten. Why would she ask Door for the key? For anything?

'The police have go-to special teams now,' said Kristina. 'They can do tests, trace evidence.'

The rain continued to fall.

'Even if they came when you called – in your dreams – it'd be a complete waste of my time. Priority for me is get the grit and stuff out of my face. First night of *Earnest* tomorrow.'

They helped Ruby sit up then, very carefully, supported her to her feet. Ruby was tall, Oscar was taller, Kristina wasn't quite as tall as Ruby but she was strong. Oscar took his parka off and put it around Ruby's shoulders. It was one of those really light expensive ones in a mustardy colour. It was surprisingly warm.

The world shimmied and she shut the eye that wasn't already closed.

'Lean on me,' said Oscar.

'I'm okay,' she mumbled.

'Your face is a mess,' said Kristina. 'You're bruised all over. You are not okay. Don't bother arguing.'

Kristina was right. Ruby's body and legs were screaming. Each step was a walk into fire. They stopped every few seconds to let her recover but finally, blessedly, they got to the gateway, and she saw the little yellow Getz.

'My car. He threw my key away.'

'You wouldn't be able to drive it anyway,' said Kristina. 'We'll go with Oscar. I'll contact Martin at the garage and he'll sort the key.'

'My bag?' said Ruby. 'Laptop. Wallet. Boot.'

Oscar looked at his key ring. Chose a key. Pointed it towards the Getz. Clicked. Lights flashed on and off.

Kristina frowned, marched along the footpath and tried the boot. To her surprise it opened.

'Christmas present from Door,' he said. 'He likes gadgets. I'll tow it to our place, so it's off the road.'

Ruby grabbed the bag from Kristina and checked. The notebook was still there. Safe. She looked up. Oscar was watching her.

'Laptop,' she said.

He got into the Hilux, drove round to the front of the Getz. He took off Ruby's handbrake and hooked up the two cars. It looked like a yellow bee attached to a large red water bug. Then he stood by his car and waited.

Ruby wanted to argue. While it made sense to have her car off the road it made no sense at all to park it at Oscar's.

The rain fell steadily – it was getting heavier. Her hair would be dancing with delight. Nothing it liked better than a chance to frizz up. You can't look cool or poised if your hair is fanning all over the place. *Lady Fate again, having another laugh at my expense.*

Oscar walked round to the front passenger door. Looked at Ruby warily. 'I'm just going to help you into the seat.'

'Don't worry,' she said, 'I won't jump you.'

His lips tightened. Kristina snorted and tried to conceal it by coughing. He put his arms around Ruby's back and legs and lifted her into the front seat. Must be fit, she thought. I'm no feather.

She shivered. She was suddenly very cold. Knew it was the adrenalin come-down, but knowing didn't make it any easier.

'Rug in back,' said Oscar to Kristina as he turned the ignition on and pulled out.

Kristina patted the rug around Ruby's shoulders. Ruby shivered despite the mustard parka and the rug.

'Won't be long,' said Oscar. 'The car will heat up and we'll soon be inside in the warm.'

'I'm not going to hospital,' she said.

Oscar pressed his lips together, pulled the car into the kerb and stopped. 'Why?'

'No bones broken. And I'd have to wait for hours.'

'Best to be sure.'

'I'm sure. I'm bruised and sore and I need the grit and stuff taken out of my face, but I can sterilise some tweezers.'

'Your eye should be checked,' said Oscar.

'It's all right. He belted me, that's all.'

'It's very swollen.'

'So, Lady Bracknell will have a black eye.' Ruby went to shrug but thought better of it.

Kristina and Oscar were silent. She saw their dilemma. If they drove Ruby to A & E and physically forced her in the door what would that achieve? An assault charge or a perfect social media opportunity for anyone with a smart phone.

'I'll ring Juno,' said Oscar. He got out his phone.

Typical Segar, thought Ruby. Always think they're in charge.

'No,' she said, 'I'll do it when I get home.'

'You have a choice,' he said, 'A & E or Juno. Take your pick.'

'Fuck you,' said Ruby.

Kristina said nothing.

There was silence in the car. Ruby shivered again.

'You're cold,' said Oscar. 'Which is it to be?' He looked like he would wait all night.

If ever Ruby had wanted to have a tantrum, it was now. But she was too sore, too bruised and too tired. Besides, no good moaning when you lost the hand you thought you were winning. Kate had drummed that into her when she was teaching Ruby to play euchre.

'No skiting when you win, no moaning when you lose,' Kate said. 'That's the rules.'

Ruby caved. Her face stung like a hundred bees had been busy there. 'Juno,' she said.

Oscar tapped his phone, spoke to his twin, listened, clicked off. 'She'll meet us at home.' They pulled out onto the road again. It was really dark now; the grey curtain had changed to black. Ruby clutched the rug to her. Okay, she thought, why should I be the only one to suffer? Time to give the bad news. Her swollen lips almost screamed as she forced the words out.

'Two things,' she said. 'One – the interviews have to be done again.'

The others considered what she was saying.

'All of them?' said Oscar.

Ruby felt a wave of hot anger so strong it could probably fuel a Boeing 777 take-off, no trouble. *Who did he think he was?*

'Dull as ditch water,' Ruby said, 'and all the same. What happened? Did she give everyone ten questions and ask them to say their answers into the recorder? And people have been left out. She didn't interview me. Or Kate.'

Kristina said, 'The ten questions were Pete's idea. He said it would save time doing the interviews and writing them up for the book. I assume she didn't ask you and Kate because Kate was dying and you were spending all the time you could with her.'

'Hester? Why didn't she ask Hester? Auden?'

'I only learned about the omissions after she left,' said Kristina.

'Two –' said Ruby, 'Delia Clarence. Says she'll sue me and the theatre for every penny we've got if we publish anything in the book about members of her family.'

There was a brief silence. Then Kristina spoke. 'If that woman was a dog she'd be put down. How did Hester manage to be so talented and so basically kind when her sister is such a bitch? A mystery.' She shut her eyes for a moment then said, 'Okay. Committee meeting tomorrow morning, eleven. You don't have to be there.'

'You crazy?'

'But if you don't get there, no worries.'

'Three –' said Ruby, because she felt like being a nark, and two whinges wasn't enough, 'why the hell did I take on the job?'

'Ruby, it's okay,' said Kristina, leaning over from the backseat. 'I've asked Oscar to do the support work for the history of the Players while you work on it – that's what we were meeting about before. He'll sort the extra stuff. Find the photos you need, and the cast lists and programmes for the back of the book. He can work in the other office at the Swan. Handle Delia.'

'I haven't accepted the job yet,' said Oscar.

'But you will,' said Kristina.

Ruby could almost see the moment when Oscar decided not to have an argument.

'It makes no difference whether you work from the office at the Swan or at your father's workroom at home,' Kristina persisted. 'You can think at the Swan just as well as anywhere else and the theatre *is* an advertiser and a good one, bills paid on time, so it won't hurt you to do us this favour. Look at Ruby,' she squeezed her friend's shoulder, 'she needs some help –'

'I'm sure Oscar's got enough on his plate now he's got the *Star* to get up to scratch before he sells it,' said Ruby. 'And he won the house in that poker game –'

'I didn't win the house,' said Oscar, 'I won the right to make decisions about it.'

'Whatever,' said Ruby. 'You're going to be busy.'

She knew she sounded like a bitch but she really didn't care. She didn't want to work with Oscar on the history and that was that.

He flashed her a look somewhere between hurt and surprise. He and Door and Juno hadn't told anyone about the poker game but it had been a hot topic of gossip around town within half an hour of the game ending. Porohiwi had a superior social gossip machine well before Mr Zuckerberg had his flash of inspiration.

It was Kristina who'd told Ruby, and Ruby's first thought was how pleased Oscar's dad would have been. The poker was his idea apparently – he reckoned it was better than the kids fighting over who did what. Oscar loved the house and would look after it, and while none of Robert and Olga's kids had ever shown any interest in the garden, their youngest son was the one who would keep it going.

Would Oscar sell the *Star* though? The gossip machine said he'd already made up his mind. The only reporter, Fiona Forrest, had given three months' notice, wanted to do some travel before she got too old. The rest of the paper was a combination of garden notes, club or society meeting reports, rugby results and the Porohiwi Library column. Advertisers were retreating, preferring local radio. No doubt about it the paper needed a new look, but people still needed it around here, didn't they?

Ruby had wondered about Door. Was he okay with the poker game? As the eldest he'd probably expected to be the one who made the decisions. Not that he'd be any good with the *Star*. Oscar was the one with experience in journalism and editing, and the obvious one to take over the newspaper. Although being a staff writer and co-founder of online news source *Nek Minit* was probably not much help to Oscar when it came to running a country newspaper. One that still published in proper hand-held printed pages – twenty-eight A3 to be precise – its only income, small advertisers. Juno would probably be easy either way, but then there were Door's twin daughters, Rissa and Jess. How did they feel about all this?

Robert wouldn't have wanted it sold. The first time Oscar's dad had rung and suggested Ruby join him for a coffee, she'd been apprehensive, but then they'd met and talked about everything and anything except Oscar, who was long gone – living up in Auckland. She didn't ask Robert why he kept up the connection with her and he never said. She suspected that it wasn't out of duty, that he really liked her and liked the way they were both writers and that she was a reader. There was plenty to talk about without bringing his son into the conversation.

'Country newspapers matter,' he'd said to Ruby, 'although some-times it seems like we're fighting a losing battle against the big guys. We need to talk about the *Star*. I need some new ideas. Maybe you and Kristina could meet with me some time? You're younger, you'll have different ideas. Good ideas.' Had Robert talked to Oscar about the paper since she and Kristina had that session with him?

Ruby could feel his son sitting stiffly beside her in the car. She thought about her and Oscar all those years ago. Everything could appear so clear-cut at eighteen. You met someone, fell in love, got married and lived happily ever after, right? Wrong. And the proof was in the driver's seat. Still tall and strong with too many curls for a grown man, still thinking he was in charge, still a pain in the arse.

Okay, she wasn't being quite fair. She'd loved that pain in the arse once and he'd loved her. And if there was a competition for best pain in the arse now, she'd probably be in with a good chance of winning.

3

'If ever I get married, I'll certainly try to forget the fact.'

The house looked the same: large, wooden and painted white, a deep verandah around three sides. Lots of windows. Built by the first Oscar and his brother Herman 140 years ago. Even in the dim light the gardens looked like they needed attention. Ruby almost laughed. Gardening had never been Oscar's strong point so what was he going to do with them? Maybe he'd changed now that Robert was dead and he was running things.

Whatever, thought Ruby, as the car stopped. I don't want to go inside. On the other hand, Oscar was right about getting attention for her face – it was throbbing like an old school bus.

He got out, came round to the front passenger side and helped her onto the driveway.

Light flared from the house as the front door opened. Ruby took a deep breath. Her body was saying, *You want me to move? You gotta be joking.* Then Juno was there in the doorway and beside her a grey shadow went rigid and whined in a series of high-pitched moans.

'Karl?' said Ruby. '*Karl?*'

The old dog sounded like he was crying, a keening sound that held disbelief and joy. Ruby and the dog limped towards each other. Tears she hadn't shed after the attack stung Ruby's face. She bent over the grey head.

'Hello, you.' She reached out and placed her hand on the dog's shoulder. Karl whimpered with pleasure as she went on to rub his neck. The last time she'd seen him, he was a pup, small enough to be held. When he'd walked out, Oscar had a backpack on his shoulder, three plastic bags of gear in one hand, the dog in the other.

'Why would I leave the pup with you?' he'd said. 'A month or so and you decide you don't want him after all and get rid of him too?'

Karl had whined but Oscar kept walking. Fourteen years later that pup was an old dog, crying out his surprise at seeing her.

'Karl,' she said.

He pushed his head into her hand and trembled as her arms went round him.

'Darling Karl,' she said, 'darling boy.' She patted his head and he looked like he was smiling.

She stood up and the dog leaned in to her.

'Hello, Ruby,' said Juno. Tall, blonde curls, skinny, smile like her twin's.

'Kia ora, Juno,' said Ruby.

'I thought we'd be better in the kitchen,' said Juno and led the way.

Ruby followed her along the hallway. She could hear Kristina and Oscar behind them. She patted the head of the old dog, who seemed to be glued to her. 'Where's your bed, boy?'

He recognised the word and padded over to a large basket in the corner of the kitchen. He climbed onto it, legs a bit wobbly and uncertain, flopped down, turned around twice and settled. He looked over at Oscar, who nodded and smiled.

'Good dog,' said Oscar, 'good boy.' His voice was calm and quiet.

'I had no idea,' said Ruby. 'Shepherds don't usually live this long, do they?'

'He's not been well,' said Oscar, 'but he's comfortable now. The vet says any time … but he's happy, aren't you, boy?'

Karl nuzzled into Oscar's hand, then relaxed back on the rug and closed his eyes.

The last time Ruby had spoken to Juno was the day after Oscar had walked out. Juno had knocked on the door of the flat. Ruby, needing a shower, eyes swollen and red, opened it, saw who it was, said, 'What?'

'Is there anything I can do to help?' said Juno.

'Yes, fuck off,' said Ruby and slammed the door shut. After a moment or two, she'd heard Juno walk away.

'Kristina,' said Oscar now, 'you remember my sister, Juno? Gun card player.'

'Just saw each other last week,' said Juno warily. 'The community meeting – Kristina had some questions.'

'On behalf of some senior citizens,' said Kristina.

'What happens in ambulances is not my area,' Juno said, 'although of course I'm happy to investigate.'

'Someone should,' said Kristina. 'These are important issues. Older people being made to feel like they're a nuisance.'

Oscar looked from Juno to Kristina, said nothing.

Juno turned her doctor's smile on Ruby, said, 'Just going to have a look.' She held Ruby's face, touched the area around the swollen eye. 'Mmn.' Then, 'Get me a high stool, Os? Dad's workroom.'

The workroom must still be operating as his, thought Ruby. She understood that. It was the reason she hadn't moved into Kate's house after she died but sold it instead. She guessed the family might also not have repurposed the room because it was too much of a mission to clear all the papers out. Robert kept every piece of paper that came his way – every receipt, every scrawled note.

Where was Olga? thought Ruby. Hopefully settled in bed or in front of TV. The last person in the world Ruby needed to see ever again was her old mother-in-law. She looked over at the dog. His eyes were closed, but as if he felt her gazing on him, he opened them briefly then closed them again. She recalled the pain of not having Karl in her life, entwined in the same wrenching hell caused by Oscar no longer being there either. He'd believed the lie he'd been told about her. Seeing the dog again made Ruby suddenly remember how much those events had affected her.

Fourteen years. Only a blink.

She supposed that anyone who'd suffered that kind of breakup never quite lost the memory of the pain, but seeing Karl again made her feel more shaken than she already was. She hurt all over.

You'll survive.

The large kitchen looked much the same although the stove was new. The table was still there.

'I love that table,' she'd said once, 'beautiful tōtara, and the generosity of the size –'

'When we get our own home I'll make you one,' Oscar had said, sliding his hand over the wood. 'Dad'll help me.'

Oscar came back into the kitchen now with a bar stool. Juno looked at it. 'Need something with some support,' she said, 'otherwise Ruby's back will get more painful than it already is.'

'Lean on me,' said Oscar and stood behind the stool.

Ruby sat down, but she didn't lean against Oscar.

Juno put her hand on Ruby's chin and turned it to the side that was swollen and pitted with livid red and purple blistery gouges. The purple gouges were the ones with little stones in them. There were a lot of them. Ruby found her body instinctively moving back from the probing fingers in their latex gloves and towards Oscar.

'I can give you a local,' said Juno.

'I'll be okay,' said Ruby. 'Just get it over.'

'First a good slosh with saline solution then I'll have a closer look.'

'I'll get a couple of towels and a lamp,' said Oscar. He moved like he couldn't get out of the room quickly enough. What was up with him, thought Ruby. Not like Oscar to be squeamish. Although how would she know? A lot could change in fourteen years.

'You want a drink of water, Ruby?' asked Juno.

'Thanks.'

'Here's the lamp,' said Oscar.

Ruby wondered how he liked being Juno's gofer. His sister's hand, in its latex glove, gently prodded her face.

'Mmn.'

'And a straw,' said Juno, then looked at Kristina. 'If you could hold her head steady? And see that she sips water every now and then. Here's a couple of paracetamol, Ruby. Probably won't do much but you never know.'

Somehow Ruby got the tablets down her throat.

Oscar turned the lamp towards Ruby's face then walked back to the stool, held the pillow in front of him and repeated, 'Just lean on me, Ruby.'

'Thanks.' Ruby's lips felt like rubber cushions. She didn't lean back.

'When I've finished,' said Juno, taking out one of the tweezers from the sterilising solution, 'we'll have some food. You must need some and I'm starving.'

Like hell, thought Ruby. Once this is over, I'm off.

After a few minutes she admitted, but only to herself, that it was good to have a support for her back.

Juno was gentle, careful and efficient, but it still hurt like hell. She stopped every few minutes so Ruby could have a break and a sip of water.

'Okay,' said Ruby, during the first break. 'Sunday week. Committee members ring members. Others. Make interview times.' She cut out all unnecessary words because every word hurt her face.

She knew they were looking at each other again and she didn't care. 'Ten digital recorders,' she said, 'supervisor organise.'

'Holy Mother,' said Oscar. Religious instruction had not taken with the younger Oscar but appeals to a higher power had. '*Ten?*'

'I'll use my phone,' said Kristina. 'Got an app.'

Was that a smile in her voice?

'So, nine,' said Ruby. 'Unless everyone gets an app.' She grinned at her friend. It hurt.

Delicious malicious. That two-word, in-your-face line she and Kristina had coined when they were ten. Then Ruby stopped feeling smart as Juno started again, and the world shrank to probing tweezers and a face that felt like it was rare steak on the grill being poked with a fork. Unbidden and unstoppable tears slid from under her eyes.

'Sorry,' said Juno, 'I know it's sore and I'm making it worse.'

The old dog lifted his head and made a sound that could have been a question.

'S'okay,' said Ruby, 'okay.' And willed herself not to react when the tweezer pushed a little further, but she couldn't stop a quick momentary reaction when it went deep. The tears continued to leak down.

Karl made a noise like he was hovering somewhere on the way to a deep sleep.

Kristina held Ruby's head still. Ruby hoped it wasn't going to take too much longer. Torture by tweezers.

'Got it,' said Juno. 'That bit was determined not to come out.'

Ruby thought if she ever got her hands on that guy he'd be sorry. She'd rub his face in the dirt, see how he liked it when it had to be tweezered out. And she'd do the tweezering.

'We'll take a break,' said Juno.

Thank god for small mercies, thought Ruby.

'I'll ring around,' said Kristina, 'and I'll ring Daisy. We'll organise afternoon tea. They'll be fighting to be interviewed.'

'Juno's a great baker,' said Oscar.

Juno said nothing.

'Any good at sponges?' said Kristina.

There was a slight pause then Juno said, 'How many do you want?'

'Well, well,' said Kristina. 'A good sponge maker and a gun card player. Interesting combination.'

'That's just the start,' said Juno, concentrating on the tweezers.

Ruby would have grinned if her face hadn't been so sore.

They had been fifteen when Kristina told Ruby she thought she was a lesbian.

'Shit, it's not me is it?' said Ruby.

Kristina had put her first two fingers in her mouth and made gagging noises.

Be careful, Kristina, Ruby thought. Juno's a Segar. Then she decided that Kristina was an adult. If she wanted to take risks it was her business.

4

He picked up the phone.

'Problem,' said Club's voice.

'What?' His worst nightmare. Spade's fingers pressed the phone like if he squeezed hard enough he could make the words come out quicker.

'Parked around the corner.'

'On my way.'

He stood for a moment thinking. Then went into their sitting room where her bed was now. She was watching The Crown. *For the third time. As far as he was concerned if it took her mind away from her condition she could watch it a hundred times for all he cared. He smiled at her, kissed her cheek.*

'Just going out for a stroll. Want to come? I can get the chair. No problem.'

He knew she would say no and she did.

'Don't be long.'

He kissed her again.

She smiled. 'Hurry back.'

'Winged feet.' He smiled at her although he wanted to yell and roar at fate for giving her that damned disease. She was so brave he wanted to cry sometimes. But crying wouldn't help. One thing he was set on though.

Whatever it took, however much or little time she had left would be happy.

No one would be allowed to get in the way of that.

Certainly not Ruby Palmer.

Club was sitting in his latest acquisition, a shiny red EV. Club cared about the environment. He belonged to a group that helped clean up the sea and river shores too.

Spade opened the door, climbed in and said, 'What?'

'Diamond.'

Spade breathed out. 'Jesus. Thought it might have been Heart. Have you heard from him?'

'No. But it'll be at least an hour before he's back from Wellington. And he won't ring till then. Diamond thought he'd have a look around the old place, and while he was there he saw her coming up the drive, so he got out the front window. Waited in the bushes.'

'Don't tell me he spoke to her.'

'Worse.'

Club told him.

Spade went quite still. 'For fuck's sake. We had a plan. Why the hell couldn't he stick to it? Heart'll be fucked off. You let him know?'

'He won't be answering his phone until he's back from Wellington.'

'At least he won't have to worry about her coming home early.'

'Heart says he'll do something, he does it.'

'We need to meet.'

'You know what Heart said.'

'Heart's not the boss.' Spade sounded as fed up as Club felt.

Neither are you, thought Club.

He said, 'We're all in this together. But we need to tell Heart about Diamond and then we need to meet and impress on that fuckwit that he's not fucking James Bond. He needs to keep to plan.'

'Not sure Diamond'll want to come out again tonight. He's a bit sore.'

'Who the fuck cares?'

They were going to have to do something about Diamond. He was too quick off the mark. Been a mistake even letting him know what was going on. Spade had said so the first time Heart called to tell him there was trouble. He'd even said, straight up, 'Don't tell Diamond.'

The other two overruled him. Now they might understand what he was on about.

Diamond was the weak link.

Spade had known it thirty years ago. Heart and Club had shrugged his warnings off then as well. Then Diamond proved the truth of Spade's assertions by doing what he did. What else did they need? Sure, thirty years is a long time. Sure, the case was closed. Well, never really a case as such. Fifteen-year-old brown girl tops herself, who cares? Turn the page.

That bloody notebook, thought Club. God knows what was in it. Who knew that little bitch could even write? Might be nothing. Poems from school perhaps. When Dinah was little she used to show him her poems in a notebook. The teacher had encouraged Dinah and the other kids to have their own notebook. Keep a journal. But Dinah had just wanted to write poems in hers. He smiled. His daughter had always been very clear about what she wanted. She'd shown him her poems. And the one she'd written to him …

I love you Dad
I would be sad
If you weren't glad

He couldn't bear it if that changed. And it would. Everyone up in arms about that stupid 'Me Too' thing. If Dinah even got a hint that her father had been involved in that sort of crap she would hate him. That couldn't be allowed to happen.

As if that thirty-year-old mistake hadn't been bad enough, now bloody Diamond had done his best to put them back in the shit again.

'The one thing we don't need,' said Spade, 'is publicity. Until we get this whole mess sorted, we need to keep our heads down and not invite attention.'

'We have to get that notebook.'

'Agreed. But the reason we want it is to prevent the kind of public airing of what happened thirty years ago. Right?'

Club sighed. Spade had a habit of stating the obvious.

'Maybe,' said Spade, 'we could just say we were young? Didn't realise what we were doing. Everyone knows men don't start using their brains properly until they're at least twenty-five. And clearly, thinking of Diamond, some never do.'

'It is what it is,' said Club. 'We did what we did. And now we have to fix it.'

'I'm determined nothing will mar whatever time Marcy's got left.'

'Tell me about it – we're off to Antarctica,' said Club. 'Everything's planned. Trip of lifetime. Me and the kids. Might be our last big trip together. They'll be off doing their own thing.'

'I know it's been hard raising the kids on your own.'

'I don't want anything to get in the way of the trip.'

'Tell that to Diamond.'

'Don't worry. I will. How's Marcy?'

'Same.'

'If there's anything I can do just sing out.'

Spade ignored the words. Everyone said that. Some of them meant it. He thought Club probably meant it.

'Looks like you were right. We made a mistake calling Diamond in but mistakes can be rectified.'

'We need to get that notebook.'

'Ruby Palmer's not stupid.'

'Good. That'll make it more fun.'

5

'Mr Worthing, is Miss Cardew at all connected with any of the larger railway stations in London?'

'No thanks,' said Ruby, when Juno offered food, 'Better get home. Need a good night's sleep. Get myself in gear for Bracknell tomorrow night.'

Ruby stared at Kristina, who got the message. 'You should have told him,' Kristina had said all those years ago. 'He should have believed me,' Ruby replied. And she still thought that.

Oscar came back into the room with his parka on, said he'd drive her home. When she demurred because it was a long drive into Wellington and back, he said it was no problem. He'd always had good manners. What she didn't say was that sitting next to him, making awkward conversation or worse, feeling anxious in the silences, wasn't at the top of her to-do list.

She'd heard all the stories about his drinking and his lovers, but then they'd changed. He'd stopped the excessive drinking and taken up cycling and, it seemed, celibacy as well. Ruby had not had too good a record herself in those first years, but time and the realisation that she was bored with it all kicked in. She thought she'd probably known this for a while but had refused to recognise it. This is what sadder and wiser means, she'd decided.

Pity she hadn't learned that before Connor Kelly.

Oh well, even slow learners got it eventually.

'You won't be able to drive tomorrow either,' said Kristina. 'You'll be even stiffer than you are now.'

'Cheer me up, why don't you?'

'How will you get out here? To the theatre? Will you ring Reilly?'

'I'll see. I planned to go to Meg's for the weekend to organise the briar patch, so I could be close by.'

'Found someone who'll lend you a chainsaw?' said Kristina.

'A chainsaw?' said Juno. 'I thought you used pruners.'

'Well past the stage of pruners,' said Ruby, not caring whether that made sense to a non-gardener or not. She'd read of a competition between two men, one using a chainsaw, one pruning shears. The next season the roses were glorious on both sites, which had proved, to Ruby's satisfaction anyway, that roses needed cutting back and they were quite relaxed about the method.

She thought of a deep hot bath. Of lying in it until all the aches and pains vanished. Although her Wellington apartment was small, dark and ugly, at least there was a bath. She would half fill it with water as hot as she could stand, then get in, add as much more water as the bath tub would take, and stay there for a long time, adding more hot water as needed. Just thinking of it made her feel better.

'Night, old boy,' she touched Karl gently. He raised one eyelid, then shut it again, something like a smile on his face.

♥

The night sky was dark, almost menacing, hard pellets of rain tossed by the easterly stung her face as she walked to the car. She shivered.

'Here,' said Oscar, pulling his jacket off again and putting it back around her shoulders, 'I'll put the heater on high.'

He helped her into the front then got in the driver's side. Kristina and Juno settled themselves in the back. It was silly them coming all the way in to town, thought Ruby, but they'd seemed determined so Ruby wasn't stopping them. She knew Kristina was trying to make it less awkward for her. And Juno, well Juno seemed to want to do whatever Kristina was doing.

The rug was still on the seat so Ruby tucked it around her legs, then she tried and failed to think of something to say. Nothing occurred to her except, 'Why the hell didn't you believe me, you arse?' Which would be a complete waste of time. A fourteen-year waste of time.

Forget it. The sour taste of old anger burned. She would never forgive him. Never. She burrowed into the rug.

If she hadn't been starting to feel really sore and tired, she would have been very depressed. She relied on her car. No trains or buses between Wellington and Porohiwi except the InterCity on its way to Palmerston North. Maybe she could stay on at Meg's for a few days instead of just the weekend? Walk to work at the Swan from Duggan Street? Only a K and a half. How would she get to Meg's tomorrow? She'd said Reilly would do it when Kristina asked, but could she really ask Reilly to drive her from Wellington to the Swan in the morning then drive back to work and back again for the performance? No. Had to be the InterCity bus. Sparrow's-fart early and no doubt there'd be rain and wind, but it couldn't be helped.

All was quiet in the backseat. Juno and Kristina appeared to have lost the power of speech. Maybe they were trying to think of what to say as well?

The sooner she found a house the better.

Tomorrow.

Don't think about *Earnest*. Or Bracknell.

Staying at Meg's for more than a weekend was high on her list of things she didn't want to do but she would ask. Just for a few days until Martin replaced the car key. And being close to the river was high on her list of things she loved, so not all bad.

> *Ko au te awa*
> *Te awa ko au.*

She had loved the Porohiwi River from the first time she'd seen it, at seven, when Kate had taken her to meet Meg. Meg had not bothered to hide her irritation at her daughter's stupidity.

'Are you crazy? What do you know about raising children?'

'About as much as other people when they first start,' Kate had said. 'I'll find out by doing it.'

Ruby caught herself sliding, jerked upright, realised she'd dozed and been leaning against Oscar's shoulder.

Sweet hell on a plate. It'd be the final straw if she fell asleep and snored. She didn't think she snored but who knew?

Her hair was definitely frizzy. The rain had seen to that. Oscar had loved her hair. Liked that it had a mind of its own and that no amount of combing, cutting or cursing would make it any more pliant. Like its owner, he said. She thought about Karl, about the dog's reaction to seeing her. That was the thing about Shepherds. Long memories. In theory, she supposed, the dog was half hers but not in reality. Definitely Oscar's dog.

Maybe it wouldn't be so bad with Oscar working at the theatre for a few months? He'd stay out of her way, sort the cast lists and the photos, read through the treasurers' reports, keep any contact with her on a work-only basis. And he could fit all this in between seeing advertisers, interviewing people, trying to organise a replacement for Fiona, learning how the *Star* worked.

Five months to get the book done? Bit of a stretch, but with Oscar's help she could do it. She already knew a lot about the Players, could look up stuff online and there were some written records – although the bulk of those had been destroyed in that fire in the eighties. She would have to talk to Oscar about the fact that the Segar family had refused her access to their private collection of Porohiwi Players memorabilia. Was it Door? *You're going to marry a Māori girl from nowhere?*

Their great-grandmother Johanna had been at the first meeting of the Players in 1919 when it was decided to hold a public play-reading to cheer people up after the ravages of the influenza epidemic. They would hand out parts, have a couple of rehearsals and then present the reading to a public audience in the local hall. They'd serve supper afterwards and perhaps ask the local music teacher, Mr Lascelles, to play some light music on the piano during supper. Eventually the play-reading group wanted to do full productions and so the Porohiwi Players Inc was born. It had been Johanna's idea to collect the records and the family had been doing it ever since.

The silence in the car was lengthening. For god's sake say something, she told herself. But nothing came to her.

Eventually they curved into the harbour from the Ngauranga Gorge and Wellington was in front of them. Rain, icy and driven by a southerly, announced the city was living up to its reputation. Water hit the windows with a ferocity that felt like it was deliberate. The swells were menacing. Ruby was glad she wasn't on the ferry tonight.

'You heard about the tree?' she said to Oscar.

'Everyone's heard about the tree,' he said.

'I haven't,' said Juno from the backseat.

'Okay,' said Kristina. 'Meg's approaching ninety, decides it's time to sit around in the sun on her verandah, but the pōhutukawa blocks the sun. It was planted the day she was born, so it's her tree. Which means, to Meg's way of thinking anyway, that she's got the right to cut it down if she wants to. Some of the neighbours disagreed and got a group together called, with great originality, Save the Tree. It all got a bit out of hand. Someone was proposing to sit up in the tree and call the media in.'

'She wanted to cut down a *pōhutukawa?*' Juno sounded horrified.

'Five other pōhutukawa on the property, so she figured cutting one down was not a major. Anyway one night when half of Porohiwi's at the race course for a free showing of *Poi e* and the other half's at a reading of *Macbeth* at the theatre, someone turns the lights off on Duggan and the streets around it, bowls up and cuts down Meg's tree.'

'No clue who did it?' said Oscar, sounding interested.

'Spider was in police custody overnight,' said Ruby, answering his unspoken question. 'A misdemeanour. He conveniently backed into the neighbour's front fence, liquor on his breath.'

'Good strategy,' said Oscar.

'Surely Meg heard something?' said Juno.

'Apparently not,' said Ruby.

'She still sleep in the front bedroom?' asked Oscar, looking like he was trying not to grin.

'Always been a sound sleeper, she says.'

There was silence while Juno seemed to digest this information. 'So this Spider …?'

'My uncle.' Kristina got in quickly before Juno said anything she'd regret, but Juno's question was about something else entirely.

'… is he the one who used to play cards with Dad sometimes?'

'Mmn.'

Ruby thought if anyone could organise the cutting down of a tree in the middle of the night it would be Spider Porohiwi.

'Still on Fraser Street?' Oscar asked Ruby.

'Yes thanks. Hopefully not for long.'

'You're moving? Where?'

'Should have done it before. Kate went on about it all the time and she was right. I know it's a dump but it's central.'

'Where?' he repeated.

'Somewhere I can make a garden,' she said. *And where I can stretch out in a bath instead of having to bend my knees.*

Oscar guided the car through the wet Wellington streets, pulling into the kerb outside Ruby's apartment block. They were on a taxi rank, but he walked up and spoke to the driver of the sole parked taxi. They'd only be a few minutes.

'You don't have to come in,' said Ruby.

Oscar ignored her and started walking. She knew why. First rule drummed into him by Robert. Never leave a girl to walk to her door on her own. Ninety-nine times she'll be okay but there was always the hundredth. Kristina and Juno got out of the car too and followed them.

The young Chinese man on reception was watching TV. 'Hi, Ruby.'

'Hi, Henry. Quiet night?'

'As usual,' he said.

They got in the lift and went up to the sixth floor, walked along to number 7A. She really had to find a house. It was just stupid for someone like her to live in an apartment the size of a shoebox. She pushed her key in the lock and the door gave way.

'Fuck,' she said, 'someone's been in.'

She pushed the door wide open and walked inside.

'Ruby,' said Oscar, 'taihoa. Could still be in there. I'll ring the cops.'

She ignored him, turned on the lights, stood and stared, her heart beating a jarring rap. Everything was on the floor. All the contents of the fridge, the store cupboard, crockery, plates, pots, pans. Jams, honey, sauces, lentils and rice, everything, except the oysters. She knew this because there was no smell. Behind her she heard Juno's gasp and then felt Kristina's hand on her arm.

'Wait a minute,' said Kristina, 'let me go first.'

'Piss off,' said Ruby.

In the little sitting room the table was pushed over, chairs and books thrown about. Her only vase, a red glass lily, had been crushed under a foot. Oscar had given it to her on the day they were married. The bedroom and bathroom were the same. Everything that could be broken or spilt or crushed was broken and spilt and crushed. The drawers and wardrobe had been emptied of clothes and shoes, which were now strewn around the room. It was like a cyclone had swept through leaving nothing whole in its wake.

Thank god I had the notebook with me.

Thank god I wasn't here.

Ruby realised she was trembling. Bloody hell, she thought. For one terrible moment she felt like she'd pass out. *Stop it*, she ordered herself, that's not going to help.

'Sit down,' said Oscar. He pulled stuff off the couch, felt it to see if was wet, then said, 'The police are on their way. I'll have to find a park.'

'He took the oysters,' she said. 'He took my bloody oysters.'

She fumbled in her wallet. 'Here.' She handed Oscar her card for the residents' car park. He rang reception.

'Hi, Henry,' he said, 'apartment 7A has been broken into. Better inform the owner. We're waiting for the police. I'm going to park my car downstairs in Ruby's car park, okay?'

Ruby stared at the mess. Incomprehensible. Why would anyone break in? The landline rang. Automatically she picked up the receiver. Reilly. She pressed the little button.

'Fabulous dress rehearsal,' said Reilly. 'You're gonna be a great Bracknell.'

Ruby stared at the phone but she couldn't speak. She was crying. She felt in her bag for a tissue. Couldn't find one.

'Here,' said Kristina. 'Tea towel but better than nothing. Give me the phone, Ruby.'

Ruby ignored her. Got her voice under control.

'Break-in,' she said, 'my apartment. Someone's wrecked it.'

'I'll come,' said Reilly.

'No,' she said, 'nothing you can do. The police have been notified. Oscar's here, and Kristina. I'll ring you tomorrow.'

She put the phone back on the cradle, cutting off his surprise. Wiped uselessly at her face. Hopeless. The tears kept on coming. She felt the sting on the grazes. Thinking of Reilly made her feel worse.

He was missing Kate as much as she was. Dear Reilly. He had no skills with wood, held a hammer in a way guaranteed to bang his thumb, a screwdriver as though he was going to stab someone, but for Kate's funeral he did all the paperwork, saw to all the legal requirements, talked to the funeral director, set up the hall for the wake, organised the programme.

Oh, Kate, thought Ruby, I need you now.

Oscar was speaking to her. She sniffed stupid tears.

'Adrenalin,' said Oscar. 'The effect of adrenalin. We all get it in some form or another when we've had a shock. You need a hot drink.'

Ruby frowned – did he think she was an idiot? Then she remembered that he'd been a volunteer paramedic and had helped out on the ambulances sometimes. He'd know about shock reactions. Talking about it to the patient was probably part of the patter. And if he didn't, no doubt his sister, the doctor, would.

There was a noise at the door. Kristina and Juno looked up and Oscar moved back through the mess to go and get it.

'Hi, Mark,' she heard him say. 'Hey, Jojo. What are you both doing in Wellington?'

'On a six-week secondment,' said a voice. 'Finishes tonight, thank god. The travel's been a bugger.'

The two police officers walked in to the trashed room. One of them was Jojo, who did the lighting for the performances at the Swan. The other one Ruby didn't know. *Mark*? She looked at Oscar.

'Ruby, Kristina, Juno,' he said, 'this is Detective Inspector Mark James. You know Police Constable Joanna Jones. When I was a lowly year 9 at St Joseph's and Mark was head prefect, he caught me wagging and didn't tell,' said Oscar.

'What was he doing out of the classroom?' said Ruby.

'Never dared ask,' said Oscar.

'Wagging,' said Detective Inspector Mark James, which for some reason made Ruby feel better.

Mid-forties, tall, with sleepy brown eyes that no one with a brain would be fooled by, DI James was standing there taking everything in. Jojo – as supple and thin as a rose branch – was prowling the room.

'Thought my two-year-old nephew was pretty good,' she said at last, 'but this guy could trash for the Olympics.'

Ruby blew her nose and wiped her eyes.

'You okay, Ruby?' said Jojo. 'Can I get you anything?'

'Tea,' said Oscar, 'strong sweet tea. I'll find the kettle.'

'No,' said DI James, 'don't touch anything. Sorry, Ms Palmer, we'll have to put you in a motel for a couple of days. But first we need to talk. Shall we go down to the station?'

Her response was immediate.

'No. I've done nothing wrong. I'm not going to the station.'

There was silence while the detective inspector considered his options.

6

'When I am in trouble, eating is the only thing that consoles me.'

Henry let them use an office along from reception. It was only a small room but DI James made no objection to Kristina and Juno cramming in behind Ruby. Oscar had a word with Henry then sat with Kristina and Juno. Jojo stood in the doorway checking something on her phone.

On the cream wall was a calendar open at January 2015. It had a picture on it of a bowl of very red glossy apples drawn by someone who'd never actually seen an apple.

All Ruby could think was that for the second time in her life she was left with nothing. This time there was no Kate to replace – no, not replace – *supply* new clothes, pyjamas and underwear. This time Ruby would have to do it herself. Stop it, she told herself, you're not seven now, you'll cope. Then she patted the bag. Not exactly nothing, don't exaggerate. You've got cash in your wallet and some in the bank. Lots worse off than you.

And don't fucking cry.

'So,' said DI James, after he'd asked about her face and questioned her about the attack and avoided asking why she hadn't contacted the police earlier, 'anything you've done recently that could have upset someone?'

'No.'

'Ruby,' said Kristina. 'What about Stace?'

'How could asking Stace to find out the names of the staff who worked at the Home in July 1981 make someone trash my apartment in May 2018?'

'The attack was in the Home grounds. All I'm saying is there might be a connection.'

'What happened in July 1981?' said DI James.

Ruby was annoyed but it was quicker to tell him than not to. She didn't want to be here all night.

'Someone gave birth to me, slung me in a kete and left it at the back door of the Home. Up in Porohiwi. Before Kate died, I promised her I'd find my parents.'

'Kate?'

'Kate Palmer. She's the woman who adopted me. She died four months ago.'

Ruby knew she sounded angry and she was. Upset that she had to say this out loud to this cop. Why had Kristina prompted it? In any case it was a red herring. A complete waste of time. She didn't own anything that warranted someone attacking her and wrecking the inside of her apartment.

Henry came in carrying a tray with a bottle of red wine, some beers, glasses. DI James sighed but said nothing. When Oscar held up a couple of beers towards him, the cop shook his head.

'I wish,' he said, 'but no thanks.'

Henry arrived with another tray with plates of things that smelled delicious. Nachos, a creamy sharp-tasting dip, little sausage rolls and something cheesy.

'Help yourself,' said Oscar. 'Been a long day, and I don't know about you but I'm starving.'

He handed the tray to DI James, who grabbed a few nibbles.

Ruby had no doubt that Jojo had been googling Ruby Ruth Palmer, even if she'd known her forever through the Players, so it wasn't a surprise when she showed her boss what she'd found on her phone.

'Did you tell anyone that you'd made this promise to Kate?' said DI James. Obviously a man who could eat, read and ask sensible questions at the same time.

'Only Kristina,' she said.

'What about your birth certificate?'

'I have a legal document signed by a JP attesting to the date I entered the Home. Kate got it done when she was applying for adoption.'

'Any ideas?'

'No.'

'Do you have anything in your possession from those days?' asked James. 'A photo perhaps?'

'Detective Inspector James,' said Ruby, 'I ran away from the Home when I was seven because Betty …' her voice broke. Fuck that. She would not cry in front of the cops. She sniffed and took a deep breath. 'Betty was lying on the path. Drowned.' Tears ran down her face anyway. She really needed that cup of tea.

'Who was Betty?'

'A girl who looked after me.' She groped for the tissues. Oscar pushed them towards her.

'You know her second name?'

'Matron renamed every kid who came to the Home. She said their own names were unpronounceable. No surprises. School teachers did the same.'

She grabbed some more tissues, wiped her face.

DI James didn't move a muscle. He would have heard this sort of thing before. Oscar already knew. Kristina ditto. Juno looked horrified. Probably thought she was hard done by if she didn't get a biscuit with her morning tea.

Kristina handed Ruby a plate with a sausage roll on it and she grabbed it. She was past starving, she was ravenous. Kristina took the plate back, loaded it with food and handed it over again.

'So Betty was lying on the path drowned? And …'

'I screamed her name and the guy started belting me.'

'The guy?'

'All in black. Balaclava.'

'Same as the one tonight?'

She didn't answer.

'His name?'

'I don't know.'

'Why did he attack you?'

'He didn't need a reason,' said Ruby. 'None of the staff did.'

'You think he was staff?'

'Who else could it be, DI James?' said Ruby. 'It was half-past six in the morning.'

'Where was this man when you came upon Betty?'

'He was kneeling beside her, taking the big stone out of her pocket. I knew what had happened. Things had got too bad.'

'Too bad?'

'Betty told me what to do if things got too bad. You stick a big stone in your pocket and lie down under the water. Let it take you.'

There was silence in the room. Even DI James seemed to have run out of steam. But only for a moment. As Kristina took Ruby's plate, placed some more food on it, handed it back, he said, 'Was Betty unhappy?'

'Unhappy was normal.'

'So you got away from this person and ran off in the clothes you were wearing?'

'Knickers, shorts, shirt. The balaclava man stopped chasing me because Matron called.' Ruby took a breath, got her voice under control. 'I suppose I should thank the bitch for saving my life.'

Kristina put a half glass of wine in Ruby's hand.

'Have any of the staff been traced?'

'I only asked Stace on Tuesday. No online records so it takes longer.'

'That's Stace Waterson who runs the SD Agency?'

'Yes.'

'Any idea what happened to the guy?'

'Vanished. Senior Sergeant Murphy said they tried to find him but he'd simply gone underground.'

'What did he look like?'

'Tall. Strong. All in black. Scary.'

'Matron?'

'Took to her bed and her doctor said she couldn't be interviewed in her present state. When they did get to ask her where the staff records were she said they were in her office. But they weren't. Someone had burned them.'

'Why would someone burn them?'

'Senior Sergeant Murphy was pissed off. He told Kate that if the higher-ups in Wellington had got off their backsides and approved a search warrant when he asked for it, he'd have had the records.'

'I'll check,' said DI James.

'It was thirty years ago,' said Ruby.

'Anything else?'

Relentless.

She hated him.

'Only that I'd better find a bed soon or I'll be a wreck. Or more of a wreck than I already am. I've got an opening night tomorrow.'

'Oh yes,' said DI James. '*The Importance of Being Earnest*. Good play. And you're playing Lady Bracknell?'

Ruby stared at him.

'One of my sons is in Hester's drama class. And Jojo might have mentioned it.' James looked down at his feet. 'I know it's not easy going over old ground like this.'

Oh *really?* She would bet that not once in his nice head-prefect life had he ever had to do any more than give his name and address. And if he'd ever been asked for his birth certificate he would have just handed over the usual form, all lovely and legal and ordinary.

'Just find me a motel,' she said, 'with a bath. A long hot soak will make this day seem better.'

Jojo got busy on her phone, while DI James munched thoughtfully on a small meat pie and looked at his own small screen. He was no doubt checking out the Home. Ruby knew what he'd find. She almost knew it by heart.

The Porohiwi Home for Children started life around 1907. A church-run, charity-funded private home for orphaned or abandoned children. It had a committee of well-meaning women, mainly Anglicans, whose views on poverty (caused by people who didn't/ wouldn't work, who drank, were too lazy, didn't attend church) were well known. The children were a different matter. *Suffer the little children to come unto me*. And so on.

The children were housed and fed, taught to love God, be polite, keep themselves clean, do housework, sew and knit, cook (girls), garden or build fences (boys). Just after World War Two, the state took over the running of it. It was smaller than their usual state-run homes, only twenty children were housed but the state pushed it up to forty-five. All Māori. Changes in the name of efficiency, a leaner staff ratio, and no more than cursory supervision by state inspectors meant the Home became a little kingdom all of its own run by a matron – all staff chosen by her, harsh discipline, meals kept to just above starvation level. It survived longer than most.

By 1979 it was probably on the way out. An anachronism which no MP or bureaucrat could be bothered doing anything about. The records were updated each year, everything added up or balanced the way they should, inspectors said the children were happy and well cared for ... and then in 1988 Betty drowned, Ruby ran away, the police got involved, the balaclava man vanished, Matron resigned and the rest of the staff pleaded ignorance (and it was convenient to believe them).

It was decided that the Home should be shut down, the house sold, the children in residence sent to larger places. Where, as it was revealed some years later, conditions were even more appalling.

DI James took another pie. He was still scrolling through whatever was on his screen.

Ruby thought the wine she was drinking was probably the best she'd ever had in her entire life. 'Thanks,' she said, when Oscar handed her a second glass.

Oscar shook his head. 'No worries.'

James said, 'I'm sorry but I have to ask. Did Kate Palmer leave you anything someone might want?'

'She left me the house money but that's safely in the bank.'

'Do you have any idea why these incidents should happen at this time?'

'No.'

'And you're sure you don't have anything in your possession someone might want?'

Ruby repeated that she had no precious gems, no rare stamps, most of her stuff was from op shops, the only things of value, and only to her, were her phone and laptop. The phone was now drowning somewhere under the bushes at the old Home and the laptop was in her bag, along with her wallet.

'Here's my card,' said the DI, taking another sausage roll. 'Ring me any time.'

Ruby wanted to scream at him that it would be a cold day in hell before she ever rang a cop, but she just nodded instead. She was done.

She felt for her phone. Remembered. Get one tomorrow, she told herself. As for the notebook, Kristina was the only other one who knew about it, and she wouldn't say a word.

'Maybe the person who trashed your apartment was looking for something you might call "rubbish" but was of value to him? And maybe he attacked you to make sure he wouldn't be interrupted when he trashed your apartment?' DI James frowned then said, 'I'm saying he, but of course it could be a she.'

'No. The balaclava man was a *he*. No doubt about it.'

He didn't sigh but he looked like he wanted to.

'Sorry,' said Jojo, looking up from her phone. 'Not having much luck. Food Fair weekend starts tomorrow – Friday. Hotel rooms, motels, B'n'Bs, everything's booked out.'

Oscar looked pointedly at Juno.

'We have a spare bedroom,' said Juno, 'and there'll be a new toothbrush somewhere. You're welcome, Ruby.'

Ruby would rather eat live cockroaches than sleep at the Segar house but she was thirty-seven not thirteen, so she stood up, grabbed her bag and said, 'Okay. Thanks. Let's go.'

But DI James stopped her and went through all the questions one more time before he gave up. He said, 'Okay, Ms Palmer. You'll need to sign a statement. Someone will be in touch tomorrow. Please be careful. Don't walk alone, especially at night. If you have any thoughts about tonight, or anything else happens that you find unusual or suspicious, please contact me. Good luck for tomorrow.' And Jojo waved.

When they got out of the lift into the car park, Kristina whispered in Ruby's ear, 'My place is a mess and you know there's only the one bedroom but I have a fold-out bed if you don't mind a sick dog and a teenager asleep on the kitchen floor?'

'It's okay,' Ruby whispered back. 'I'll survive.'

'He didn't …?'

'No, he didn't.'

'I just thought … it made me …'

'It's okay, e hoa. He only got his hands on my face, nothing more.'

Ruby squeezed Kristina's hand.

♠

Juno was quick and slid into the backseat beside Kristina so Ruby had no option but to get in the front again. No fear of falling asleep on the ride back. She was too fired up to sleep. While it was plain to all of them that she was reluctant to stay at the Segars', she was tired to the bone, sick of this night which was now early morning, sick of this stupid drive home. All she wanted was for it to be over. When Oscar pulled up outside his front door she had an irrational and overwhelming desire to turn and run away back down the drive, out onto the road, anywhere away from this place.

'Here we are,' said Oscar. 'And here's me stating the obvious.'

For a couple of seconds Ruby didn't think she could move, but when Juno opened the car door and smiled at her she got herself out of the car and walked through the front door and into the hall. The same paintings looked down on her. The same pile of umbrellas and gumboots were on the racks by the door. The smell of privilege was the same.

Juno led the way into the kitchen.

Karl was curled up in his basket. He opened an eye, gazed a moment at Ruby and then it seemed to roll back in his head. Karl was an old dog now. Tired.

Kristina, who'd been persuaded to come in and have a hot drink, stood beside Ruby looking enigmatic.

'Tea please,' she said.

Now they were in the kitchen, Ruby relaxed.

'Spa, anyone?' said Oscar, 'I turned it on before we left. Should be nice and hot by now.'

'Wonderful,' said Juno. 'I can lend you some knickers or T-shirts if you want. I don't usually wear anything but it's up to you.'

Ruby could have cried with pleasure. She'd forgotten the spa.

7

'Well, what shall we do?'
'Nothing.'

Ruby sat in the very warm water and thought paradise had to be a spa pool. The steam, like a mist from some ancient site, turned the line of windows at the far end of the room into misty barriers. Her body began to relax as she gave herself to the water, her aches and bruises easing to barely felt impressions at the edge of her consciousness.

It was like the world had stopped for a moment and the only reality was the warmth and comfort, and the easy movement of the water.

Juno and Kristina, faces softened by the steam, were also silent, letting the water do its work. Oscar, eyes shut, head leaning back, was quiet. He looked fit, all the cycling no doubt. His hair was wet, curls like question marks all over his head. Had he had other plans for tonight? Something he'd had to ditch because of Ruby? If so he was keeping any disappointment to himself.

'Wine?' asked Juno.

'No,' Ruby smiled to soften her rather abrupt refusal. 'Nighthawks time.' Juno nodded. She knew the painting.

'Aaah,' sighed Ruby, moving lazily in the water. 'If every household in the country had a spa, domestic violence would go down to almost nothing. The cost of installing them would be recovered from the savings in police, hospital and welfare time.'

No one commented on this hypothesis, but no one disagreed with it either. Too blissed out, thought Ruby.

'We could make up a four?' said Juno lazily into the silence. 'Haven't had a game of euchre for ages.'

'Now there's a challenge,' said Kristina. 'Up for a game?' She looked across at Ruby and then to Ruby's annoyance, without waiting for a reply, said, 'Course you are. Do you good.' And she winked.

Ruby was irritated but not prepared to have an argument in the Segar spa pool at one-thirty in the morning. Her friend was pushing an agenda she knew Ruby didn't want.

'And I can help with the interviews,' said Juno. 'I've got two weeks before I start at the hospital.'

Kristina grinned. She was too good a card player to show surprise but Ruby knew her very well. She was surprised all right. She'd been interested before, now she was hooked.

Well done, Juno.

'I should never have taken the job on,' said Ruby, 'that's very clear.'

'Don't moan,' said Kristina. 'You've got a nice office. We even cleaned the couch.'

'Were they really having sex on it?'

'According to Barbara.'

'Barbara?' said Oscar, without opening his eyes. 'She new?'

'Runs the ticket office, a royalist, twinset and pearls. Hasn't had sex since her husband died forty years ago. Probably thinks it should be banned.'

'That reminds me,' said Kristina. 'You still run first-aid courses?'

'No,' said Oscar.

Ruby wanted to smile but didn't. She remembered that day. 'Oh come on, Oscar, that was a long time ago.'

'Two women resorting to a punch-up to settle who went first to be my "patient" is not something I want to see again in a hurry. So, no thanks.'

'Look,' said Kristina, 'the Porohiwi Health Trust will give us a defibrillator but we need to have people who know how to use it. They won't go to the St John's courses. They will come to the theatre courses because I'll round them up.'

Oscar said nothing. Ruby thought that was very wise.

'I'll send you the proposed timetable, and you can think about it, okay?'

'Go on, Ossie,' teased Juno. 'Do you good.'

'You do first-aid courses?' said Oscar.

'No way.' Juno's grin disappeared instantly.

'Good. You can help me do the course,' said Oscar.

Ruby yawned and it hurt. She put her hand over her mouth, looked up and Oscar was looking at her. For one moment the world narrowed down to just two people sitting naked in a pool. He smiled at her and something inside her that had been frozen for a long time, eased.

Stop it, she told herself. It's just the time and the place. Nothing's changed. But her body took no notice, every sense sharpened to red alert. She took a deep breath.

Like hell, she thought, get a grip. Deliberately, she looked away. Felt like she'd escaped from some kind of danger.

'Come on,' said Kristina. 'Time to get out. You're just about asleep.'

Ruby thought about the shit who'd trashed her flat. Probably sleeping peacefully. Job done.

You wait, she thought, your turn's coming.

8

*'In matters of grave importance, style, not sincerity
is the vital thing.'*

When Ruby woke the next morning she felt for her phone, then remembered.

Her body had loved being in the spa but once in bed her brain had refused to shut down, the events at the Home and then her apartment playing like a film set on perpetual, events happening over and over, the man running out of the bushes, intent on hurting her, hating her enough to smash or wreck everything in the apartment. What had she done to invite such a brutal rampage?

She felt tired and grumpy. Definitely not in the mood to go shopping, but she'd have to go and buy a couple of things to wear at least. Jeans. Some knickers. Socks. And she'd need something to wear when she went out into the auditorium after the show tonight. Jeans, T-shirt and track shoes probably wouldn't cut it. Hester liked her casts to mingle.

'They've paid for the seats,' she'd say, 'they like this little extra.'

Shit. First night tonight and Kate won't be there.

Don't think about it.

Those first few months after Ruby's arrival had coincided with Kate's production of *Julius Caesar*. As well as the rehearsals, Kate had to teach each day and prepare each night, and there was the drama club after school three afternoons a week. On top of all that, she suddenly had a child to look after.

Kate would come home, make dinner, clean up, supervise Ruby's reading, look over her homework and then go to rehearsal, where Ruby would be tucked up in a rug in the cossie room. Once home again with her daughter settled – which sometimes took a long time in those first months – Kate would have a shower, a cup of Milo and a quiet read, time to herself. Over the years Ruby had never missed Kate's first nights and Kate had never missed one of hers.

It took nearly a year before the adoption went through and Ruby was legally Ruby Ruth Palmer, but Kate said that as far as she was concerned Ruby was her daughter right from the moment she saw the hunger and hurt on the girl's face.

'You're welcome to live with me,' Kate had said the next morning. 'I'm a lesbian, which means I'm attracted to women not men. Is that a problem?'

'No,' said Ruby.

Kate had fed her, showed her the bath and left her to it. There was a clean warm bed, and Kate and Daisy had bought new clothes and new pyjamas, so if that was what being a lesbian meant it was okay with Ruby.

'How did you get your name?' Kate asked.

'They were up to the Rs on their names list.'

'I like Ruby Ruth,' said Kate.

Kate was in a league of her own, thought Ruby. If a kid ran up the drive to any place I lived in, I'd run out the front.

One thing had been resolved for Ruby in those wakeful hours after the spa. She knew for sure now that she wasn't going back to the apartment. The invasion, the furious mess, the violence of the search and the deliberate smashing of anything that could be smashed would always be there every time she entered the place. She just couldn't do it, and thanks to the inheritance from Kate, she didn't have to.

She would ring the landlord from Meg's and tell him, but first she would ask Meg if she could stay for a week. Surely she'd be able to find somewhere new to rent in that time?

It was just one more thing to do, she thought. On top of keeping her promise to Kate, Meg's garden, the Players history and *Earnest*, there was finding somewhere to live. I'm a juggler, she thought, and if I don't watch it one of the balls will fall and the whole lot will crash to the ground.

Maybe I could leave a note for Oscar and just sneak out? No. Kate would rise out of her ashes at such blatant rudeness. Politeness was high on the list as far as Kate was concerned. And Ruby knew she couldn't go without saying goodbye to Karl.

She smiled, remembering the pup and his inability to keep still when they first brought him home. 'Only a flat,' Oscar told the pup, 'but we'll get a house to rent soon. Dad's on the case.' And look at Karl now, thought Ruby.

Were Kristina and Juno a disaster waiting to happen? Just because two people came from different backgrounds didn't mean they couldn't be happy together. Ruby had believed that, and she'd been right, up until the day Olga told Oscar something about Ruby that was utter shit and made him hate her – and he'd believed his mother. He hadn't believed Ruby. Didn't want to listen. That their relationship had ended had nothing to do with class. They *had* been happy together. No one had ever been so happy.

Enough, she told herself, enough. It's because of last night. Seeing Karl again. Makes it all come back.

◆

The bruises looked fairly startling this morning but more colour than real damage. Her face was a mess though. Oh well. A bit of makeup and some net floating over it and Bracknell would be fine.

Reilly reckoned Oscar Wilde meant *The Importance of Being Earnest* to be done by queer males, that it was coded. Which could be true. But you could suggest a lot of things about people's motives after they were dead and couldn't answer back. You could twist almost any line in a play and make it mean something else. And it was not always because a director wanted to make her mark. Kate used to say each generation brought a different view, a different set of values to a script. You only needed to look at the history of audience attitudes towards Shylock to see that.

If you prick us, do we not bleed? Shakespeare's lines weren't all great by any means, and he gave most of the good ones to stupid adolescent Hamlet, but Shylock's speech had to be one of his best. Whatever Oscar Wilde's motivation in *Earnest*, he'd had some fun at society's expense, and in doing so created a play that had been loved by hundreds of playgoers ever since. This would be the Players' fourth production of *Earnest*. One for every generation it seemed.

Ruby walked silently down the hallway and through to the kitchen. She needed coffee. The sun was shining. Maybe she could walk to the shops on the highway?

'Morning, Ruby,' said Oscar.

He looked like he'd slept for ten hours rather than six, but Oscar was lucky – his hair did what it was told and that blue top brought out his eyes.

Karl climbed out of his bed and stood shakily. She would swear he was smiling.

'Hello there,' she said, scuffing her hand through his fur. 'Good boy, good boy.'

She sat at the table. Karl slumped beside her feet. She wondered whether getting up would hurt as much as sitting did. Karl lifted his head, nudged her leg, sighed, put his head back down.

'Messages for you,' said Oscar. He was standing by the kettle waiting for it to boil. 'Stace says there are some clothes that might help until you get some new ones. She'll meet you at the theatre either before or after the committee meeting, your choice. Hester rang to say there's always a bed at her place. Daisy ditto. And there's a phone on the table you can use till you get a new one. It's an iPhone 4 so not the latest but it's all clear.'

'That's very kind of you,' she said, picking up the phone. 'It's all ready to go,' she said, surprised. Or it would be once she added some social media. She put the phone down. Later.

'I put your name on it,' he said, 'stuck some credit on. Put in a few contacts.'

'Fabulous. How much do I owe you? I'll get one as soon as I get my car back.'

'No worries,' he said, 'I keep a couple of spares. This was Rissa's old one. She has to have the latest. When you've finished with it, give it back. Always someone who wants one. Coffee?'

It was like they'd only just met yesterday and he was being polite to a guest.

'Yes please.'

Oscar poured boiling water into the plunger to warm it up, tipped it out and spooned in coffee from the grinder. More hot water. Got some eggs out of the fridge.

She wanted to insist on paying him for the phone but it seemed a bit churlish.

'I'll take you to the theatre,' Oscar said, 'I'm going there anyway. Said I'd give Rissa a lift. Her turn to clean the dressing room, she says. Have it looking good for tonight. I've got a few things to do then I can take you to Meg's later?'

'Thanks,' she said, 'that'd be great. You want me to do the eggs?'

When they were together Oscar's greatest culinary treat had been burnt toast.

'Scrambled or poached?' he said.

'Poached please.' He must have learned how to cook, and Ruby wondered who'd taught him. The acid test for a cook – if he could do good poached eggs he could do anything. Those poached-egg holder things were for amateurs. All you needed was hot water, eggs, a knife, and a spoon with holes.

Oscar carefully broke four eggs onto a plate, slid them one by one from the plate into the water, separated the eggs with the knife. 'Free range,' he said. 'The neighbour's got chooks.'

They were perfect. Firm yellow yolks, no bits left behind in the pan, good shape. Ruby said so as she ate. She was starving.

'My tutor would be pleased,' he said.

Don't ask, Ruby told herself, *do not ask.*

'Who was it?' she said.

Door's daughter, Rissa, came in, leaned down and patted Karl, smiled at Ruby. 'I don't know whether I said it last night but the dress rehearsal was really cool. You were great.'

'Thanks,' said Ruby. 'So were you.' Which wasn't quite true but would be once Rissa got into her stride. She was eighteen, blonde, blue-eyed, clever, a perfect Cecily. She smiled at her uncle.

'Just toast,' she said.

'Nervous?' said Oscar.

'Scared stiff. Jess is coming tonight.'

Oscar patted her on the shoulder. He knew all about being a twin, thought Ruby, and the inability to be anything but truthful with each other. Oscar and Juno, Rissa and Jess – they've all suffered the loss of a parent, but they seemed to be managing, why can't I? Grief's over when it's over, she thought. It's only been four months. Ruby didn't expect to ever not miss Kate, but maybe in time it wouldn't be so damn … sharp? Wouldn't ambush her with those bloody tears. As though tears would ever … oh, come on, she told herself, get a grip, there was all those months of looking after her before she died. It's reaction, tiredness, whatever. It will pass.

What would never pass was the knowledge that if Ruby'd run into anyone else's woodshed and been sent back to the Home and lived there without Betty's protection, she'd have known sexual or physical abuse like most of the other girls. When she turned fourteen she'd have been sent away, expected to find a job and somewhere to stay and no doubt ended up on the streets, or jail for stealing or soliciting.

And in spite of the hoo-ha about setting up the Royal Commission so far nothing had been done. Not one abuser had been charged, not one. No one from the state institutions, or the Catholic church, the Anglican or Salvation Army homes, had ever been held to account.

Rissa was poking around in the bowl of bananas and oranges.

'Any avocados?' she said.

'Seven dollars each,' said Oscar, 'so no.'

'They're very good for your health,' said Rissa. 'I try to have one every day.'

'Then you buy them,' said Oscar.

'I had to put in more for the flat electricity bill this month, we all did, so I'm a bit short.'

'You'll have to wait until you can afford avocados then.'

'I'll ask Dad,' said Rissa.

'You need to learn to manage your money,' said Oscar. 'Some people only have seven dollars a week for a whole week of breakfasts.'

'Maybe they should learn to manage their money,' said Rissa.

Oscar turned round swiftly and Rissa saw his face.

'Sorry, Uncle Os, sorry, I was just being smart.'

Rissa took a banana, peeled it and began eating. Her face was pink. Oscar poured himself another coffee and Ruby stared into space.

9

'It may be necessary to do something desperate. That of course will require serious consideration.'

Ruby looked up at the Swan. It really was a good example of art deco. Light clay colour, blue and yellow stylised sunbursts across the front. A bit on the shabby side now, but still worth looking at and it didn't matter how many times she saw it, this place always made her heart lift. She'd been coming here since she was seven. Made a nuisance of herself, showed off, trod in paint, made up her face with greasepaint, pranced around in someone else's high heels, ate pies and numerous packets of fish and chips before guilt overcame Kate and she'd put them both on a regimen of salads, fish and eggs. Until the next getting-close-to-first-night performance time. Ruby already knew some of the Swan's history, and working on the book meant she was finding out more. The Swan knew all of hers.

It was relatively easy for her to say, 'I'm not going back to the apartment,' unimaginable to say, 'I'm not going back to the theatre.'

Inside, the committee members were sitting around the kitchen table. Five of them out of seven. Apologies from Auden, who'd got a moving job that morning, and Jojo, who was on duty. Kristina looked like she hadn't slept much. The place was sparkling clean and smelled of coffee. Daisy was in charge here and everyone hoped she'd live forever.

'Your poor face,' said Jen Bailey, committee secretary, plump, fair-haired and formidable. Jen managed her own accountancy firm, would be overseas at a conference when the history of the Players came out and had pre-ordered ten copies already.

'It's fine,' said Ruby, 'I'll live.' There were murmurs from the others.

She looked around the table at the familiar faces: Kristina, Jen, Hester, Patsy, Pete. Except for Pete, Ruby had known them all since she was seven years old. Daisy and Ronald Hugh were there too, included in the meeting as a self-preservation move. If the committee made a date for something that needed food, tea and coffee, Daisy needed to know. There had been one occasion when she'd been rung at eight one night and asked where the supper was. *What supper?* Getting food and drink on the table for fifty people by ten o'clock had been a miracle, but Daisy, along with the three women she'd rung, had achieved it. She wasn't going to let that happen again. Ronald Hugh looked after the backstage gear, kept it orderly, knew where every flat, screw and hammer was. His motivation was the same as Daisy's. He didn't like surprises.

Joining them were Oscar, Jake and Ruby. She had no idea why Oscar and Jake were there but maybe they'd decided to maintain a watching brief on their contracts.

Ruby felt herself relaxing. For a little while she could ignore yesterday, forget the soreness that made every movement an effort. She was safe and secure in this place, among these people. Could any of them be the apartment trasher? Or hate her so much they organised someone to do it? Stop it, she told herself, you know these people, they wouldn't.

But the thought lingered like an undercurrent in a river.

In a minor way Ruby's life at the moment was what it must have been like for a citizen during the war in Britain. She knew someone was trying to hurt and upset her, but what could she do except carry on as usual? Ridiculous to be sitting here as though life was going its ordinary way when someone out there wanted to, at the very least, muck up her life completely, and at very most … who knew?

'Delia Clarence,' said Kristina.

Everyone knew Delia, Hester's half-sister, hadn't recovered from her rage at discovering that the house she'd thought was her mother's, and therefore Delia's when the mother died, had in fact belonged to Ronald Hugh Morrison, Hester's dad. For some reason known only to herself Delia blamed Hester for this and was set on revenge.

'Publish and be damned,' said Hester.

'I don't want to lose all that lovely money we got from *As You Like It*,' said Jen. 'Don't want to have to catch a plane back for a special committee meeting to organise a loan from the bank.'

'What is there to find out anyway?' Patsy asked Hester. 'What did your grandfather do?' Patsy was thin with slightly bulging blue eyes. She wrote bad plays and was very sensitive, with one layer of skin less than everyone else.

'Oscar?' Hester said.

'In the late seventies, yours and Delia's grandfather, Henry George Clarence, was charged with stealing money from a trust at Montague & Montague where he worked. He was found not guilty. Caused a real stir at the time. Some believed he was guilty.'

'Oh, that old stuff,' said Patsy, 'I thought you meant something really bad. But I'm like that. I have a very broad and generous view of human nature. I can't help it. I had a French grandmother.'

Hester ignored Patsy. 'He was found not guilty. Why should Delia object to that being mentioned?'

'After he was found not guilty he sued the firm, the police and the other side's lawyers, and he lost. Cost him a lot of money,' said Oscar. 'No one in Porohiwi would speak to him after that. He was forced to resign as treasurer on the Porohiwi Players' committee, then from the Players themselves, as well as the country club and the euchre club. Must have been very hard for his wife and his daughter, Joan – your mother, Hester.'

'Marissa,' said Hester, 'Joan changed her name to *Marissa*. But everyone knows about him. Public knowledge. Not like it's breaking news. Anyone can look it up.' She drummed her fingers on the table.

'Okay, Ronald Hugh,' she said to her father, 'what have you got to say?'

Ronald Hugh immediately looked guilty, blushed right to the top of his balding red hair. His freckles stood out like traffic lights.

'Nothing,' he said, 'it all happened before my time. The first time I met Joan, I mean Marissa, was when she played Amanda in *Private Lives* in 1976. I don't remember much detail. I was depressed.'

'So depressed you were shagging every woman in sight,' said Hester.

Ronald Hugh said nothing.

'And,' said Hester, 'we all know the result of that. Me.'

'Joan, sorry, *Marissa*, had just divorced her first husband,' said Ronald Hugh. 'I cheered her up. I was feeling very down and she cheered me up.'

'So much that you took off and didn't come back for forty years?'

'Could we keep to the point?' said Jen. 'I, for one, have other things to do this Friday morning.'

'The point is,' said Pete, 'we had no plan for this history book. The committee were supposed to be supervising the writer. If we'd made a *plan* and followed it, we'd have found out sooner.'

What the hell has lack of supervision got to do with Delia's threat? Ruby's lips tightened over the words and she said nothing. Her face still hurt.

'Why is your sister doing this?' asked Jake.

'Give me time,' said Hester. 'There'll be a Delia reason.'

'So,' said Kristina, 'why don't we leave this till Ruby has completed her research and written a first draft, and then make a decision about what could be left out.'

'Left out?' said Ruby. 'Are you suggesting we *tamper with history?*' She grinned at Kristina.

'I'm suggesting we wait and see,' said Kristina, grinning back.

'Just saying,' said Ruby.

Everyone except Patsy appeared thankful that Ruby had got in before Patsy began a more dramatic and lengthy conversation along the same lines. Even though it was some years ago everyone in the room had vivid memories of Patsy playing Gertrude, Hamlet's mother, and ignoring the lines Shakespeare had written in order to give a long and tear-ridden soliloquy on the right of older women to have sexual feelings.

'I may have a layer of skin less than everyone else,' Patsy had dramatically concluded, 'but if I want to fuck Claudius I will.'

The audience had clapped. Half of them thought this Shakespeare bloke should have had his mouth washed out when he was little and the other half thought Patsy was on the right track.

'Okay,' said Kristina, 'the interviews.'

'What's this about the interviews having to be done all over again?' said Pete.

'The recorded interviews we've got so far are boring and repetitive,' said Ruby. 'I understand everyone was given a piece of paper with some questions on it and told to say their answers into a recorder?'

Pete looked across at Ruby. 'I don't know if you understand the science of time and motion?' he said.

Oh boy, let the good times roll. 'Probably not,' said Ruby, 'but if you keep to words of one syllable I might be able to grasp it.'

A frisson of uneasiness rippled around the committee. Oscar looked into space and Jake glanced at the ceiling. Ronald Hugh was just glad he wasn't getting the blame for anything.

Ruby didn't care.

Pick up the fucking gauntlet, Pete, see how far you get.

'I apologise if I spoke out of turn,' said Pete, 'it was just a passing comment.'

Okay, if you won't I will.

She said, 'I understand you're a good coach, Pete, but I don't think writing is your field.'

Whoa.

The committee members as one looked at the chair. Kristina looked at Ruby.

'Maybe you could explain in a little more detail what's wrong with the interviews?'

'The interviewees state their name, age, the plays they were in or connected with, whatever else they've done, and that's it. A total *waste* of time, repetitive and dead dull. Boring. The Players might have had their ups and down over the hundred years, but if Kate's stories are any indication it was never boring, never dull. Any one of you would do better if you'd been given a little more time and a lot more interest.'

'But some things, well, you don't want the world knowing, do you?' That was Jen.

Ruby sighed. Some people wanted the fairy-tale version of their life and some went for warts and all – fact of a ghost writer's life. 'Look,' she said, 'I'll write it using the material from the new interviews we're going to do and from whatever else I find when I do my own research. I'll make a judgement about the content, and if you don't like it then you can have your fee back and I'll keep the book.'

'But then we won't have a book,' said Pete, like he'd just discovered the moon revolved around the sun.

'And I'll have done five months' hard work for no fee,' said Ruby. Then she went for it. 'I'm not being dictated to about my work by Delia or Pete or anyone else. You have rights, you're my employers, but I have rights too. You either trust me or you don't. If you don't then sack me. Now. Up to you.'

Ruby thought that Pete was right when he said that if they'd organised themselves properly and done regular checks on the previous writer and the renovator over the last six months, they wouldn't be in this fix but the situation was what it was. No good agitating over what might have been. Delia must have gotten to the previous writer. No doubt about it. Ruby thought she'd actually be quite happy if they sacked her right now. But that was because she was sore and tired and had a first night tonight. That was the thing with community theatre, no one waved a wand and said, 'First night tonight? Take the day off.'

Now she was hungry. Why? She'd had a good breakfast. Oscar's eggs. But as always when she was tired, she got hungry. And when she got hungry, she got irritable. A hangover from the Home. If she got hungry and there was no food, she got anxious. The anxiety turned to irritation in a heartbeat. It also made her deeply annoyed with herself. She usually carried a little tin of biscuits she could nibble on at these times but that tin was sitting in her car at the Segar place.

She should be over these things.

Same with running. It wasn't that she couldn't run. Just that the minute she started to run, she was so overcome by fear she became a gibbering wreck. And the only people who understood that were Kate and Kristina. Or maybe 'understood' was the wrong word. Maybe it was that they *accepted* her fear as a reality like they would accept someone else's physical or mental disability. Kindness sounded such an ordinary thing – we all tried to be kind, right? Wrong, thought Ruby. Kindness is an extraordinary thing.

'I say leave it to Ruby,' said Jake. 'You'll all have time to read the draft before it goes to the editor. And what is the point of employing Ruby to do a job then putting some kind of embargo on the content? We either trust her judgement or we don't.'

'I second that,' said Daisy.

'Hear, hear,' said Ronald Hugh.

'None of you are on the committee,' said Jen Bailey, 'so you have no say. I propose that we leave it to Ruby, and when she's finished we read the draft and make up our minds then.'

'I second that,' said Pete.

Ruby could have swiped him. Why had he wasted time arguing?

They started to make 'thank god now I can leave' noises but stopped when Ruby said, 'Five minutes? What were you all doing in 1981?'

'Jeepers,' said Jen after a minute, 'not sure I want to go there. At one stage I was a hysterical mess because Phillip Borley reneged on taking me to the Town and Country Ball and took my best friend instead. What the hell else did I do in '81? I must have done something. Marched of course. That was a time. One half of the town yelling at the other half who yelled back.'

'God knows,' said Hester. 'What would I have been? Two? Being bullied by Delia's a pretty good guess.'

'I was in Auckland and in between marches wondering what the hell I was doing with my life,' said Daisy.

'Was '81 the year I did Gertrude?' asked Patsy.

'No,' said Jen, 'that was the year you played Miss Prism in *Earnest*. Marissa directed it. Stace played Gwendolen and no … sorry, that was 1980. Pete, did you play Jack?'

Pete looked irritated. 'Badly,' he said, 'I'd hoped everyone had forgotten about it.'

'You were what we'd now call hot,' said Jen. 'How could I forget?'

Clearly Pete didn't see her words as a compliment.

'Who played Algernon?'

'Colin.'

Colin? He'd have been a very mournful Algernon, thought Ruby. Maybe he was more cheerful when he was young?

'Oh that's right,' said Jen, 'and Garth played Lane then too. Now I think of it he must have been quite young for Lane back then, although I suppose butlers have to start some time. Jake, you were around,' said Jen, 'what were you doing?'

'Allegedly helping with the set,' said Jake, 'but actually snogging anyone who'd let me.'

'Oh yes,' said Jen, slight colour on her cheeks. 'Jesus. The things we do.' She turned to Ruby. 'Why do you want to know? Not for the book I hope?'

'Context,' said Ruby. 'Just trying to get a feel.' She smiled around the table. 'I'll talk to Mrs O'Rourke about the earlier decades. Her husband played piano I think?'

'Don't believe a word she says,' said Jen, hastily. 'I only met her granddaughter once. I had nothing to do with the shenanigans at the river.'

'Well, whatever she says about me will be true,' said Jake. 'I was an up-myself, tongue-hanging-out-for-it little shit.'

Ruby smiled. 'See you all Sunday. Nine-thirty.'

'Could it be the following Sunday?' asked Patsy.

You could always rely on Patsy, thought Ruby. She would wait until every meeting was virtually closed and then ask a stupid question.

'Patsy, you know as well as I do that the following Sunday is the first-aid course. Oscar is running it with Juno.' Kristina looked around the table. 'Members of the committee are expected to attend. Death is the only excuse and then I want to see a doctor's certificate.'

'So this coming Sunday, nine-thirty, half an hour before the interviews start, my office. Okay?' said Ruby. What about her sleep-in? She thought of the Home. She'd still be able to do the search in the afternoon after the interviews.

'When we get our marching orders.' Hester grinned.

'Don't forget the Circle Market the following Saturday,' said Kristina. 'Yes, I know, but they're great supporters. We need to return the favour.'

Hester appeared beside Ruby. 'See you for five minutes?'

Ruby was at screaming point with hunger, but she said yes.

'Coffee?' asked Oscar. 'Something to eat?'

'Don't mention food or I'll start eating my hand.'

The office was a good size, two windows overlooked the car park, the red couch along the wall almost glowing after its clean. What could Hester possibly want?

'I'm pregnant,' said Hester. 'Four months on. I just about passed out when the doctor told me. My first pregnancy I was as sick as a chook all day every day for months. This time the only symptom I had was I felt really good, and then over the weekend I weighed myself and whoops … so I went to the doctor to get a diet sheet and he did some tests, actually one test, and I'm pregnant. Auden is over the moon and so am I but …' she paused.

Ruby knew exactly what Hester was going to say next, and she said it. So after Hester left expressing huge thanks about a hundred times, Ruby sat at the table in her office and stared into space. No doubt about it, she told herself, you're certifiable. You'll be carted off any day soon.

How old was Hester? Forty-one? How would that go – having a baby at forty-one? Especially after her first one, to Hester's previous husband, had died at birth. Lots for Hester to be happy about, thought Ruby, and lots to be said for having a baby when you were a bit older. Ruby could only be thankful that she hadn't wanted any babies when she was twenty-two for reasons that had seemed good at the time.

Ruby had never planned on having a baby, but Oscar had wanted one. Made noises about it before they broke up. She'd joked that it would be a bad idea – genetic inheritance wasn't the only factor to take into account when thinking about the pros and cons of raising a child, but what child would want to inherit Ruby's hair? He hadn't laughed.

There was a tap at the door.

'Ruby?' said Oscar. He'd made her a coffee and thrust it into her hands. 'I'm going to get a pie – you want one?'

'Is the Pope a Catholic?'

'You've got ten minutes before Stace comes,' he said, turning. But stopped. 'What's the matter?'

'Hester's pregnant, so she can't do the last-term drama classes or the end-of-year kid's show,' said Ruby.

He stared at her. 'You didn't.'

'Yes,' she said, 'I did.'

'Right,' he said, 'you'd better have some food before you promise to save the world from climate change. Back in five.'

10

'The fact is, Lady Bracknell, I said I had lost my parents. It would be nearer the truth to say that my parents seem to have lost me.'

Stace arrived in a rush. 'Sorry, sorry, sorry,' she said. 'Traffic on the coast is a pain.' She threw her bag and a couple of cartons on a chair, stared at Ruby.

Stace was slightly taller than Ruby, fifty-three, short dark hair, brown eyes, thin face. She could have made a living as a dressmaker, but she only sewed for herself and a few select others. Charged a mint. Bright patchwork jackets and embroidered kimonos, each one different and worth every penny she charged.

'You look like you've been in a round with Muhammad Ali,' she said at last. 'Showing my age, aren't I? Should have said Joseph Parker. How are you?' She nodded awkwardly and glanced at herself in the mirror. 'Bethany thinks the attack and the trashing is the ghost's doing. Apparently she saw it last night after the dress rehearsal, when she was waiting for Colin.'

'I'm fine apart from looking like a colander,' said Ruby. 'Bethany sees lots of things and most of them aren't real.'

'Yeah, but there've been sightings of her? The '88 fire? And at other times before something bad happened. Not that I believe in them of course.'

'Should I try and find the first mention for the history?'

Stace shook her head. She looked irritated. 'Look,' she said, 'why would a ghost, supposing there was one, only appear before a bad thing happened? Why would it appear at all in a little country theatre? A load of rubbish. In any case the theatre history is supposed to be about real events isn't it? Not silly whispers and suppositions.' She tapped two of the clothing racks.

'If there's anything you want, take them, list them in this book and when you bring them back, clean and in good order, tick them off, okay?'

Stace to the rescue again, thought Ruby. Stace had always helped her with clothes.

Thirty years ago Kate had called her in, with Daisy and Marlon.

'I don't know anything about bringing up a child,' Kate had said, 'so you'll have to help me.'

'I know bugger all,' said Marlon.

'Less,' said Stace, 'but I can sew. Help out with clothes?'

'We'll muddle along,' said Daisy, 'that's how most people do it.'

It was Stace who discovered Ruby the time she stole Kate's lighter and a cigarette and snuggled down in the ditch next to the Catholic church, accidentally setting fire to the dry grass. The word flew around like a bee zizzing from flower to flower. *Nearly set the Catholic church on fire. Congregation just escaped with their lives. Kate will never live it down. Ridiculous, her adopting that girl.*

None of it was true. For a start, it was a Saturday so no congregation, and if that boy hadn't come nosing along and told his mother, who was doing the flowers, it would all have been all right.

'Go get the police,' the woman had told her son. Well, Stace had put a stop to that.

She was right as usual, thought Ruby. Some good clothes here.

'So you stayed at the Segars' last night?' Stace said. 'Had a spa even.'

Ruby, her head inside a shirt, breathed heavily. She'd been doing this with Stace since she was seven. It hadn't stopped her then and it wouldn't stop her now.

'Interesting,' said Stace. 'And Kristina Porohiwi and Juno Segar? *Really?*'

Ruby didn't answer. No use asking where Stace had got the information. She just had.

'Why won't the Segars let you look at their archive of Players' stuff?'

'They'll have their reasons.' Ruby grabbed two jeans, two shirts. Jacket? She moved along the rack. Yes, a kind of blue check. Jersey? That red one would do for a week or so. A bit on the big side but warm and the jacket was rainproof. She stared at herself in the mirror. Looked like she'd walked into a bus. She could see Stace behind her busy looking through cartons of clothes assessing them for costumes.

Stace had female lovers but as far as Ruby knew, none of them lasted beyond a few months. It would be hard for someone like Stace to sustain a long-term relationship anyway. Her mind was always on the SD Agency work. She loved technology because she said it made her life so much better. The downside was that she was forever checking her phone, her laptop, receiving emails, sending guarded replies, having long conversations in the early hours of the morning with someone on the other side of the world; the upside was that if you wanted to know anything, Stace would either already have it or would find it for you.

'Dykes get a discount,' Kate had told Ruby, 'but because Daisy and I started the SD Agency, my discount spills over to include you. If there's any information you want that you can't find or you don't have the time to look – Stace will find it for you. That's what she does.'

Until now Ruby hadn't needed Stace to look for her. Writing life stories on behalf of other people always involved research, sometimes a lot, sometimes hardly at all. And when records had been lost or destroyed and answers couldn't be found from the subject or through Google or Wikipedia, Ruby didn't mind searching through old papers, archives, diaries. Some jobs took a lot of work, others were very straightforward, all the relevant papers and newspaper cuttings already sorted. In these cases she felt like an impostor taking the money. It was an immutable law where work was concerned – ninety per cent had to be like digging into concrete with a fork so the other ten per cent was coffee and lamingtons.

Asking Stace to trace the staff from the Home had been common sense given Ruby's workload. Whether knowing the names would lead anywhere was problematic. Would any of them have been working there when she was dumped at the door? Long call. Maybe been there when Betty arrived at the Home eight years before? Even longer call. Know Betty's real name?

Now, thought Ruby, running her hands over the clothing racks. Something for tonight. She looked at a black shirt. Maybe a bit sombre but it felt like real silk, black suited her and hopefully it would mean she'd merge into the background where her swollen face and bruised lips wouldn't be so noticeable.

'I've got a spare kimono you can have,' said Stace. 'Never been worn. Red, with gold embroidery? I'll bring it tonight.'

Ruby was surprised into a smile, then thought – Shit, that hurt. 'Great,' she said. 'I can pay.'

Stace ignored that, said, 'How did it go? The spa.'

Kate used to say Stace was either born without the ordinary radar most of us have or life had taken it away. This was an asset when ferreting out facts people didn't want found but when it came to something like a friendly chat, her antennae simply didn't register the red *stop* signs.

Ruby began looking through the shoes. Unlikely there'd be anything much, but there might be something she could wear tonight instead of track shoes.

'Must have been a great poker game when the Segar kids played for the house,' said Stace. 'Poker's not Oscar's favourite game, I'm told, but there you go, he won. Wonder if he'll sell the *Star* now it's his?'

Ruby wished Stace would stop talking. Maybe it was a habit. Or maybe when her hands and brain were caught up measuring and thinking about turning clothes into cossies, it was an accompaniment. The way bass accompanies the treble.

Stace had made two piles of clothes – and was searching through pockets now, turning out cuffs, testing zips, and continuing a conversation only she was having.

'Olga's in chronic pain,' she said, 'had her bedroom and bathroom fixed up so she can look after herself as much as possible. Taken Robert's death hard.'

Ruby thought about Oscar's mother. Did she feel sorry for this woman who had shafted her fourteen years ago? Broken up her marriage? Thank god Olga hadn't been up and about when Oscar was feeding her eggs in the kitchen or Ruby might have had trouble being polite, and the nice time they'd had around the breakfast table would have been ruined.

It struck her that Olga Segar now had exactly what she'd always wanted. Her younger son, home and under her thumb, where he would have been years ago if God had only listened to her, and Ruby Palmer hadn't come along. Olga loved Door and Juno, Rissa and Jess, but the world began and ended with her younger son and that was that. It was a wonder Door and Juno didn't hate Oscar, but they didn't.

'I know you and Olga didn't exactly hit it off,' said Stace into the silence.

Opinions might differ about Stace Waterson, thought Ruby, but the one thing everyone would agree on was that she was persistent. *Fuck it.*

'Olga and I both wanted Oscar, Stace,' she said. 'I offered sex, so I got him. Temporarily.' Which was a smartarse comment but she was sick of the probing.

'Why didn't you divorce him?'

Ruby's body tensed. What the *hell*? She'd never said a word to Stace, or to anyone except Kate. It wasn't that she would have contested a divorce but at first she'd been too heartbroken, in too much pain. Organising a lawyer seemed impossible. A year later she decided that as she was never going to do *forever* again, it didn't really matter what her legal position was. If Oscar had asked of course she'd have agreed immediately, but he hadn't.

Stace, thought Ruby, not only knows everything, she likes you to *know* she knows everything.

Ruby wondered again where apartment trasher was. Having Saturday coffee with a wife? A lover? A friend? Somewhere looking out at the rain. Thinking of Ruby? What had this bastard really wanted from her? What if she'd been home when it had happened? Would she have been trashed in the same way as everything else in the apartment?

What was the trasher's motivation? What had he – or she – wanted?

Someone knocked on the door. 'It's Pete. Want to check the windows before tonight. Okay to come through?'

'Five minutes,' called Stace.

'I'm on a short time frame,' said Pete.

'Five minutes,' repeated Stace.

Ruby didn't smile but she felt like it. She liked the way Stace wasn't fazed by Pete. He should have more sense anyway. If it came to a showdown Stace would win. Must have known why the door was locked. He knew everything else.

'Right then. What have you got?'

'Two jeans, two shirts, two T-shirts, and a couple of large ones to sleep in, jerseys and a jacket. These black shoes. Got any earrings?'

Stace handed her the exercise book. 'Write the list in here,' she said. Then went to a shelf and pulled out a box. 'If you choose anything don't bother to bring it back,' she said. 'In fact take the whole box. I've got six others all crammed.'

What would be the motivation for attacking a stranger's house? Orders if you were a soldier or a cop, Ruby supposed. Fear? Guilt? She became aware of a lengthening silence. When did Stace stop talking?

Ruby took a deep breath. 'What were you doing in 1981?'

Stace frowned, stood quite still for a moment as though she was thinking. Then she said abruptly, 'Why do you want to know?'

'Research,' said Ruby. 'Trying to get context.'

Bland enough to sound authentic. If Stace thought it was for background on the Players history, even better.

'You were living with your mother in Porohiwi?' Ruby prompted.

'Probably more truthful to say arguing with my mother in Porohiwi,' said Stace.

This was Stace. You got really fed up with her and then she'd say something laconic and funny and make you smile.

'Did that a lot in '81. Why I moved out. How long have I known you now?'

'Thirty years,' said Ruby.

'Wow. Of course. Of course. Thirty years.' She paused, looking off into the distance. 'I must have been twenty-three when I went to Kate's and met you. You looked at me like you hated me on sight. Kate said it wasn't personal, you looked at everyone like that.' Stace stared at Ruby as if she was remembering that day, that little girl, who'd now turned into this grown woman asking stupid questions.

'What was your favourite song back then?' Ruby had discovered a while ago that if someone thinks you're talking bullshit, or is suspicious about where your questions are leading, asking them another question in a completely different area is always a good move.

'Something by ABBA? The Stones? Sobbing along to Aretha Franklin or Roberta Flack was a favourite pastime. Carole King? Who knows? Now.' She checked Ruby's notes in the book. 'Sure this is enough?'

'Yes. Thanks, Stace.'

'I'll bring the kimono to the dressing room tonight. And I'll let you know as soon as I've tracked those names. There's a bag over there you can use.'

Ruby opened the door to leave and Pete, practically breathing fire, pushed his way in.

There was a man behind him.

Who? Then it clicked. 'Hi, Fritter.'

Late fifties or maybe early sixties, hair that could do with a wash, looked fit. She supposed lugging gear up and down ladders kept you fit. His clothes could do with a wash too. He'd recently come back to Porohiwi to take over what had been his mother's bach, which was bad luck for Hortense Spenser, who'd had to vacate the home she'd lived in for the past fifteen years. Ruby knew those baches well. They were just round the corner from Meg's.

'*Fritter?*' Ruby had said to Jake.

Jake shrugged. 'Likes whitebait,' he said. 'If I'm gonna get these renovations finished by September and he can do the work, I don't care what he's called. Bit of a rip and blaster, but I can tolerate that for a few months.'

Ruby knocked on Oscar's open office door. Karl lifted his head then went back to sleep again. 'You want to give me a lift to Meg's?'

'Half an hour?'

'I'll be in my office.'

She crossed the foyer and unlocked her office door. The red couch looked inviting so she lay back on it and thought about DI Mark James and his questions. If he was right, and Ruby had something that someone else wanted it couldn't be Betty's notebook. It just couldn't.

♥

'Kate said you were to be given these when everything was settled and sorted.' Elliot Montague had called Ruby into his office after the funeral and held out two envelopes to her. One had a letter in it and the other had a notebook. 'I'm sorry about Kate,' he said. 'You must miss her.'

Ruby had nodded, taken the envelopes, sat in the car and read the letter. Put it in her bag. She would keep it forever. She opened the other envelope, looked at the notebook for a while then wrapped it in the red scarf she was wearing because she couldn't bear to look at it anymore.

Only three people had known about the notebook. Betty, Kate and Ruby. Betty and Kate were dead. That left Ruby.

Once Kate put the notebook into that envelope Ruby had felt safe. 'You can have it back whenever you want,' Kate said. 'Just ask.'

Ruby never asked. All she wanted was to do what Betty said – hide it so no one would find it. To forget? Maybe, she told herself. Seven-year-old Ruby and her motivations were lost in time. What she knew now was that the sight of that notebook had brought all the memories rolling back. And they brought some unpleasant luggage with them, the biggest of which was guilt. How could she have let all this time go by without trying to find out who Betty really was? Useless to say she'd been a terrified kid and that all she'd wanted was to forget.

Ruby wondered if Kate had known what a load of self-recriminations would follow when she saw the notebook again after all this time. Probably.

Reilly had been present when the will was read but that was a different meeting. This later one was between Ruby and Kate.

Everything had been done. The house cleaned, furniture given away, grounds tidied up, house put on the market, sold. So from Kate's point of view it was exactly the right time for Ruby to be given a letter saying … well, saying what it said. And the notebook.

Even if, long shot, someone else read those twelve lines of symbols they wouldn't know, apart from the obvious, what they meant. The obvious was what they'd see and understand. No names, no identifications, so no worries.

Only Ruby knew what the symbols were really saying and that was because Betty had told her. And what had Ruby done? Pushed it away. Couldn't get rid of it fast enough. Betrayed Betty, that was the guts of it.

Enough, she thought, enough.

Think of something else.

The Players, 1919. Though the influenza epidemic had thankfully waned, hardly anyone in Porohiwi was untouched by it. Oscar's great-aunt Joanna's idea that reading plays would cheer them up had been a good one. The first play they read was *Earnest*. One of their number, a Samuel Markis, had bought a copy in London when he was waiting for a berth on a boat to become available. Had to be related to our Sam Markis, thought Ruby. His family might have a diary or something. She would ask him tonight at the Swan. Assuming that Samuel senior was around twenty-three when he was in London, he was probably thanking God he hadn't copped it at the Somme.

> *What passing-bells for these who die as cattle?*
> *– Only the monstrous anger of the guns.*

Good old Wilfred Owen, thought Ruby. Enough of the patriotic fairy tales of Brooke et al, he told it like it was. Died in 1918. Too young, too young.

So there's Samuel waiting for a berth, perhaps convalescing from a wound, or suffering from the effects of that terrible gas, maybe Samuel Markis wanders down Piccadilly to Oxford, sees a bookshop and goes in? Liked plays perhaps? Or, and this was more likely, there'd been a production of *Earnest* on in London at the time? So he bought the script?

Ruby would check.

How long after the scandal and jail term did it take for producers to forget the furore and start doing Wilde's plays again? Oscar Fingal O'Flahertie Wills Wilde died in 1900. Silly, silly Oscar. He should have ignored that note. *Oscar Wilde, posing sodomite.* But no, he had to challenge it. Two court cases. *The Importance of Being Earnest* was enjoying a huge success and its author was being sentenced to two years' hard labour for having illegal relations with men. Served his time but it broke him.

Who was there for him when he left Britain, wrote 'The Ballad of Reading Gaol', lived and died in poverty in Paris? Not Lord Alfred, that's for sure. Was Lord Alfred Douglas worth it? Of course not. A lethally attractive, vain, selfish boy. Hardly worth wrecking your life over. But who can tell when sex is involved? Certainly not someone from a distance of a century or more.

She thought of Connor Kelly. Sighed. Instead of blaming herself for her stupidity, she should be asking why the hell does a man of twenty-eight meet a woman of thirty-seven and then decide he's found the love of his life? She was pretty sure both she and Connor had started from the same place. A bit of fun with no strings. Never mind. He hadn't been in touch for at least a week. No texts, no flowers, no phone calls. Must have got the message.

Sex. Sometimes so much pleasure, sometimes on reflection, such stupidity.

Maybe he'd keep out of her way from now on?

Yeah and that was a pig flying up in that bit of sky out the window.

◆

'Ruby? Ruby?'

She opened her eyes. Oscar was looking down at her.

She smiled sleepily. 'Darling,' she said, 'you came back.'

And then she woke up. Properly.

Shit. Fuck. Bugger.

'Sorry,' she said, 'sorry.'

Which only made it worse.

Rissa was standing in the doorway, eyes wide. What the hell would she be thinking?

Fuck. Ruby scrambled off the couch, brushed past Oscar, face burning like beetroot on a barbecue, and yanked on her shoes. Of course the bloody laces got tangled. She strode across the room, grabbed her bag and the bag of clothes and waited for Oscar to leave.

'Right,' she said, and marched out of her office, locking the door.

It was only eleven-thirty on a Friday morning but Ruby had had enough of this day. She walked out of the foyer, down the front steps and into the car park. She waited by Oscar's car and wondered where the fucking ghost in the blue dress was when you needed her.

11

'Do not speak slightingly of the three-volume novel, Cecily. I wrote one myself in earlier days.'

Porohiwi. A small country town with its own share of the heartless, the hopeless, the helpless, all attracting the same mix of kind or cutting comments as anywhere else. The rest of us, Ruby decided a long time ago, just get on with it. The bulk of the population lived on this side of the main highway, the rest up on the other side which everyone who didn't live there called the Other Side. Which sounded a bit like an expression a medium like Ramona Kelly might use.

The highway separated the two sides but wasn't the cause of the divide that existed. Everyone on this side agreed that to live on the Other Side you had to have money, luck, think you were better than anyone else and eat organic.

People who lived on the Other Side thought those who lived on this side were lazy, bludging beneficiaries. Unsurprisingly, these deeply held beliefs didn't seem like prejudices to the ones who owned them. There were exceptions. Daisy Carter for one. Daisy's view of humanity was not sidetracked by where they lived, or how they looked, only by what they did.

Give me a child until he is seven and I will show you the man. Ruby knew now that either Aristotle or St Francis Xavier had first said this, but the first time she'd heard it was from Senior Sergeant Kelly in Kate's kitchen. Ruby had allowed him to see the bruises because Kate said it was evidence. But she didn't like it. Daisy was uptown buying Ruby some new clothes but she wasn't back yet so when the sergeant arrived Ruby had to get out of the bath and back into the old ones she'd worn all the long night in the woodshed. They smelled of sweat and sick although she hadn't actually chucked up.

When Senior Sergeant Kelly said thank you, she glowered at him. Then he said the quote about the child and grinned at Kate.

'Good luck,' he said.

Kate said, 'Luck's got nothing to do with it, sergeant. Three meals a day, a decent bed, soap and warm water and a bit of kindness, that'll do the trick.'

She smiled across at the skinny sullen little girl with the bruised body. 'Right, Ruby?' Ruby glowered back.

'And you'd have more chance of getting permission to adopt her if you're a married woman,' said Senior Sergeant Kelly. 'Know anyone who'll go through the motions?'

'Marlon,' said Kate.

Senior Sergeant Michael Patrick Kelly, staunch Catholic, happily married father of five, had looked across at Katherine Margaret Palmer, lesbian feminist and political stirrer, and said, 'If you need a reference, Ms Palmer, ring me.'

♣

Oscar spoke. 'You got hold of Meg?'

'She hates the phone,' said Ruby.

'You want me to buy you some knickers?' said Rissa from the backseat with Karl. 'I'm going to the highway shops later. There's a special if you buy three.'

Ruby smiled back at Rissa. 'Thanks,' she said, 'get me three threes. I'll give you some money.' She grabbed her wallet. 'I'll have to do a grocery shop for Meg but not up the highway.'

'How will you do that?' said Oscar. 'You can't drive.'

'I'll think of something,' she said, trying not to look at Oscar. Handed some notes to Rissa.

His turn to look cheesed off. Ruby looked out the car window.

There was the Mimosa Café – the goss was that it was for sale. She hoped someone bought it. It was true that Porohiwi had a main street full of op shops and cafés but the Mimosa had memories. Hester

76

organised annual poetry readings there so her drama kids could get a feel for performing in public. Ruby wondered if she might have to do it this year with Hester's pregnancy, but then she thought that Hester would probably still want to organise it. Some poor kid would have to do 'The Highwayman'. That ballad by Alfred Noyes with its seventeen verses was a yearly challenge for whichever poor drama student got the nod.

> *The wind was a torrent of darkness among the gusty trees*
> *The moon was a ghostly galleon tossed upon cloudy seas.*

The miracle was that they did it. Always attracted a good crowd too, most of whom chanted along with the student for the last two verses. Everyone over a certain age had a story about having to learn 'The Highwayman'.

There was a pub either end of Main Street, and a library, a town hall, a bank building that had been turned into an exhibition space, and at the end a couple of ATMs the rats left behind when they deserted the ship. Off on a side street there was a supermarket.

Strolling up and down Main Street was not like promenading along the banks of the Seine, thought Ruby, but it had the same expectation. Everyone said hello, mōrena, kia ora or ni hao. You were thought to be up yourself if you didn't greet people you passed with at least a nod. If you were in a car, you tooted. Porohiwi was linguistically varied but you didn't necessarily need to use words to convey message or meaning.

The upmarket women's clothes shop had gone, the bookshop, even the $2 shop. There was something both sad and heroic about towns like this, thought Ruby. They didn't know whether they were waving or drowning.

She checked to the right. Shayne's Music was still there, thank god. All was okay in Porohiwi then. Shayne had inherited the business from his father. That he kept it going was down to Shayne and his wife, Maria. Miracle workers. Must pop in and say hello, thank them, she thought. They'd played all the old songs at Kate's wake. Kristina and her cousin, Matiu, and Jake and his sister Sophie, had got up first, danced, then when the music stopped, separated and each asked someone else to dance. This had gone on until the whole room was up and dancing. Kate would have been so pleased.

Ruby decided she'd go in and see Shayne and Maria tomorrow. No, not tomorrow. Tomorrow was Saturday. She had to start organising work on the garden and it was second night of the play. She'd pop into the music shop on Monday, buy a pie for her lunch on the way back. Steve Martin stocked great pies. Perhaps not quite as good as the lamb shank pies from that shop in the south of the South Island but close.

Oscar stopped because the car in front stopped. Over on the footpath was a large sign. Porohiwi was big on signs. Someone from the car in front shouted, 'You there – *mate*.'

The young Māori guy, track pants, black hoodie, turned, frowned. Roly. Kristina's nephew. Jeepers, thought Ruby. Last week he was a tall bony teenager playing Romeo in the school play, now he was nearly a man. Young but definitely shoulders of an adult.

'Hold the sign up, mate?'

Roly rolled his eyes at his companions but walked across, grabbed the sign, held it up: *Ramona Kelly Circle Retirement Village Annual Market.* There was quite a queue of cars along Main Street by now. Drivers tooted. On a scale of one to ten, with ten being totally pissed off, these toots were an eight. You had to wonder why the guy in front was driving if he couldn't see a sign that large, thought Ruby.

The market was Saturday week. They had the sign out in plenty of time then. Still, if you wanted people to come to out-of-the-way Duggan Street, you had to start advertising early. It took Porohiwians a little bit of time to think about whether they'd go to the Circle Market. The retirement village was on Duggan Street. Meg lived there too.

At the bottom of the sign it said: *Tarot, tea leaves, palm-reading, all questions answered.*

'Well there's a claim,' said Ruby. 'Maybe I should go to the market and ask them who the apartment trasher is? And who my parents are, while I'm at it.'

'You believe in that stuff?' Oscar looked amused rather than sceptical.

She told him about Ramona and how when *The Spirit Soars* hit the bestseller list and stayed there for three weeks, Ramona sent her a bonus. The only one of her clients ever to do so.

'You enjoy the work? Writing other people's lives?'

'What's not to like?' she said. 'Probably the oldest profession.'

'I thought that was prostitution,' said Rissa, watching Roly.

'Who wrote the Gospels? I bet Paul's letter to the Corinthians wasn't penned by Paul. The books in the Old Testament? The *Odyssey*? Who knows? And what about all the monks who wrote screeds and it was passed off as the prior's or the lord of the manor's work? The prime minister doesn't write all her own speeches. Neither does the queen. And China? The wise men who were supposed to be writing all those wise thoughts would definitely not have actually *written* them.'

'The Magna Carta?' Rissa smiled. 'Is that suspect too?'

'Why not? Ghost writers have been around forever. Gertrude Stein is probably our most famous, although she ruined it by putting her name on *The Autobiography of Alice B*. So probably not strictly a ghost writer.'

Oscar looked behind them. The queue of cars now trailed along out of sight down Grace Road.

'Only pays around the same as waitressing but I don't have to deal with drunks. And it suits me. I like being my own boss.'

Oscar smiled.

You'll get yours, she thought. Then remembered her stupid, stupid words. Over, she told herself, *over.*

Roly put the sign down, went to stroll back to his mates, saw Ruby, gave a flick of recognition, no smile of course, wouldn't be cool, then he saw Rissa.

'Babe.' He was smiling now. Rissa rolled her window down.

'Fuck *babe*,' said Rissa.

'Sorry,' said Roly. 'Sorry. *Rissa*. Coffee?'

'Cool,' said Rissa. She got out of the car. 'Pick me up on the way back, Uncle?'

'I'll toot,' said Oscar, 'but I'm not waiting. Have to get the hedge finished.'

'Bye, Ruby,' said Rissa, 'see you tonight.'

And she and Roly went off down the footpath and into the Mimosa Café. *Interesting.*

'You've got something in your bag.' Oscar looked like he'd made up his mind that this had to be said. 'Something that's not a laptop or a wallet. Something that I suspect whoever trashed your apartment wants. What is it?'

Ruby thought for a moment. Decided. 'Betty's book,' she said, 'but no one knows about that except me and Kristina. And now you.'

'Betty's book?'

Ruby sighed. This is what happens. You answer one question and it's never enough.

Karl made a little breathy sound and wagged his tail.

'It's all right, boy,' she said.

'If anything happens what am I supposed to say to Mark James? Or to myself?'

'Nothing will happen,' said Ruby. 'No one else knows about the book.'

Oscar looked unconvinced.

'Just give me a week,' said Ruby.

'What difference will a week make?'

'Jesus,' said Ruby, 'and they say women nag. If Stace finds some names and one or two of them agree to talk to me it's just possible they might know something about my parents. If I tell Mark James now he'll go off on a tangent, and no one will talk to me if there's a cop hanging around. And anyway, *as I said*, no one but me and Kristina, and now you, knows that a notebook even exists.'

'So how do you explain the assault and the trashing?'

Ruby tried again. 'Betty gave me the notebook thirty years ago. Only she and I knew about it. Then Kate. Been among Kate's papers at the lawyer's in an envelope with my name on it since the day after I hid in her woodshed.' Ruby swallowed.

'What's in the notebook?'

'What is this? The inquisition?' She watched a man instructing a little boy, who was sitting on one of those learner bikes with extra wheels on the back.

'Lines of playing-card symbols.' And that's it, she thought. All I'm going to say.

'Lines of hearts, diamonds, spades and hearts?'

'Yes.'

'And you've asked Stace to find the card players?'

'No. I've asked Stace to try and trace some *staff*. In the hope that one of them might have been there when I was left at the door. But if I get the chance I'll ask them about the card players.'

And then I'll find the bastards and face them with what they did to Betty.

Oscar turned in to the older part of town. She didn't think he was happy with her reply, but tough.

Why the hell had she been so stupid when he woke her up?

♠

Oscar drove down Bethell Street. You can smell the sea from here, thought Ruby. Mrs O'Rourke was out in her garden bent over like a croquet hoop. Ruby waved but she didn't look up. She would ring and make an appointment to interview her about the theatre.

'What's this thing with Door?' Ruby said to Oscar. 'He asked me to write the Segar family history and I said no. So now I can't have access to the Swan collection for the Players history, is that it?'

'Be a good contract. We'd pay well.'

'We? So you're in on it too?'

'Door suggested the family history. He suggested you write it. You said you didn't want to. End of story.'

'Then you all agreed to use a little blackmail to make me do it?'

'Of course not.' He looked irritated. 'A separate matter. We all have to agree to anyone seeing the collection. Door didn't.'

Ruby wondered what game Door was playing and why neither Oscar or Juno had stopped him. Why should he have everything his own way? Although obviously Oscar's brother had not had *everything* his own way. He and Josie had met on the school bus when they were thirteen. They married at twenty, had the twins, led a charmed life and then Josie got sick, and nothing Door could do stopped the inevitable. His siblings had been unable to do anything to make the pain any less. Three years since Josie died. It had been hard on fifteen-year-old Rissa and Jess but they seemed okay now.

Seemed is a good word, she thought, everyone, including me, *seems* okay but I'm not really so they're probably not either. But whether she'd agreed to write the Segar history or not should have no bearing on whether she could see the Porohiwi Players collection owned by the Segars.

'In fact you don't need anyone's permission to view the collection,' said Oscar, staring straight ahead. 'We're still legally married so you're a member of the family, which means you can check, search, spend time, make notes, whatever you need, at any time.'

'Is that a worry?'

'What?'

'That I haven't gone for a divorce.'

'I haven't either,' he said. 'Laziness.'

She had to smile. 'Same. But you knew if you'd wanted one I'd have said yes?'

'Yep,' he said. 'I knew that.'

There was a little silence, then he said, 'I'll give you a spare key to the house so you can come and go as you like. You know your way around the kitchen if you want coffee or anything.'

'What about Door?'

'He'll live.'

From the backseat Karl sighed heavily.

12

'Child, you know how anxious your guardian is that you should improve yourself in every way.'

It was the end of May and in spite of the chilly rain and wind, the Porohiwi gardens weren't looking too bad. As they drove Ruby could see a few heart-lifting flashes of yellow here and there. Those who'd planted their bulbs in pots or gardens a few years ago and then left them to do what they willed were reaping their annual reward. Bulbs liked being undisturbed. She'd stick some in pots for Meg, Ruby decided, add to the perfumes she planned.

Over some of the fences, one or two clumps of small pale pink buds. Cécile Brünner. Once established they always flowered early and long. When they were in bud and flower, you could see why the settlers' wives had grown them. Not only were they attractive but they grew easily from slips which is why they survived. If Ruby got closer she'd probably see little pinky-red tips on all of them. One day Meg's garden would flourish like these – once Ruby got the chainsaw to it.

Some gardens had lots of native plants. Mānuka, harakeke, kōwhai, probably ferns she couldn't see. Good for birds. Down this end of town there was more evidence of gardening. Hardly a place that wasn't over sixty years old, most were older. This was the desirable part of Porohiwi, if you couldn't live on the Other Side that is. Some of these houses were set right back from the road, down long driveways, tree-lined. Some had been in a family for at least three generations. You couldn't see them, but you knew they were there. Some houses looked like they'd been done up by new owners, but only in the best possible taste, according to the real estate ads. Insulated, new kitchens, new bathrooms, terraces added, glazed windows, woodburners had replaced open fires … but they'd very wisely left the roses.

Which made her think of Olga and the Segar roses.

Lady Fate must have laughed herself silly when she saw that Oscar was with Kristina during last night's attack at the Home, and that he was the one who gave Ruby a ride into town after Juno did the work on her face. In fact Lady Fate had enjoyed a fair few laughs at Ruby's and Oscar's expense.

◆

'You'll go to the Combined Schools Dance,' Kate had decreed. 'You need to learn some social graces.'

'It's a patriarchal plot,' Ruby said, fresh from reading *The Female Eunuch*.

'Jesus,' said Marlon, 'she's fifteen. Where will it end?'

Ruby wore a cream dress and silver sandals.

'Your dress looks beautiful,' said Kate, 'and so would you if you'd stop scowling.'

The Porohiwi College Hall was gleaming from the efforts of the parents' working bee, determined that no student from St Joseph's School for Boys or St Mary's School for Girls would be able to say that Porohiwi College parents weren't proud of their school. Those who weren't part of the clean-up had been blackmailed into providing supper. Those who complained were told it only happened every three years, so suck it up.

Students were lectured for weeks about the necessity of best behaviour. Mr Hartley didn't actually say why. He didn't need to. The St Joseph's and St Mary's opinion of Porohiwi College was not that high.

'They count on beads when they're praying,' Kristina said, 'so they won't lose their place.'

They were fifteen. They knew everything.

Porohiwi College might be a drag but at least all kinds of students were welcome. Any religion, even those who said, 'Blessings,' and kissed you on the forehead if they met you up the street and you couldn't dodge quickly enough. Or those who had no religious beliefs at all.

Kristina and Ruby sneaked a look in the supper room at the laden tables. Ruby nipped in, grabbed two lamingtons, and they scoffed them instantly. Then they sat down on one of the seats along the wall of the hall. When the band launched into 'Blueberry Hill', which had been popular about a century ago, it confirmed Ruby's worst fears. Kristina's whānau loved it and had taught her to dance to it – she knew all the words too – but that didn't make it any less of a blah at a school dance.

The boys from St Joseph's marched across the floor like they were the NZ Second Expeditionary Force advancing on El Alamein.

'Lost the toss,' muttered Kristina, when she saw two boys heading their way.

Someone had told someone that their older sister had been told by someone that the St Joseph's boys would motor through the Porohiwi girls first so they were free to launch themselves at the St Mary's girls. They'd seen them on the buses under the eagle supervision of a teacher but been unable to make more than eye contact. The dance gave them a chance to approach the girl of their choice and organise a way to exchange more than just a glance.

They'd set their targets but first they had to ask the Porohiwi girls to dance. Father Francis had decreed it. Those who were late staking a claim to a particular girl had to toss a coin, and the losers had to choose from the girls no one else wanted.

'There are two strikes against us,' said Kristina. 'We're too tall and, quoting Mum, we've both got too much to say for ourselves.'

A tall thin boy, suit trousers already down at his hips and half his shirt hanging out, fair riotously curly hair, blue eyes wary, stopped in front of Ruby, recognised her, lost the prepared greeting, settled for, 'You wanna dance?'

At that same moment she recognised him. This was the boy whose mother had threatened to ring the cops during the ditch-smoking episode. No doubt he was thinking, this was the girl adopted by a *lesbian* who *allowed* the girl to *smoke*.

If she hadn't been scared of Kate's wrath Ruby would have said no and walked home, but she shrugged and said, 'I guess.'

Not the most enthusiastic of answers. He stopped looking wary and started looking like he'd heard a fire alarm in the next room.

Ruby stood up. He put his left arm round her waist and held her right hand up high like he was pronouncing her Champion of World Wrestling. Then he began a kind of skating motion around the floor. He took long strides, and she had to keep up by taking little skips backwards so she wasn't trampled into the floorboards. She was furious. She should never have given in to Kate. Who cared about social graces?

'Read any good books lately?'

'What?'

He looked even more alarmed. Was she *deaf?* 'Read. Any. Good. Books. Lately?'

'*The Female Eunuch*,' she said, and he missed a step. 'I'm a feminist,' she added.

He missed another step and she could almost see the words 'Holy shit' coming out of his mouth in one of those balloons. She felt very pleased.

He steered her a few more steps while he gave his predicament some serious thought. Had another try. 'Play sport?' he said.

'I hate all sport,' said Ruby, 'especially rugby and boxing.' These were the two sports St Joseph's boys excelled at, won cups for. 'I only play cards.'

His eyebrows shot up. 'Which game?'

'Euchre.'

'You any good?'

She looked at him. She was able to do this quite easily because she was tall and he was only slightly taller. Lightning bolts flashed from her eyes. 'Are you?' she said.

'Won the junior championship two weeks ago,' he said and immediately went scarlet. No boasting, no moaning. He'd just broken this rule.

'Huh,' she said, thinking if you can, I can. 'That's just kids. I won at the marae against a senior last Sunday night.'

'*Liar*,' he said, 'they don't let kids play against seniors.' And he smiled, a superior smile that seemed to be saying this is exactly what you can expect from Porohiwi College students.

A splash of red stars appeared in front of Ruby's eyes. She wrenched her right hand out of his and slapped him across the face. 'Don't you dare call me a liar, you stuck-up Catholic *skite*,' she shouted.

He yelled and put his hand up to his eye, which seemed to be swelling as she looked at it. Ruby didn't care. Who the hell did he think he was?

The music stopped. Everyone stared. Father Francis and Mr Hartley must have flown from wherever they'd been standing. They were right beside Ruby, faces carefully impassive, knowing all eyes were on them to see what they would do.

'The office,' said Mr Hartley.

She kept her head down, didn't dare look in Kristina's direction, but heard clearly the delighted gasps from the other students. This had lifted the dreary Combined Schools Dance out of its relegation to the most boring social occasion of the year to a place right at the top of the events tree. Those who'd managed to persuade their parents to let them stay home would never forgive themselves.

In no time, Kate (jeans, red jersey, striped scarf, ankle boots), and Marlon (stylish jeans, black jersey, Doc Martins), swept into the office quickly followed by the boy's parents: Olga (stylish black dress, high-heels) and Robert Segar (jeans and jersey, track shoes).

'Oscar,' cried the woman and embraced her son.

The only Oscar Ruby knew was Oscar Peterson, the best jazz pianist ever, according to Marlon. Privately Ruby thought that Oscar Peterson played the kind of music where the listener sat and waited for something to happen and it never did. It took a few years before she recognised the subtlety and imagination at work when Peterson played.

The two women nodded at each other, Robert and Marlon grinned then stopped, conscious that Kate and Olga's eyes were on them. They all sat in the chairs indicated by Mr Hartley, and waited. Kate was best at it. She sat quite still with an interested look on her face. Olga held the cross on the chain and put it against her lips, which Ruby knew Kate would see as very bad overacting.

Marlon looked up at the ceiling and Robert stared at the floor. Oscar looked straight ahead and Father Francis was definitely praying. Mr Hartley described the 'incident' and said that Ruby had refused to explain her behaviour. Then he looked at Kate who didn't muck around.

'Why?' she said.

Ruby took a deep breath and went for it. 'He asked me if I'd read any good books lately and I said *The Female Eunuch* and he said did I play sport and I said no I played euchre and he asked was I any good and skited that he'd won the junior trophy for euchre and I said that was nothing I'd won against a senior at the marae and he said I was a liar so I hit him.'

Marlon's hand came up and covered his mouth. He looked like he was dying to laugh but knew Kate would kill him if he did. He didn't look at Robert whose lips were firmly clamped and who had moved his gaze to the ceiling.

'*Oscar?*' Olga's voice was throbbing with fury and disbelief.

Oscar looked at the floor and mumbled, 'They don't let kids play against the seniors.'

There was a brief silence, then Robert's head came down, he cleared his throat, looked at his son. 'You *boasted* about winning the junior? Then you called this young woman a *liar?*'

He got up, marched across the room and held out his hand to Ruby, who was so aghast she took it.

'Congratulations,' Robert said, 'you must have played well, they're gun players.'

'A fluke,' said Kate, 'but yes – she played well.'

'You taught her?'

'Me and a friend,' said Kate, which was true, because Daisy had spent as much time teaching Ruby as Kate had.

Ruby now felt bad. Really bad. And worse, she knew she was going to cry. She stared straight ahead and said, 'I'm very sorry, Father Francis and Mr Hartley. I behaved badly and I won't do that again. I'm sorry, Mr and Mrs Segar. I'm sorry, Kate and Marlon. Sorry you all had to come out because of my actions, and I won't do it again.' This was the hard part. She took a deep breath. 'I'm sorry, Oscar. I lost my temper and I hope it doesn't hurt too much and that you'll forgive me.' She didn't add anything about not doing it again because she was never going to see him again. She would sooner walk naked up Main Street.

Oscar remained silent. She didn't blame him. Keeping his mouth shut was definitely the best option.

Ruby walked out of the office, across the passage and out into the cool night air. Kate's car was out front on the no-parking zone. Ruby stood in the shadows on the other side of the car and cried. 'Fuck social graces,' she sobbed.

She was a slow learner though.

Her eighteenth birthday. July 1999. Kristina and two other flatmates. It was all organised. A couple of beers at a pub on Cuba Street, before they caught the bus to Porohiwi for a birthday dinner. She'd just lifted a glass of beer to her lips when someone behind her said, 'Read any good books lately?'

She swivelled round. Oscar. Grinning. Beer brave. Also, it turned out, celebrating *his* eighteenth.

'Want a game?' he said. 'Bet you I win.'

So she went back to his hostel and played euchre. He said he'd be happy to play any game she chose – smartarse, she thought – so she chose euchre because that was one she was best at. She won the first game, he the second. Naturally they had to play a decider.

Oscar was expected in Porohiwi for dinner. Ruby was expected home for dinner too. Neither of them got there. Ruby had enough sense to ring home straight away. Kate was annoyed but philosophical, and definitely didn't want Oscar driving her in his old banger.

Oscar rang Olga, who was furious. And when she understood that they'd drunk half the bottle of the crab apple liqueur she'd made especially for Oscar's birthday, it was strike three as far as Ruby was concerned. Obviously the girl had *lured* poor Oscar into behaving like this. Ruby never knew what Robert said but all Marlon said, according to Kate, was, 'Eighteen. What do you expect?'

They didn't finish the third game because lust intervened. Ruby might have had one too many crab apple liqueurs but she still had enough sense left to say, 'You got a condom?'

'Six packets,' said Oscar. 'Happy birthday.'

♥

Ruby looked out the window and smiled. They'd been so *young*. She wondered what Lady Fate had in store for Rissa and Roly.

'Something funny?' said Oscar.

'Just thinking about fate,' she said.

13

'I don't think that you should tell me that you love me wildly, passionately, devotedly, hopelessly. Hopelessly doesn't seem to make much sense, does it?'

Oscar indicated right, and there was the river, wide as an expressway in parts, deep as Mount Taranaki in others. Two boys were throwing a stick for a dog to fetch. Ruby knew who'd get sick of that first and it wasn't the dog.

'Got time for a stroll?' said Oscar. 'I haven't said hello properly to the river yet.'

'Cool.'

He pulled the car over, and Ruby got out slowly, stretched her legs. They weren't too bad but sitting made them stiffen up. A walk would be good.

The waters were clean, the rain yesterday hadn't been strong enough to push any unwelcome silt down the current. When you got to ten years old swimming across the river was the focus of every kid's dream. Once you were old enough to swim that river, you considered yourself, and were considered by the other kids, as having crossed a line. You were not a little kid any more. Little kids didn't swim across that river. Only big kids did.

Every year parents said, 'Don't go swimming across that river. The current's dangerous.' And every year those sons and daughters did exactly what their parents had done when they were young – ignored the grown-up's warnings and swam across the river. Ruby and Kristina were not the first girls to sneak out at midnight and do it, but the exhilaration remained a bubbly and lasting high.

'Do you know anything about your parents?' said Oscar, 'Anything at all?'

In the middle of the water a boy was rolling a log. Arms outstretched he moved the log with his feet, maintaining balance with the kind of casual grace that said this wasn't the first time he'd done it.

'No,' she said. 'Only suppositions.'

'Suppositions?'

Ruby hesitated then thought *what the hell.* 'The Home's in Porohiwi, which suggests a local. Maybe someone on foot? Or someone who parked on the public road down at the end of the drive – walked up to the back door? Wellington was over an hour away then, other places on the coast were closer but the odds are in favour of a local.

'I could go round asking if anyone remembers seeing a girl in 1980–81 who looked pregnant but didn't have a baby. I'm not putting that out into the ether, though. The most likely explanation is that I'm the result of an encounter at a drunken party, or an affair which went wrong, maybe one of them was married to someone else? Could have been rape? Or worse, incest? Any number of possibilities. Most of them bad. And then the other question – which one was Māori?'

Ruby knew she sounded like she was reeling off these surmises as though there was no personal connection, but she'd decided a long time ago there was no sense in showing anger, hurt or outrage. To someone like Oscar who'd known not only his parents but had either known, been told or heard about the generations of Segars who'd lived in the same big house before him, her situation was incomprehensible. Or Kristina, whose whakapapa went back forever. To them the idea of not knowing where you came from was an unfathomable concept.

'Are you worried about what you'll find?'

'My situation is what it is,' said Ruby, and she meant it. She wanted neither pity about the past nor protection from the future. 'I'll find them or I won't.' Her tone said it wouldn't be a big deal either way.

'Some records haven't been computerised.'

They watched the boy roll the log to the bank where another boy waited. This was the tricky part where the boy on the log had to slide off and his mate had to manoeuvre his way on without falling in.

Oscar's voice was carefully casual. 'I could look them up? Might be something in the old Social Security records? Not that they'd let you see them without a lot of barriers. You'd have to get the ombudsman to intervene and that always takes time. Still, might be worth a try. Or Archives? On microfiche probably, which is a pain, but might be worth it?'

They walked along the path worn by the feet of generations into two uneven tracks. The willows and the taller poplars, some of them dating back to those first Pākehā settler plantings, had lost their leaves a month or so ago and sunlight showed little knobs that would soon become buds that would soon become leaves.

Ruby ignored his offer, and asked the question that had been on her mind since Oscar's father died. 'Will you really sell the *Star*?' Sounded peremptory but couldn't be helped.

'Why? You want to buy it?'

'You'll sell it. *Jesus*.'

'It's losing money. I've never run a business. I've always worked with or for someone, occasionally for myself. I'm not sure I want the responsibility of a monthly newspaper. The responsibility of other people.'

'Community newspapers are really important.'

'Don't people rely on TV or online news?'

'None of them do community news. People like to know what's going on where they live.'

'Do they? Rissa and Jess don't read it. Door sometimes.'

'Rissa and Jess are eighteen,' said Ruby. 'Door lives mainly in Wellington. Go up Main Street, ask people there. Where else do they get college news, and rugby, soccer, athletics results. Garden Club, the library book group? You go into Mimosa the morning the *Star* comes out and no one is talking. They're sitting, heads down, reading the paper. It's how they keep up with themselves. School fairs, church stalls, sports sausage sizzles – they're all there. The *Star* is the only link without strings. It has no axe to grind, it simply reflects the community back to itself. And the community likes that.'

'You sound like you think it's a public duty,' said Oscar.

'Robert said there were times when he wanted out and there were times when he knew he was in exactly the right job.'

'When did Dad say that?'

Damn. Why didn't I keep my big mouth shut?

'The last time we met for coffee.'

'You met for coffee?'

'He'd ring me occasionally and suggest … coffee. I liked him.'

'So did I,' said Oscar.

'He loved you,' said Ruby. 'I know he did because he told me.'

Oscar was silent.

'If you do decide to sell …' she said, pausing to watch as the second boy managed to get himself upright on the log without falling in. His mate was swimming around giving instructions. Perhaps it was the first time the boy had rolled logs? Keeping her eyes on them, she said carefully, 'Robert would understand, but would you?'

'Dad knew I might not carry it on. He said to do what was right for me.'

He sounded defensive. Ruby knew he'd worked as a paper boy, hung around his father's workroom after school, aware there were times he could play around with paper and pencils and other times when he had to sit and read and not say a word. He would have seen something but not much of the transition from big machines to computers, from the smell of hot lead and linotypes to one room, a long desk and a mess of copy waiting. He would know the design programmes and how to work them.

She thought what was really worrying him wasn't how much he already knew about the *Star* but more what he didn't know. And how he'd manage living and working in Porohiwi.

Like rolling logs, thought Ruby. You're scared, but if you want to do it you do it.

It had been a blast for her and Kristina talking with Robert about which direction the paper could go. 'Just say anything that comes into your head,' he'd said, 'doesn't matter how way out, whether it makes sense or not, whether you think I'd like it or not.'

As Ruby and Oscar walked back to the car and climbed in, she thought about how Robert had written it all down. Everything they'd talked about. Thanked them. Looked happy. No doubt put it on one of his piles of papers to consider when the time was right. He was the messiest man ever but he knew where everything was. Then a couple of days later Kristina rang to say she'd heard Oscar's dad had died.

And Ruby drove out to Kristina's and they had a little private wake for Robert Segar, a man they'd both liked.

'Did he ever say anything to you about me and Oscar?' Ruby asked Kristina.

'No,' said Kristina, 'but he was very fond of you. He told me.'

Now Oscar was driving Ruby along Duggan. The street was divided into three large blocks which were criss-crossed by skinny side roads. On the first block on the left were some mean grey boxes called pensioner flats, built as far away from the bus stop and the shops as they could get. The people who lived in them had done their best. Little gardens edged with pansy seedlings just about to take off and become clumps. Geraniums poked through or hung over fences, neat little lawns. An array of pots of succulents around the front door. She supposed the occupants felt lucky the council had not sold off their housing for older people.

Past this little straggle were old houses behind hedges. Some of the hedges were smartly clipped and the houses well cared for, others needed a paint and some maintenance. One of the cared-for houses and sections, number 12, was Bax Tallison's. His mother lived in a small house on the same property. The other gardens looked like their owners had given up the unequal battle with the weeds. Sore backs, sore legs, sore everything.

And here was the Ramona Kelly Circle Retirement Village that covered the whole block. The Circle looked like it should have been called Paremoremo or Alcatraz but the people who lived there loved it. There was one large building, three storeys, plaster exterior. It was surrounded by a circle of small houses crammed against each other round the large house, like pāua clinging to a rock. There was another stretch of houses opposite those. All the windows looked into other windows. The retirement village block stretched from Duggan Street across to a scraggy-looking reserve and then down to the stony beach that edged this part of the river. There was a ramp with a wooden rail sloping gently down to a boardwalk so anyone who wanted to get closer to the water would be safe.

Ramona said it was good for the inhabitants to walk alongside water. Good for their inner peace. Contact with the earth, even the part of it that grew flowers, was to be avoided. Ramona bought this block because it was near water. Not close but close enough. It didn't seem to be an issue to her that further along Duggan there was a dangerous bar between river and sea. The people who bought a home at the Circle were unlikely to be interested in swimming or boating, she said, but everyone liked to look at water. Spirits, Ramona said, like to float over water.

Which sounded lovely but made Ruby wonder how the spirits coped with the changing nature of the Porohiwi bar. It might be out of sight around the bend but when she was a kid it had fascinated her. In those days, when she and Kate went to Meg's, and after she'd said hello and endured Meg's grilling about schoolwork, Ruby would go for a walk either around the corner to the bar or down Devanny Road to look at the river.

'Don't get over the fence,' Kate always said, and Ruby always said, 'Okay,' and always got over the fence. Those who lived in the four baches on the beach a little further along had to park up on the road and walk down to their bach over the shingle. Which reminded her – how was Hortense managing? They were both in the same boat. Suddenly homeless. Must ask Daisy, thought Ruby. Daisy had known Hortense's mother, the drunken violent woman who'd made her daughter's life a misery before she died suddenly at fifty. It was not easy being a teenager at college when your mother sold sex on the street for money to buy booze.

Sometimes the river flowed into the sea, no trouble, sometimes the sea flowed back into the river, like an old friend greeting another, but other times they clashed like two large frustrated taniwha each wanting the same piece of crab. The river heaved and bashed, butted and crashed against the sea, which thrashed and kicked, wrestled and heaved back.

Adults talked about boats that were out, hoped the fishermen or boaties would not try to get home, would leave it till the storm settled. There'd been many lives lost in the early days when boats and communications were less certain and skippers had less knowledge and therefore less skill with this particular bar. The Porohiwi bar was famous. Or infamous. Depended on your experience.

Over the years the unlucky ones were mangled by the bar and then flung out along the coast. How those four old baches had survived was a miracle but at least one of them must be liveable because Fritter was living in it. Great fishing on a fine day though.

The Circle residents would not be encouraged to venture around to the bar or even onto the boardwalk on a bad day. Ruby wasn't sure about the spirits, but she thought any that hung around there had to be hardy. Ruby had played Madame Arcati in *Blithe Spirit* in a school production and helped Ramona write her life story, but neither of these experiences had converted her to a belief in spirits. Even though Ramona sent that bonus.

Ramona Kelly had made a reasonable living as a medium and had the good luck to be the only child of John Kelly, who'd made a fortune in building houses. According to the kindly parishioners of the local churches, Ramona was as crazy as a coot. So when she decided to invest her fortune in building a retirement village for those who appreciated spiritualism, their worst fears were realised.

Ramona's vision was that here in their old age people who believed could indulge in Ouija boards, cards, crystal globes, could contact spirits, whatever, and be content in the knowledge that no one would mock or jeer at them. They would be, perhaps for the first time in their lives, among their own.

Oscar parked the Hilux outside Meg's place behind the large red monster of a truck with a big SweetAz Real Estate sign on the side.

'Could I see Betty's notebook?' said Oscar.

It never ends. Did she want anyone else to see Betty's book? Read the story that was there. Did it matter? You had to know what Betty had said to know the real story. To anyone else the lines of hearts, diamonds, clubs and spades would just be a record of card games, the surface story. Oscar was bright at codes and puzzles, but even he wouldn't know the real meaning because he didn't know what Betty had said. Only Ruby knew.

She fished in her bag for the red-wrapped package. Handed it to him. Waited while he carefully extracted the notebook, looked at the one page that was written on, at the lines. Each line had four symbols with an equal sign followed by one of the symbols. There were twelve lines.

She looked out the window while he worked out the story. Didn't take long.

'Okay to take a photo?'

She sighed. 'Okay.'

She'd taken a photo on her old phone too. Just in case. And now it was lying in those damn bushes, wrecked. She wished she hadn't told Oscar about the notebook.

'So this is a record of weekly card games over three months?' he said.

'Yes – 1988. Stopped in July. Betty died on the twenty-seventh, the Sunday. Just over a week after my birthday.'

Betty had taken Ruby over the other side of the stream and they'd sat behind the blackberry bush and Betty had sung happy birthday and then said, 'Shut your eyes and hold out your hand,' and when Ruby did, she dropped a Mintie into her palm. Ruby wanted to share the sweet, but Betty shook her head.

'Your birthday,' she said, 'your treat.' And for a few glorious moments as Ruby sucked, the world became good.

'So,' said Oscar, 'each line represents a game or games and then the equal sign and then the overall winner for that night. Four players. Right?'

'Saturday nights,' she said.

He waited a moment but she said nothing.

'So why is the book so special? Why don't you want to show it to Mark James?'

She didn't answer. She didn't want to lie to him but she would if it came to the wire. For the moment silence would do.

'I'm wondering what they played for,' he said. 'Do you know? Did Betty say?'

Fuck. Trust Oscar. He was too damn clever by half. Or maybe it was the obvious question? She supposed it was. She felt the sour wash of saliva rising in her mouth. She should never have shown him the book. She didn't need anyone else barging in. She would find those men and they would be outed. She would see that they paid.

'Ruby?'

She grabbed the notebook and the scarf, got out of the car. 'Thanks for the lift,' she said.

She saw his lips tighten over his impulse to persist, his decision not to.

'What time do you want to be picked up tonight?' He saw her hesitation. 'I have to come down anyway.'

So she said, 'Ten to six?'

Oscar nodded, turned the car around and drove off.

14

'Never met such a Gorgon ... I don't really know what a Gorgon is like, but I am quite sure that Lady Bracknell is one.'

She looked away from the perfectly maintained houses on the right and towards the big old villa on the left. It stood on its own on one corner of the large block of land, surrounded by the mess she'd been stupid enough to say she'd clean up. If there was one kind of house she disliked and would never consider living in, it was the old villa. The most popular house for moneyed people in New Zealand from the 1880s to probably the thirties, it was sent away with a flick in its ear by the bungalow. Well, not quite. Large and draughty the villa lived on as a haven for students or for anyone with the will and the money to capture the style these villas once had and make them beautiful again.

She knew all about villas from the harsh experience of living in one with three other girls for two years in Wellington. It had cost a fortune to heat and she never got warm. The ratio of cold air to slightly warmer air was too great for the warmed air to survive. Each room had one power point, usually low down on the wall by the door. Which meant they needed an extra cord if they wanted to use a lamp on the desk. If you shared the room and you used a bar so you could both plug in a table lamp for each desk, you blew all the wiring in the house and had to ring the electrician. Again.

As for paying to have more power points put in, an electrician would have to charge you double what they charged anyone in a different kind of house because the electric wiring in these old villas was very shonky or, as the sparky put it, completely fucked. Living in a villa again was not a nice thought, but it would be a place to live until Ruby got the history written and the garden done.

Like the Ramona Kelly Circle Retirement Village block, this section with the old villa on one corner of it sloped down to the river, but here was no boardwalk, no cluster of newish buildings, no neat gardens, not even one lavender, just a mess of brown prickly branches, all that remained of what had been Kate's mother's rose gardens. Every couple of years or so Ruby got someone to hack them back but they were unstoppable.

When Kate first suggested to Ruby that she resurrect Meg's garden, she was immediately interested. She liked the idea of testing herself against the odds. Would she be able to identify the old out-of-control roses? Most, she decided. And she could always call in the big guns if she got stuck. Sophie, Kristina's mother, had grown roses for years and years and what Ruby didn't know, she would. And there was Hortense. She was pretty good too, although roses were not her favourite flower. Olga Segar had been an old rose devotee too, before her bones began to crumble. Had she been a judge even? Not that Ruby would be asking Olga for help identifying roses, or indeed for anything.

'I'm not pruning that mess,' she'd told Kate. 'If I can do the first cut with a chainsaw I'll give it go.'

'My grandmother spent a fortune and a hell of a lot of time on that garden,' said Kate. 'Meg kept it up for a while.'

The pōhutukawa tree stump looked a bit rough, thought Ruby. Clearly it had been done in a hurry. Must have been a big truck or two small ones. And not a solo job, that's for sure.

Meg's house matched the tree. It could have done with a paint and a thousand other things. She sat in her house while it crumbled around her and didn't lift a finger to stop it. It wasn't lack of money, for according to Kate her mother was comfortably off.

'She didn't get anything from the arse she was married to because he died penniless, but she had the house, her share of her parent's money, and she got her brothers' share when they died, both unmarried.'

'Were they queer?'

'No. One was a drunk who died when he drove his car into a tree, and the other roamed about and lived on weeds, and one day one of the weeds turned out to be poisonous. Shame. Mad as a snake, my uncle, but harmless.'

'So why?'

'Because she's a stubborn old fool,' said Kate. 'She'll probably tell you if you ask nicely.'

The front path should have had a sign saying 'Danger – Keep Off'. The uneven bricks were hidden under masses of red clover. Once you have red clover in your garden you know what frustration means, thought Ruby. There was a fine crop around the wooden steps going up to the verandah as well. The steps rocked a little as she walked up. The paint on the house had been white once and she assumed that at that stage the roof was red and the sills green. Kate said Meg's parents had moved in the day Meg was born. It must have looked good then.

Standing on the verandah, her back to Ruby, talking to Meg, was Corrine Sweet, one half of SweetAz Real Estate.

Corrine hadn't noticed Ruby's approach. The red clover had muffled her track shoes.

'It's a good offer, Mrs Palmer,' said Corrine, 'I'd advise you to accept it.'

'Told you,' said Meg, 'I'm not selling.'

'With the money you could buy a little place in the new complex? We could even make it part of the deal. Live very comfortably, rent and rates free, for the rest of your life, which we hope will be a long one.'

'I'm not leaving this place. I'll never sell. Piss off.'

'Mrs Palmer, you're not listening,' said Corrine.

'She's listened,' said Ruby, 'now do as you're told.'

Corrine turned and her right hand slipped into her pocket, where it stayed. She saw Ruby was holding a phone, smiled, took her hand out of her pocket and offered her card.

'Hi, Ruby,' she said, 'you been in the wars? Apologies if there's been a misunderstanding. SweetAz has been hired by the Circle Retirement Village. They said it was clear Mrs Palmer wasn't able to care for the section or the house so they hired us to make an offer on their behalf. Just helping out really. The offer stands, Mrs Palmer,' she said. 'Call me any time.'

Corrine directed a flashing smile at Meg, who was already walking away, another at Ruby, then stepped off the verandah and down the path to the red monster.

Interesting, thought Ruby. It's obvious why they want the extra land but surely the Circle could have approached Meg themselves? They're neighbours after all. I'll ask Ramona. Or even better ask the cards or a spirit at the Circle Market. They've got all the answers apparently.

Meg was wearing old corduroy trousers that had once been black, tucked into thick grey socks and brown sandals. Her red-checked shirt hung loose over a navy jersey and there was another jersey sticking out around the navy neckline. Her white hair looked like it had been cut by a drunken shearer in a hurry. Her thin face was lined, but the eyes behind her glasses were bright and keen. She might be physically deteriorating, but there was nothing wrong with Meg's brain or her determination. She had endured Kate's illness and dying without a tear, at least in public. She'd been monosyllabic at the funeral and the wake.

It was Spider who knew how to look after her when she was like that. He'd just got out of jail so while Meg stood between Ruby and Reilly at the wake, and sniffed or grunted at people who wanted to tell her what a wonderful woman her daughter was, Spider loitered by the eats table, keen to grab some whitebait fritters while they were still hot. He was entitled. He'd supplied the whitebait.

He'd taken half a dozen fritters and the same number of slices of buttered bread, a couple of lemon slices and salt and pepper. Then he'd cut everything into bite-sized pieces and gone back to Meg, offering her a fork and the plateful.

Meg had looked at him, a half smile on her face, and Spider had grinned back and made a clicking sound with his tongue.

He had a nice smile – missing a couple of teeth but you didn't really notice that after you got to know him – but was as hard as a bank manager's heart, believed in nothing and trusted no one except Meg. They'd met in 1981 on Molesworth Street marching against the Tour. Meg grabbed a cop's truncheon and in the struggle a skinny Māori guy grabbed her arm, pulled her away and ran her up Molesworth, onto Pipitea and down a drive of a large old house.

'For Christ's sake,' he said, when he got his breath back, 'don't you know cops don't like anyone else playing with their toys? And these are young cops. Scared shitless so they're lashing out.' Then he said, 'Any chance of a ride home?'

'Where do you live?' asked Meg.

'Round the corner from you,' said Spider. He was thirty-six and she was forty-five.

So Meg Palmer and Spider Porohiwi, having lived around the corner from each other all their lives, became friends. He didn't go home that night and the next day he moved his gear into Meg's place.

'Lovers?' Ruby asked Kate.

Kate had shrugged. 'What does that mean?'

Now Meg looked at Ruby's damaged face and said, 'What's the other guy look like?'

'Kia ora, Meg,' said Ruby. 'Did you get my phone message? No? Someone trashed me then trashed my apartment, so is it okay if I stay with you till I find somewhere else? The play opens tonight and plays tomorrow then it's a break till next Thursday. I'm working at the theatre during the week. So, a week or so? I can start organising the briar patch and the garden while I'm here.'

'Huh,' Meg grunted, thought for a moment. 'Suppose you could take over the back half of the house. Don't want you under my feet.'

Ruby was surprised. Coming from Meg this was almost effusive.

'I'll pay rent,' she said.

'Don't talk rubbish,' said Meg. 'Organise and cook dinner six nights – that'll do.'

'It's cold,' Ruby said, stepping inside.

'You can make yourself useful and get some wood in. That'll warm you up. If you want a cup of tea you'll have to make it.'

Meg turned and stopped, took a deep breath.

'*Christ*,' she said.

She put a hand out but wasn't quite close enough to the wall. Ruby offered an arm and Meg grabbed it. She had to. Otherwise she'd have fallen.

'Been to the doctor?'

'I don't need a doctor to tell me I've got arthritis and I've put my back out.'

'What about some Panadol?'

'Don't believe in drugs.' Meg took another step and stopped again. Took another deep breath. 'It'll pass,' she said, more to herself than Ruby.

The hall wasn't lit by anything except the light that filtered in through the dirty windows. The first big room on the left was Meg's bedroom. Should she help her to bed? She'd be better lying down. Meg made the decision.

'Couch,' she said, 'couch. Just give me a minute.'

It was a long, long minute but she was finally able to move. Ruby held her around the waist – it was easier and she didn't object. Progress was agonisingly slow and painful, but with lots of stops and starts they got to the couch and Meg almost fell on it. If there'd been another one Ruby would have fallen on it too. Sweaty stuff.

'Got a hot-water bottle?'

'Don't believe in them.'

Don't say a word.

'You need a pillow,' she said, and went through to the bedroom. It stank. She located the source of that and emptied the bucket down the toilet. The flush sounded like Niagara Falls on a bad day.

You can do this.

She filled the bucket with hot water and left it sitting in the bath. Looked under the sink for some disinfectant. *None. Deal with it later.* She ripped the pillowslip off the first pillow and opened the cupboard in the hall. Only bottles. Empty ones. The next cupboard was stuffed with towels, face cloths, pillowslips, some grey-looking sheets, more towels. She found a pillowslip, shoved the pillow into it, thought *to hell with the cold*, pushed up one of the long sash windows in the bedroom, shut the door behind her and went back into the sitting room.

She couldn't blame the Circle Retirement Village for thinking Meg wasn't managing because quite obviously she wasn't. Not surprising either that they had their eyes on this place. The perfect extension to their property. Pull down the old villa and build a new crop of houses, extend the boardwalk. The only stumbling block to this exciting and financially rewarding plan was Meg's refusal to sell.

She knew from Kate that Meg would not go into a retirement

home. Ruby could hardly blame her. There'd been more than a few reports online of ill treatment of the old, frail and disorientated being hit, pushed or left to lie in their own faeces. No one responsible was ever named publicly and often the home wasn't named either. Same old dance. To be expected, especially with state-run institutions. None of the staff who'd sexually abused, beaten and starved state wards had ever been held to account. Being a government employee, while not well paid, had its advantages.

If Ruby ever found out who those card players were she wouldn't wait for the state to bring them to justice, that's for sure.

'You been long enough,' said Meg. 'You been snooping?'

'So much beauty,' said Ruby, 'I could hardly tear myself away.'

'You got a smart mouth.'

'Have you had anything to eat? Want a cup of tea?'

Meg didn't bother to answer such a stupid question. Ruby looked at her phone and reminded herself again to get a new one. Be a waste of time putting stuff on this. First thing tomorrow she'd get online and organise it. Deliveries were pretty quick.

She went down the hall and through to the kitchen and outside, got some wood, dealt to the fire in the sitting room. Meg ignored her. There were no gloves in the kitchen so Ruby poured hot water into the sink, stuck some dish wash in, sloshed the grey rag she assumed was the dishcloth and wiped the kettle all over. Then she filled it, boiled it, tipped that lot out, filled and boiled again. This second lot was a big improvement. Teabags? There were three teabags in a tin that was made for five hundred. No hot scones, no home-made biscuits, so she made some toast, crossed fingers when she put the bread in the old toaster and shut the sides. It didn't burst into flames although there was a funny smell she decided to ignore. She put everything on a tray large enough to hold a sheep and went back to the sitting room.

'Took you long enough,' said Meg.

'Well,' said Ruby as she sat down, 'here we are. Hot buttered toast, a cup of tea and good company. What a treat.'

'I suppose you think you're funny.'

'No, I think I'm crazy.'

'I only like cold toast.'

'I can see we're going to get along just fine.'

This room, the largest room in the house with three long sash windows on the curved end, could be beautiful if it just had a clean and polish, thought Ruby. New wallpaper. Ceiling painted. Windows cleaned. The couch and chairs were covered in some fake (or maybe real?) velvet, old and a bit tatty, but the dining table and chairs, while needing attention, looked like they'd been made by someone who knew about wood. Ruby wondered how old they were. The curtains would have been reasonable too, if they'd been cleaned.

There was an oak sideboard and she knew that inside the top left drawer the cutlery nestled in rather grubby dark blue velvet grooves, and in the drawer on the right were Spider's two handguns. The drawer wasn't locked because the key had been lost many years ago.

She ate some toast. Had to admit, but only to herself, that she'd tasted better. But given the state of the toaster and that she'd had to pick out slices that didn't have any black spots on them, they were lucky to have any toast at all.

'I'll order pizza for you tonight,' she said. 'I have to be at the theatre at six. Took a couple of ducks out of the freezer for tomorrow night.'

At least she hoped that would be so. The stove matched the rest of the kitchen and she'd never cooked on it before.

'Do you know how to roast duck?' said Meg.

'Thought I'd just pour some oil over them and pray.'

'No oil,' said Meg. 'Don't believe in oil.'

'That'll be a surprise to all the olive growers in Greece.'

'Duck fat in the back of the fridge.'

That'd be the smell, thought Ruby. 'How's the port situation?'

'What are you implying?'

'I'm going to the supermarket – if you need some I'll get some.'

'Spider got me some a few weeks ago. How you going to the supermarket without a car?'

'I rang Jake.'

'Huh. What're you going to the shops for?'

'Bread, milk, you name it. And I'll call in at the medical centre. You need a commode, much better than the bucket.'

'Who do you think you are?'

'Still the sixty-four-dollar question, Meg,' said Ruby, 'and I still haven't got a clue.'

15

'Oh, before the end of the week I shall have got rid of him. I'll say he died in Paris of apoplexy.'

She opened the narrow door that said 'Players Only' and limped slowly along the badly lit passage to the dressing rooms, carrying the black trousers she'd borrowed from Stace over her arm. It was like entering a cave but the dim light at the end showed Daisy Carter, in a bright green shirt and stylish jeans, checking props. She saw Ruby, smiled, came over and hugged her.

'You okay?' Daisy said.

Ruby nodded.

'Kate'll be here somewhere,' she said, 'cheering you on.'

Ruby nodded again. Tonight was the first time since she was ten and stepping on stage as Cinderella, that Kate wouldn't be here, wouldn't send her a card saying, 'Here's looking at you, kid.'

Casablanca was Kate's favourite movie, although *The African Queen* was a close second. She'd been into old movies, so a large TV gave her lots of pleasure in those last months when indulgence was the only way to go. Ruby thought she'd probably never watch either of those movies again.

She walked along to the dressing rooms. The backstage area of the Swan looked like a small wooden box had been placed inside a larger one and they'd both been set on their sides with the open tops facing the auditorium. The smaller one was the stage and the space between the small box and the larger one was the rest of the backstage including the passageways which went right round like a U on its side. This passage allowed for exits and entrances to be placed wherever the set designer decided and for actors and backstage people to walk around behind the stage and not be seen by anyone in the auditorium.

Tonight the main entrance onto the set was from the back. The two side entrances indicated internal doors except when the indoor scene was being changed to the garden scene and then all entrances were used in a kind of slow choreographed set of movements.

'Shabby' was the word for backstage at the Swan, but like all theatres the Porohiwi Players put their patrons first, so the front of the Swan was getting most of the money they'd put aside for refurbishing. It was all thanks to Hester's hugely successful production of *As You Like It* and all the Getting to Know Shakespeare workshops she'd done for schools. Not that the renovator they'd employed had done all that much before he was fired for fucking the history writer, but Jake and Fritter had stepped up and the auditorium was starting to look smarter already – the walls and skirtings nearly all stripped back and ready for painting. Once the season of *Earnest* was over Jake and Fritter could really get into it. Ruby couldn't wait.

Reilly appeared out of nowhere, hugged her. 'Go for it,' he said. 'Bracknell's an old cow but a very funny and notable old cow. You've got her sussed.'

He was wearing a blue scarf with little butterflies all over it. It matched his blue shirt. He didn't look the slightest bit concerned that he was soon about to walk on stage and play Jack/Ernest. On the other hand Bax – their usually unflappable stage manager – looked a bit flustered. He smiled at Ruby, though, and said, 'You're the first Bracknell with a black eye. Well done.' And he hugged her and Reilly laughed.

When Ruby had texted to thank him for setting up the emergency text that had brought Kristina and Oscar running, all he said was that he was just happy that it had worked. Now he lifted a thumb to wish her well, then he and Reilly moved towards the men's dressing room. Ruby could hear them talking.

'I'm not interested,' Bax was saying, like he'd said it a few times already. 'Besides he might be straight.'

'Yes and I'm George Clooney,' said Reilly. 'He's been hanging around for weeks looking at you like you're a spaniel who needs a home. Time to take pity on him.'

'He's not the one,' said Bax.

'Bax, Bax, *Bax*,' said Reilly, 'there is no *one*, there are only possibilities. If you don't stick your toe in the water how are you going to know if it's hot or cold?'

'It's all right for you.'

'You don't understand, Bax.' Sam Markis was walking along the passage towards them. Black hair, beautiful features, like one of those sculptures of a Greek god, but at the moment a Greek god in a very bad temper dressed to play Algernon Moncrieff. 'Reilly's giving you his manifesto,' he said, 'lovers are disposable items. You should lap it up like the nice little puppy dog you are.'

Whoa, thought Ruby.

Reilly said, 'Now listen, Sam –'

'No you listen, you fucking shit,' said Sam. His face was that deep red-wine colour that dark skin becomes when its owner is angry.

Bethany, holding Miss Prism's cap, and Jane, halfway through pinning her hair up for Gwendolen, appeared at the doorway of the women's dressing room.

'You said you loved me. You think it's okay to say you love someone and then send them an email saying it's over? Like you're cancelling a lunch date or something? So – how did I rate? Ten stars? Do I get a reference?'

'I'm sorry,' said Reilly, 'I'm sorry, Sam. I messed up. It's not you, it's me.'

'Here,' said Sam. He chucked a plastic bag down on the floor. The contents flew everywhere.

'As for you,' he turned to Bax, 'you reckon if you hang around long enough he'll see your tongue's hanging out for him? Well, cheers with that.'

'That's enough.' Daisy's voice was loud and authoritative. Any early audience members might think it was a lines rehearsal.

Sam looked hard at Daisy like he wanted to say, 'What the fuck's it got to do with you?' wisely decided against it, turned and walked along the narrow passage and into the men's dressing room.

Trust actors, thought Ruby, on stage they get to say wonderful lines, off stage – you want melodrama and clichés? Here they are. Two ripped books, loose pages fluttering back to earth like doves surprised by a footstep, a T-shirt that Sam had cut into jagged pieces, and a china mug smashed by a discarded lover. Maybe Sam could trash an apartment too?

Jane Martin, her hands busy with her dark hair, nodded at Ruby. Her eyes were bright, as if tears were threatening. 'You okay?' she said.

'Bracknell now has a limp,' said Ruby, 'and a swollen face plus a black eye, but otherwise okay.'

Jane slipped back into the women's dressing room. She was wearing an old buttoned-up man's shirt and faded jeans. She'd have her dress-up clothes for later hanging up ready to wear. Which reminded Ruby of Stace's kimono. Had she left it for her? Don't be silly, she told herself. It's Stace. Of course it'll be here.

Would Jane be okay? Ruby hadn't thought to ask. She followed her into the dressing room. Jane was obviously upset about her own breakup with Ra. Should I do something? thought Ruby. Say something? She became aware that Bethany Clark was speaking.

'I had a *feeling*.' Bethany's beautiful green eyes with their long dark lashes looked soulfully up at Ruby from her seat by the mirror. She was whispering loud enough to carry, 'you know, *uneasy*. I have a *sixth sense* you know, it was *passed on* by my Scottish grandmother. There was a sort of *dark cloud* hovering over the Swan when I got here yesterday for the dress rehearsal. I didn't say anything. Well, you don't, do you?'

No, thought Ruby, especially if you've just made the whole damn thing up.

The dressing room looked great. Rissa had done a good job. The long mirror on one side of the room was spotless, and the bench in front of it was clear, except for vases of flowers in four places – one each for Ruby, Bethany, Jane and Rissa aka Lady Bracknell, Miss Prism, Gwendolen and Cecily. Someone had put the heater on so it was warm. The paint was faded and the carpet dingy but clean.

'This place is haunted,' said Bethany, staring at herself in the mirror.

Jane sat down and peered into the mirror too. Breathed. Good, thought Ruby. She'll be okay.

'A woman in a dark blue dress,' said Bethany. 'She appears at moments of great crisis. She was seen backstage in 1981, and she appeared just before the fire in the backstage area – 1988? – when all the records were burned. How are you getting on with your research?'

'Okay,' said Ruby, deciding to make no other comment whatsoever. Not one syllable.

'Must be difficult to write a history when most of the records are missing.'

Ruby was working on the assumption that the less interest she showed the more likely it was that Bethany would stop. This hadn't been successful previously but, apart from strangling her, was the only option. And Ruby knew if she started talking about the history she'd been stupid enough to sign up for, she'd explode. Although now that she had been given access to the Segar collection, life would be much easier. Forget about the history, she told herself. In about three-quarters of an hour the lights will go up and you'll step (limp) out on the stage and play one of the most loved ogres in British theatre history. Getting into any discussion about the damn history or the supposed ghost was out of the question.

'I caught a whisk of *blue* around the back of the set last night after dress rehearsal. I do hope that isn't an *omen*. Have you seen her, Ruby?'

'There are no ghosts, Bethany.' *So much for not saying anything.*

'Well, you have to be sensitive to feel the *aura*,' said Bethany. 'You're probably not sensitive to it.'

'That's me,' agreed Ruby, hanging the dress-up black trousers and shirt on a clothing rail, which held three costume changes for each of them and their clothes for later, 'made of solid brick.'

Jane turned to Ruby, her dark eyes bright with sudden laughter. Then she quickly returned to staring into the mirror, but this time the stare was Gwendolen's – cool, distant, watchful.

Stace had left the kimono. Ruby ran her hands over it. She didn't know how anyone found the patience or the time to make these gorgeous garments but she wasn't going to worry about that now.

'You are *so* lucky,' said Bethany, brushing her hair. 'I've always been sensitive. Oh, what lovely flowers. Oh, and a card. *Colin.*'

She kissed the card, beaming.

Colin and Bethany deserved each other, thought Ruby. Bethany was the admiring ditz to Colin's creepy Uriah Heep, for like Heep, Colin was always hanging about, constantly downplaying his more than adequate playing of Merriman and deferring to Ruby and Jane in a manner that made Ruby want to shout at him. Somehow he and Bethany had become close over the three months of *Earnest* rehearsals. Nice for him, three years a widower, but how could Bethany possibly like such a man? Wasn't he old enough to be her father?

'It's not easy being a *receptor*.' Ruby realised Bethany was still talking. 'But my grandmother was a receptor too. So that's how it's *passed on* ... Oh, sorry,' said Bethany. 'I do apologise.'

'For what?'

'I'm so sorry. *Truly* I didn't mean anything. I'm such a klutz. Being adopted doesn't mean you don't know about *other-world reception* does it. Silly me.'

Jane stared at Bethany like she was some strange creature from another world. Maybe she was.

'Did you hear that man on the radio?'

Would someone stop this woman? Where the hell was Hester when you needed her?

'He's been trying to talk to extraterrestrials for years and years but they don't answer. So *sad*. And he's a psychologist.'

Bethany shook her head at the folly of extraterrestrials.

Ruby sat down at her area of the mirror and decided that Hester knew a thing or two when she cast Bethany as Miss Prism. If anyone thought Oscar Wilde had gone too far in creating a character who sticks a manuscript in a pram and a baby in a handbag they would only have to meet Bethany Clark.

As if on cue, Colin popped his head around the dressing-room door. 'How are we today, Miss Prism?' His jowly face was pink with exertion.

'Darling,' Bethany breathed, and blew him a kiss.

He dipped his head and left.

Reilly walked past the door with a broom and shovel and began sweeping up the mess in the corridor. Behind him came Bradley Peters, ex-drama student of Hester's and one of the scene-changers. He was carrying a carton. Tall, dark and undeniably handsome, he leaned around the doorway.

'Drink afterwards?' he said to Jane.

She looked up, smiled. 'You don't have to,' she said.

'I know,' said Bradley, and winked. 'Hey anyone seen Bax? Can't find him anywhere.'

Where was Bax? It would be difficult if he'd walked out, thought Ruby. With three scenes, including one garden, they needed a stage manager as capable as he was to make it work. Poor guy. He'd be feeling like shit. He knew, none better, how Reilly behaved. They'd been friends for at least ten years, and nobody it seemed had noticed Bax's attraction. He was very good at being the friend. She hoped Sam hadn't wrecked that. Spoilt little rich boy, she thought, used to getting his own way, considered himself the answer to every gay man's prayer. No good Bax looking for sympathy from their director over this one. In Hester's view, if you said you'd do something, you did it, no matter how much of a drama your private life was.

Forget Bax, forget Sam, forget Reilly, think about the play. Focus.

'Forty-five minutes till show time,' called Hester. 'Elsa's here, Ruby. Come along.'

Jane and Bethany immediately went back to the mirror, and Ruby started undressing. The room was originally one long room until a few years before when someone on the committee suggested they cut it in half with a folding door, so half could be the women's dressing room and half the men's. Which allowed the room they'd used as the men's dressing room to become a space for storing everything except the flats they used to create the scenes. It worked well and no one seemed worried that conversations could be heard by everyone.

Usually there was a loud chatter of cross-talk until Hester gave the fifteen-minute call. The men talked when nervous. The women, unless you were Bethany Clark, didn't. Tonight a stark silence was all that emanated from the men's side of the folding door.

There was a faint perfume from the spray of flowers in front of Ruby's part of the mirror. Tonight the pitiless light shining down showed every scratch and gash on her face. The left side of her face looked what it was – a battered mess. The black eye was simply part of that mess. Thank god her hair would be under a hat.

Oh hell, orchids. Typical. She opened the card. *Just back from a business trip to Hawaii, missed you, all the best, see you later xx*

She hadn't really needed to look inside. If Connor Kelly was going to send her flowers it would have to be orchids, the flower whose bulb was said to represent male testicles. But the fact was she loved orchids. She might grow some in pots once she got a place.

What she needed to do was decide when she would murder Connor Kelly. God knows she'd tried everything else to make him stop. The trouble was she'd been bone tired and not able to cope with the torrent of pleading that would ensue if she said no to him. So she'd said yes. Actually she hadn't said anything, just allowed what happened to happen. And it had been fun. But.

'At some stage everyone says yes when they should say no,' Kristina said when Ruby told her. 'Part of the deal. No worries.'

She opened another card. An apricot rose on the cover. Beautiful Christophe. Looked for the signature. Hester, who hated gardening but liked roses.

Another envelope, she pulled out the card inside. Daisy.

There were some other cards too. Ruby quickly opened and skimmed. The senders were probably here tonight so she needed to be able to thank them. Kristina, the committee, Ramona. She smiled, picked up the apricot rose again. It wasn't an old rose, but maybe she could bend her ideas a little and include some choice modern roses in Meg's garden? Maybe have a bed of them just as a salute to the ongoing history of roses.

'Once you're into your cossie, Ruby, please.'

Elsa, a former Porohiwi College student with large beautiful blue eyes and now a talented makeup artist to the stars of TV and film, happened to be in Porohiwi, so of course Hester had called her in to check Ruby's makeup.

Ruby put the other cards down unopened. She took off her shoes, jeans and jersey, and went over to the rail where her costume was hanging. For the first act she was wearing a tailored blue jacket over a white frothy top, a darker blue skirt with a light train, a blue hat with feathers, a small purse hanging from her left arm, and brown boots.

She reached for the hanger, pulled it out, said, 'Oh *fuck*.'

The jacket had been cut into ribbons that fluttered from the shoulder seams as she held the hanger out in front of her.

16

'In any case, she is a monster, without being a myth, which is rather unfair ...'

Hester's bright red curls were fizzing with annoyance. She took the hanger from Ruby's hands, said, 'Oh *Medusa*,' pulled the jacket off the hanger, held it up. 'I'll find Stace. You get into the skirt and top so Elsa can check your makeup.'

Hester was right, thought Ruby. No time to worry about the blue jacket. Get a replacement. If she could. If there was one.

Ruby's hands were shaking. Stop it, she told herself. You don't have time to panic. Act. Act like you're okay and you will be.

Bethany sighed, shook her head. 'A *sign*.'

Ruby breathed deeply. In and out.

You're okay, she told herself, you're okay. You can go to pieces later.

Jane stared straight ahead, her teeth pressed over her lower lip.

Elsa looked enquiringly at Bethany.

'I don't mean the ghost cut up the jacket herself,' said Bethany. 'I mean, her fingers couldn't hold scissors, could they? But someone had to be deeply, deeply unhappy to do something like that.'

Ruby thought they'd be even more unhappy if she or Hester got hold of them. Who the hell would grab scissors and hack up a cossie? You might just as well say who would trash an apartment or attack a woman walking in an abandoned garden.

And why destroy the jacket like this?

Why hadn't they just taken it, thrown it away somewhere – it would have had the same result?

Oh, she thought, of course – the violence is meant to upset me. But why? Ruby made herself breathe normally. Perhaps they wanted to undermine Bracknell and the success of the play? Was that the reason for the attack and the trashing of her apartment too? Was it something to do with the history she was writing?

It couldn't be one of the Porohiwi Players. Everyone out the back of the Swan was a member of the cast or a backstage worker. Not one of them would attempt to sabotage a theatre performance. Would they? Oh hell, she thought, if I can't trust the Players who can I trust?

Think about it later. Focus. You've got a performance to do.

It took time to get into the skirt and even longer to do up the buttons on the top. Her fingers seemed particularly clumsy. She was conscious that she was fumbling, that Elsa was waiting, and although she didn't betray any irritation, she was probably pushed for time. Ruby did up the last button, flung a towel around her shoulders and pinned it in front, then began her makeup. Her face was sore and she had to be careful. She was conscious of Elsa watching every move.

'Now,' Elsa said, 'let's see.' Her touch was light.

Ruby couldn't remember her first line. *Focus.*

Elsa had brought her own makeup box and after a close inspection of Ruby's face began, carefully, to smooth a little more greasepaint over it. Ruby thought Elsa could fiddle around as much as she liked but nothing was going to alter the fact that Lady Bracknell was being played by a woman who had a brown pulverised face. Not that either Hester or Elsa thought her brown face needed any special attention. It was all to do with giving her sore skin a slightly *older* appearance without causing any further hurt.

Hester had been dismissive of the naysayers who thought Ruby was too young for the role. 'Bracknell would have been forty at the most. Look, she was probably married at sixteen, had Gwendolen's brother Gerald at the latest at eighteen, so say she had Gwendolen when she was nineteen, and now Gwendolen's eighteen, so that still only makes her mother thirty-seven or maybe thirty-eight. Yes, I know they aged much quicker in those days but Elsa can fix that.'

That was before the balaclava man messed up her face. No need to worry about looking too young. The face in the mirror looked about a hundred.

'What I suggest is …' said Elsa, 'Hester, where's Hester?'

'Here.' She was breathing just a little quicker. She must have run back from seeing Stace.

'For the first act we float some net over the hat and bring it down over this cheek, tie it under the chin. Okay?'

'Brilliant,' said Hester.

'For the third act we could use this blue scarf, fold it over Ruby's head and down her cheek and tie it then pop her hat on over it. It will look like it was *meant*, if you see what I mean.'

Elsa leaned back and stared at Ruby. Frowned.

'The problem is,' she said, 'it's hard to make brown skin look old. It ages much slower than fair skin. Genetic. If you can choose your ancestors, choose from Māori, Polynesian, Asian or Jew. You're very lucky, Ruby.'

Ruby decided there was definitely something wrong with Elsa's eyesight. Had she not seen the bruises?

'Perfect,' said Hester. 'Ruby?'

'Thank you, Elsa,' said Ruby. 'Wonderful.'

Who cut up the jacket?

The truth was it had to be someone in the theatre. A stranger would have been too noticeable. It was in one piece when she left after the dress rehearsal. So between now and then someone had sneaked in and cut it up. Ruby could dismiss Jane and Reilly. Sam seemed to have got into cutting up clothes. She thought of his anger earlier. He knew she and Reilly were close friends … so maybe? No, she thought, no. All Sam's anger was directed at Reilly. His hurt was genuine and he didn't have the maturity to deal with it in private. She remembered that feeling.

Forget it. *Focus.*

Stace appeared with a jacket over her arm.

'Black,' said Stace, holding it out, 'but it'll fit.' She shook her head. 'My big scissors are missing, which means whoever did it has a key to the cossie department. Committee better check the key holders. And we need to change the locks. In the meantime if anyone attempts to get into the costumes without me, they're in for a very unpleasant surprise.'

She helped Ruby into the jacket. She and Hester stood back.

'Mmn,' said Stace. 'Not too bad. What do you think?'

Hester nodded, 'Good,' she said.

'Whoever did this needs their arse kicked,' said Stace. 'Took me ages to sew all those little buttons on that blue jacket. I'll speak to Kristina about the locks.'

'I've rung Auden,' said Hester. 'He'll sort it. He'll ring the cops.'

Hester's husband, former Senior Sergeant Porohiwi, now owner of Movers and Shakers removal firm, was often called in by locals to handle tricky issues – not all of them trusted the police, but they trusted Auden.

Elsa smiled. 'How about Ruby using a stick?' she asked Hester. 'It'd look quite in character.'

'Thought of it,' said Hester, 'or one of those parasol sticks … but I decided against it. However, things have changed. What do you think, Ruby?'

Ruby had already decided. 'I think I should,' she said, 'just in case.'

'Good,' said Hester.

'I'll get one.' Stace vanished.

Ruby turned to Elsa. 'Thanks so much. It's so good of you to come out. You probably had other plans for tonight.'

'I'll be in the audience,' said Elsa. 'Couldn't miss my favourite play. Seen some great Bracknells.'

She inspected Bethany's makeup, then Jane's, made a couple of comments, smiled at them all and went out followed by Hester and Stace.

Okay, thought Ruby, so she's seen some great Bracknells?

There was no time to muck around. Jane finished her makeup, while Bethany told them again how she'd actually *sensed* something in the air *last night*.

'I couldn't put my finger on it,' she said, 'just a strong *feeling*, or perhaps more a *foreboding*. I wish I'd said something. I've definitely inherited my grandmother's *sixth sense*. My mother used to say, "Bethany, come into the real world." She didn't understand that it's not something I asked for, although I know it's a beautiful gift. My mother said my grandmother drank, and I'm not denying she did like a little whisky with lemon before bed, but she had the *gift* and I've inherited it.'

Jane caught Ruby's eye in the mirror and quickly turned away.

'Would you like me to hear your lines?' said Bethany. 'Your nerves must be at *screaming* point. Bracknell's such a huge responsibility.'

What Ruby would have liked was for Bethany to go and jump off a tall mountain or at least get the hell out of the dressing room, but she couldn't very well say that ten minutes before the play opened. Instead she stared into the mirror as though she was thinking deeply about her makeup or her lines. Bethany moved away.

And that was when Ruby realised there were only three people in the dressing room and not four.

When she'd asked Oscar earlier where Rissa was, his lips had tightened and he'd said, 'Made other arrangements.'

'Oh?'

'Eighteen,' he said, 'you make stupid decisions at eighteen.'

Ruby looked away and said nothing, and Oscar said quickly, 'Sorry, didn't mean that to sound the way it did.'

Yes you did, Ruby thought, that's exactly how you meant it to sound. Not as stupid, though, as the decision made at twenty-one to get married, that had to be the winner in the stupidity stakes. Equalled if not beaten by her decision to write that letter he'd never ever answered.

One day she would ask him about it.

'Rissa?' Ruby mouthed to Jane.

'Roly,' Jane said, 'not tequila this time – flat tyre.'

'*Fuck.*'

One. Someone had cut up the jacket.

Two. Rissa was late. With Roly.

She knew, *everyone* knew, the story about Roly when he was playing Romeo, drinking a bottle of tequila his Juliet had stolen from her father's drinks cabinet, and their subsequent stage performance that led to their team losing the drama competition.

'Be all right on the night,' Jane said, and smiled her Gwendolen smile, full-on for people she regarded as equals, a lower wattage for lower classes and servants. She moved to the corner where she stood quite still as if she were training to be a statue. Ruby knew she was going through her lines. Jane didn't have to worry. She and Reilly were very good as Gwendolen and Jack/Ernest. Reilly would be all right – there was an unyielding side to Reilly and he wouldn't muck up his role because of Sam's drama. But he didn't forgive or forget easily. Ruby thought that's why the two of them got on so well. She had the same streak in her character. 'Keep an eye on Reilly,' Kate had told her. She'd probably told him to 'keep an eye on Ruby'.

How would Sam be in that big scene with Rissa? She'd mucked up her lines and missed a cue yesterday during the dress rehearsal, and now on opening night she was late. And the jacket had been cut to ribbons. What else would go wrong?

Nothing, she told herself, just ignore it. Ignore everything. Fix it later. Breathe.

Rissa had been a little wary of Ruby at first. Ruby supposed it was difficult for an eighteen-year-old to know how to behave around the woman who'd broken your much-loved uncle's heart. She presumed that was still the version the Segars held to. Rissa had been great this morning, though, when Ruby made such a fool of herself.

What the hell must Oscar have thought?

When she'd opened her eyes and seen his blue eyes smiling down at her, she'd flipped back in time to that awful night after he'd walked out. Her hope had been all centred around the certainty that he would come back. And bring Karl. That he'd come running to answer that stupid, *stupid* letter.

Forget it, she told herself. Life is what it is. You'll cope. Focus. Roly and Rissa will do whatever they do, Oscar will give me the key to the collection, I'll write the theatre history in five months. I was an idiot to sign the contract, thought Ruby, but I did and that's the end of it.

Focus.

'*Aaaaah rrroooo-sesss lalalalaven-dah,*' sang Bethany, who appeared to be in another world. Perhaps she was. Or maybe she was trying to connect with an extraterrestrial?

Ruby wondered where Roly and Rissa had got the flat tyre. Roly's mother always said he'd taken nine and a half months to arrive and had been late for every other appointment since.

She could hear the buzz of people coming into the theatre, finding their seats, calling out to each other, buying drinks, talking about the weather. She wished she was there with them. A large glass of red would be perfect right now.

Ronald Hugh Morrison began playing the piano.

'No relation, different spelling,' he always said whenever he met anyone who thought he might be related to the great New Zealand writer of *Scarecrow* and other dark and funny novels. Hester's father was, like his namesake, a good pianist but, unlike him, not a drunk. Dressed in his Canon Chasuble cossie, his soft playing eased its way under the chatter and clink of glasses in the auditorium.

Where the hell was Rissa?

Jojo popped her head into the room – no police uniform this time. She was in black from head to toe. Looked like a cat burglar. 'You good, Ruby?'

'Yeah, Jojo. Thanks. Maybe soften the lighting a bit so I don't look like too much of a dragon.'

'Done.'

At last Hester paused in the doorway of the dressing room, clicked her fingers. 'Five,' she said.

Nerves of steel, thought Ruby. She's seen a lot of opening nights.

She moved to the door, Jane followed her and they walked to their entrance. In her head Ruby went through the sequence of the entries onto the stage: the butler Lane, then Algernon, Jack/Ernest, Bracknell and Gwendolen.

She'd remembered her opening line but now she'd forgotten it again. Shit, what *was* it?

What was the *matter* with her?

She looked across at Jane. Pale as death.

Rissa? What would they do if she didn't turn up?

Jane dipped her head at Ruby. She was Gwendolen now. Ruby held up her thumb and the two of them stood still while the lights went down. Ronald Hugh played the intro and Garth McGrath, dressed all in black as Lane, walked out onto the stage. He looked pale and grim. Sam, a little tense, stood still and ready, waiting for his cue. Did he know that they had no Gwendolen?

Ronald Hugh looked completely at ease as well he might. All he had to do was play some offstage music on cue and then just sit peacefully in the half-dark until the scene change.

Oh god, Ruby thought, why do I do this?

Sam entered.

'Did you hear what I was playing, Lane?'

'I didn't think it polite to listen, sir.'

Reilly made his entrance. He and Algernon talked about a cigarette case, town and country, Bunburying.

Ruby's breathing quickened but she forced it to slow down. Adrenalin overload. Just breathe, she told herself. Okay. Get ready.

Shit.

Forgotten the first line again. Too late.

How long did it take to fix a tyre?

'Lady Bracknell and Miss Fairfax.'

Ruby, her knuckles white around the stick, limped on into the light.

17

'Thirty-five is a very attractive age.'

They took three curtain calls, which was pretty good for a Porohiwi first night.

'Sorry, sorry, sorry,' Rissa hissed to the cast the moment the lights went down.

Then Hester walked out and everyone in the auditorium stood up and went crazy. Ruby knew what they were thinking. Here was this woman, little dot of a thing, born in Porohiwi, one of their own, who'd shown the theatrical world how to direct Shakespeare and was now leading the way with Oscar Wilde.

Ruby agreed with them. The Porohiwi Players were very lucky to have Hester. Fanatical, quick-tempered, funny, hugely talented, red frizzy hair and all. It was Hester's iron determination that had made the transformation from an interior of an upper-class London flat to an outdoor garden scene, work.

'If they have to see it happen they might as well have something good to look at,' she'd said.

So three drama students had dressed as upper-class passers-by and two had dressed as maid and garden boy, and they'd silently posed and pointed at Bradley, Bax and three other drama students as they lugged the heavy tubs of ferns, bushes, roses and smaller pots of violets to the various spots marked with a tiny X. The audience watched, entranced. It was like a choreographed dance. It wasn't the first time one of Hester's scene changes had got a clap but the crew were very pleased. The first time they'd rehearsed it they'd taken forty-five minutes. Now it took five, and it was a pleasure to watch.

As soon as Hester finished her speech and the cast started leaving the stage Reilly walked over to Bax, who looked at him like he was a stranger.

'I'm off,' said Bax to Hester, ignoring Reilly. 'See you tomorrow.'

He pressed his lips together to hold back either words he was determined not to say or tears he was resolutely not going to let fall. I'd like to murder that little prick, Ruby thought. As if reading her mind, Sam, looking neither to left or right, stalked off to the dressing room. He'd done well as Algernon, though, entering the stage on cue if a little flushed, and Rissa had been word perfect. Terror and shame, Ruby supposed. Works for some.

'Bax,' said Reilly. 'We need to talk. I'll just do a quick change. You want to have a drink?'

'Rather swim naked in sick,' said Bax. He looked tired. 'You were fabulous,' he said to Ruby. 'Kate would have been so pleased.' And he hugged her. Bax was good to hug. Big arms and a broad chest and he did it like he meant it.

'Ring me,' said Ruby, patting his back.

He nodded, but she knew he wouldn't. 'Love to stay but Mum's not so well. Told her I'd look in.' Then he left.

'Fuck that idiot Sam,' said Reilly. 'I'm only looking for Mr Right. Is that a crime?'

'No you're not,' said Ruby. 'You're looking for Mr Perfect. No such thing.'

Reilly looked at her as though she'd hit him.

'Did you know,' he said, 'about Bax?'

'Had a suspicion.'

'I thought he was a friend. My best friend actually.'

'One doesn't cancel out the other does it?'

'Want a drink?'

'You kidding?'

'Okay,' said Reilly, 'see you out front in five.'

Just as Ruby sat down to clean her face, she saw the scissors.

They'd been pushed, points down, into the bench in front of the mirror with enough force to push the points at least fifteen centimetres into the wood. She stood up quickly and stared at them.

Who the hell?

She realised her hands were trembling.

Sam?

No, he wouldn't. In any case he'd been on stage most of the time. He'd cut that T-shirt into ribbons but surely that was just a coincidence? Sam had never really grown out of the terrible threes tantrum stage, but he wasn't the slipping-around-corners-with-scissors type.

She stared at the scissors.

Perfectly ordinary dressmaker's scissors. How many fabrics had they shaped and cut? Now they looked evil, vicious, like all the time they'd been pretending and now they were showing their true selves. They were a weapon. Deadly, vicious, lethal. What had she done to invite this kind of violence? To push scissors into that old hard wood required some force. Whoever did it was angry. Angry with her? Why?

To send a message. To her.

She went out and around the back of the set, saw Hester, told her what she'd found. Then back to the dressing room, cleaned her face, washed her hands, changed into the black pants and black shirt, pulled on the embroidered kimono, felt the silk. Really lovely.

It'll be all right. Auden knows about this sort of thing. Ruby didn't want the cops involved again and the thought of having to deal with that up-himself-head-prefect James made her want to swear, but the scissor-wielding creep had taken it out of her hands.

She slipped her pounamu pendant around her neck, looked in the mirror and sighed. The hair. She hauled the comb through it, sighed again, threw the comb on the table. Really needs a garden rake she thought. She should try and keep the scissors thing between herself and Hester and Auden. No sense spoiling the night for everyone else. It couldn't be any of the cast. But who? And why? What was the point?

Ruby shook her head, the black mass went crazy. She grabbed it from the back with one hand, felt for the hair elastic with the other, hauled it over the thick black wiry fighting-every-inch-of-the-way rope. It was like wrestling a tiger. She twisted it ruthlessly between her hands and forced the band on. There.

'What's the hold-up?'

Kristina. Red shirt, jeans, hair smooth as glass. She looked terrific. She walked over to Ruby, hugged her.

'Fucking hori,' she whispered. 'A for ace.'

They were seven years old when Fergus Craddock called Ruby a fucking hori, and to Fergus's surprise Ruby hadn't stared at him frozen, saying nothing, or turned away and pretended she hadn't heard, which were the sort of responses he'd clearly come to expect. Instead she'd leaped on him, crashed him to the ground and belted him on the nose.

By the time Kristina had arrived on the scene, the bully was crying and Ruby was walking away.

'You okay?' Kristina was running up to catch up with her.

'Course.'

'You wanna be in my running team?'

'No.'

'Okay,' said Kristina. 'You like pies?'

'Course.'

'I'll get two then.'

They'd been friends ever since.

Now here was Kristina giving her an A for Bracknell.

'You're sure?' said Ruby. 'A?'

'Course.' Kristina grinned. 'Kate would have been ecstatic.'

'Congratulations, Ruby.' Juno came up behind Kristina. 'You were fabulous.' Oscar's sister grinned at Kristina like she was fabulous too.

'Hmn,' said Kristina.

'Juno's right.' Oscar stood in the doorway. Blue shirt, dark jacket, jeans that hadn't been bought at the Warehouse, hair ruffled. 'Best Bracknell I've seen. Although of course I didn't see your first one at the college, which I understand was electrifying.'

Ruby couldn't help it, she burst out laughing. Kristina too. The only electrifying moments about the night Oscar was referring to were when Jake, sent out by his sister Sophie, discovered Kristina and Ruby dancing on the river bank after they'd drunk a bottle of wine Ruby had stolen from Kate's supply and eaten nearly all of a chocolate torte Kristina had filched from her mother's freezer. He'd dragged them back to Kate's, where Sophie and Kate waited. That had been an electrifying moment for sure, cut short when Ruby had to run to the bathroom and throw up in the bath. It had to be the bath because Kristina was already being sick into the toilet.

'Got a table,' said Juno, 'in the foyer. Rissa's holding it but her mates are waiting for her. Don't be long.' She and Oscar left.

Ruby poked at her hair.

A table? Why would Juno? Oh, of course, Kristina.

Not everything is about you.

'Leave it,' said Kristina, 'it looks great.'

Door was at the entrance to the auditorium. He was easy to spot – tall and fair like Oscar and Juno, but unlike either of them his hair was straight and cut short, and he wore glasses. He didn't say hello, didn't say anything about her performance, just nodded past her. 'Ruby, who's that?'

She looked over at the thin woman with almost white-blonde hair. 'Hortense,' she said.

'Hortense who?'

Kristina rolled her eyes. 'She's not interested in men,' she said, then added, 'or women, for that matter. She's a loner.'

'What does she do?'

'Gardener.'

Hortense saw Ruby, and her rather severe, perhaps even gaunt face, softened into a smile. Must have decided the play would be a special treat. Or more likely Daisy had given her a comp.

'Hortense,' muttered Door, and strode purposefully over.

Hortense looked at him like she'd lifted a lid and smelled something very unpleasant.

Ruby and Kristina watched with interest. Even Juno had stopped in her rapid move across the auditorium and was staring. She nudged her twin. Oscar lifted an eyebrow and turned back to the bar.

'Auntie?' said Rissa, then watched as her father said something to Hortense, held out his hand. She said something back and didn't take the hand. Not something nice judging by the look on her face. Then Door spoke again. She shook her head. Not a good outcome for him. He went straight to the bar where he stood morosely waiting to be served.

Ruby went over to Reilly, who was also at the bar. Before she got there Connor Kelly approached with his cousin Ramona.

'Ruby,' he said, 'you were fantastic. Did you get my flowers?' He walked confidently, sure of his welcome. That beautiful maroon jacket over the white T-shirt made his eyes seem darker.

'Wonderful, just wonderful, Ruby,' said Ramona, 'but I knew you would be. The cards were very clear.'

When Ramona smiled you forgot the long grey hair hanging in a rope down her back, the faded trousers, the man's blue-striped shirt underneath an old Wanganui Cricket Club blazer.

'Would you like to go out for supper?' said Connor. 'We could go to that little place you like and talk?'

'Hell no,' said Ruby. Rude but what else could she do?

'Red?' said Oscar. He looked Connor up and down, raised his eyebrows at Ruby.

The message was clear.

'Who's this?' said Connor. 'Your new lover I suppose.'

'No, an old one,' said Ruby before she could stop herself. Adrenalin high, she told herself, for god's sake *keep your mouth shut*.

Reilly was listening. He lifted an eyebrow at her, leaned with his back against the bar. Grinned. Glad he wasn't the only one having problems.

'Oscar Segar, Connor Kelly,' said Kristina, also grinning for some reason.

'Oh,' said Connor, like he'd discovered the one ring. 'The idiot ex.'

'Half right,' said Oscar. His expression said he thought she'd really scraped the bottom of the barrel.

Ruby wanted to tell them both to go and get fucked but realised in the nick of time that it would be an unfortunate way of telling them to go away.

'Look,' said Connor, 'I can see you've heard about the interlude in Hawaii. Honestly, Ruby, it meant nothing. A moment of madness.'

'That's a good line,' said Oscar, 'have you thought of writing for television?'

The two men stared at each other like they were at the OK Corral, waiting to see who blinked first.

'Ruby,' said Kristina, 'there's someone I want you to meet.'

She let Kristina drag her away.

'Who?' said Ruby.

'No one,' said Kristina, 'but you wanted to get away, didn't you? Let's find the table Rissa's guarding.'

'Well done, Ruby,' said Jen, doing her thing as a committee member. 'Really well done. You were great. And everyone was so good. I didn't think *As You Like It* could be bettered but tonight you showed me it can at least be equalled.'

'Ruby,' Kristina urged, 'this way.'

Reilly came over and hugged her. 'You were awesome,' he said. 'Do you mind if I scarper? I'm a bit tired. Your wine's on the bar.'

'Have a good sleep,' said Ruby.

She let Kristina lead her over to the table where Juno and Rissa sat repelling people who wanted to share the table, or grab a chair to use somewhere else. Ruby smiled over at the two people who shouted, 'Great show, best Bracknell ever,' and only realised after she'd said thanks that they were Sam's parents. You could see where he got his looks. His mother was beautiful, his father very handsome. The Markis family had been members of the Porohiwi Players forever.

Oscar came along carrying a tray with five glasses and put it down on the table. 'Reilly's shout,' he said.

Behind him was Auden's nephew Ra, with another tray of plates of food. 'Hi, Ruby,' he said, 'Daisy sent you this.'

Nice, thought Ruby. She would know I was starving.

Ra put the tray down on the table and came face to face with Jane. There was a small tight silence.

'Jane,' he said, 'you were wonderful. Have a word?'

'No,' said Jane, smiling radiantly up at Bradley, who raised his eyebrows at Ra and shrugged.

You had your chance mate, now step aside.

'Ruby?'

'Kia ora, Auden.' He always looked the ex-cop, thought Ruby, wherever he was. Something about the grey buzz cut, the good jacket and tie.

'You were awesome,' said Auden, 'Talk to you for a moment?'

'Sure,' said Ruby.

'I'll just grab a chair.'

'Wine, Auden?' said Oscar, looking at Ruby. 'You okay?'

Auden sat down, said, 'Hester's told me what happened. First you knew was when you found the jacket cut to pieces on a hanger?'

'Yes,' she said.

He talked her through the rest, listened while she said that no, she hadn't noticed any strange behaviour beforehand, and she thought she got on well with everyone. Then he stood up and said, 'Thanks for helping Hester out.'

'A pleasure,' she said and meant it. 'And congratulations.'

Kristina pushed a plate of pastry savouries towards Ruby.

Rissa was sipping her wine and looking for someone. 'Ruby,' she said. 'Sorry I was late.'

Ruby smiled. 'Happens to all of us,' she said, 'but only once.'

Rissa looked relieved. A group of people who could only be university students were hovering. Rissa got up.

'Where are you off to?' said Oscar.

'Here for a bit then a party at Bradley's mum's,' said Rissa.

'Ring me if you need anything.'

Rissa touched her uncle's arm. 'Sorry. I should have come to the theatre with you.'

'*Oscar*,' said Bethany Clark.

Oh *jeez*. But Bethany took no notice of Ruby, her whole attention beaming in on Oscar.

'Oscar, how *lovely*.'

Oscar stood up. 'Hi, Bethany.'

'How *are* you?'

'Great thanks,' said Oscar.

'That was such a lovely night,' said Bethany. 'You were *wonderful*. Under the stars. *Unforgettable*.'

Someone called her name. 'Coming,' Bethany said, rushed to Ruby and gave her a huge hug. 'Wonderful Bracknell, Ruby. So *lovely* to work with you. See you tomorrow night.' And she hurried off.

'Os,' Juno stared at her twin, 'you *didn't*.'

Oscar's face looked like it had been dipped in red ink. He said nothing.

Ruby tried not to look like a cat who'd just been given a bowl of cream. So he thought Connor Kelly was a bad choice? But *Bethany Clark*? Maybe he was *tired*? Nah. Had to be unconscious.

'What was Auden on about?' said Kristina.

Ruby told her.

'You pissed anyone off?'

'No.'

'Jeepers,' said Kristina. 'I think we'd all better have another glass.'

Door came up carrying a chair that he pushed in between Oscar and Juno and sat down.

'Just in time,' said Oscar.

Door looked at his brother.

'Your round,' said Oscar.

Door sighed, but Ra was passing so he gave him the order. He didn't look like a man who was having a good night.

'You were superb, Ruby.' Hortense was by her chair.

Ruby stood smiling. 'Thank you. How's the house situation?'

Hortense shook her head.

'I just offered her a house,' Door said. 'She refused.' He was looking at Hortense like she was the prize in a treasure hunt he never thought he'd win.

'I told you. The rent's too high.' Hortense looked thin and irritated.

'I said I'd lower it,' said Door, standing again to join them, 'if you fix up the garden.'

'And what'll happen when I've finished the garden? The rent will go up.'

'Not necessarily,' said Door, 'and even if it does, you'll be able to afford it because I want you to take charge of the garden at the Home. I'm having the house pulled down and building some two-bedroom units so the grounds need to be fixed up. Make a herb garden or something. We could talk about the job. Arrange a meeting. You could make a plan?'

Oscar and Juno stared at their brother like he'd just announced he was leaving for Mars.

Door stared back at them. 'What's the matter?'

'Nothing,' said Oscar, 'except I've never heard you display any interest in gardens before.'

'The grounds need attention,' said Door. 'I've always liked lavender.'

'A fairly recent interest?' Oscar grinned.

Door ignored him, turned his attention back to Hortense. 'You want to discuss it over a glass of wine?'

There was a sharp silence. Hortense frowned. Thought. Came down on the side of possible work. 'Okay,' she said, 'but no side benefits, understood?'

Door stood up. 'Take my chair,' he said. 'I'll get you a glass. Wine's coming.'

Won't hurt him, thought Ruby. Then felt bad. Door knew what unhappiness meant. If he'd seen someone he wanted to get to know better who was she to criticise? She wondered if Oscar had told him about giving Ruby a key to the Segar house. If he had, Door didn't look concerned.

Ra came along with two bottles and a glass on a tray.

Kristina waited till they'd all taken a sip then jumped in. 'The Segars changed their minds about Ruby seeing the collection?'

'Oscar's giving Ruby a key,' said Door.

So that answered that.

Ruby took a big swallow of wine. She was starting to feel like she'd be happier under the table where no one could see her, but she kept nodding and smiling her thanks at the compliments that kept coming. With each one, she thought – Was it you? Did you sneak in this afternoon and cut up the jacket? Did you plunge the scissors into the bench?

Why hadn't Bethany, Rissa or Jane noticed them? Probably because they were still on a high from the performance and in a hurry to get out to the auditorium.

There were a few looks at Oscar, then at Ruby, some mental notes made, looks at Kristina and Juno, more notes made, both items tucked away in that part of their brain that said *interesting, keep watching*.

'Would you like another glass?' said Kristina.

Ruby thought about it. Decided it would be really stupid given everything she had to do tomorrow, said, 'Yes please.'

18

'Diamonds are trumps, your lead,' said Heart. He pushed the stack of cards to the side.

Spade led with the king of clubs. Not high enough to do anything useful, but good as an indication to his partner Club. Heart had gone diamonds and Spade only had a few rags. Club had called spades but he might have something. You never knew with Club. Diamond followed suit with a rag of clubs. Bet Heart was swearing behind that impassive face. He'd have to follow suit? Surely he'd have a rag of clubs. Heart put the ace of clubs.

Fuck.

Club put a rag of diamonds on the ace and pulled the hand towards him. Oho, so he had no clubs? Spade had no diamonds so Club was probably on his own for this hand.

Club led with the ace of hearts. Everyone followed suit. He led another heart, the queen, and Heart plonked the king of diamonds on it and won the hand. Heart led with the jack of diamonds, took the trick, led the joker, everyone threw what rags they had, then Heart led with the king of spades and club put the ace on it. Heart gave Diamond a dirty look. Diamond was supposed to be his partner and he'd stopped him. He'd been stopped from getting a march? They finished the game in silence.

Then Heart looked around at the others.

'We need to taihoa for a few days,' he said, 'Auden's sniffing round. I don't want a run-in with Auden. Not yet anyway.'

'A few days? We should keep the pressure on the bitch,' Diamond said.

'You've made one mistake already,' said Heart. 'Don't repeat it. If you do you're out.'

Diamond looked as if he wanted to tell Heart to fuck off, but he had *enough sense to remain silent. He knew Spade and Club were with Heart on this one. He wished he'd strangled the bitch when he had the chance.*

'I'm worried,' he said.

'We're all worried,' said Heart, 'but we need to keep our heads. No good getting rid of one bad thing if we're going to create another worse one. Let it settle for a week. We know where she is. We know where she works. We can take her any time we like. We just need to be sure about the book.'

'I've got an idea,' said Spade.

They all listened while he outlined his plan.

'Okay,' said Heart, 'that's good. Let it lie for a week then we'll do it. The lock on the cossie room is going to be changed but it's not a problem.'

'What about Oscar Segar?'

'What about him?'

'He's working with her on that book she's writing. His job to notice things.'

'He's her ex. Why would he even bother?'

'We're just going to have to be very, very clever,' said Heart. 'Agreed?'

They all agreed. None of them noticed Diamond cross his fingers. He knew it was childish but it had always brought him luck, so why not? Anyway, crossed fingers or not, agreement or not, he was going to see to that bitch, get the notebook, and then they'd see they weren't so fucking smart. They'd always treated him as if he was an idiot. Well, thought Diamond, you've all got a real surprise coming. We'll see who's boss.

19

'I had some crumpets with Lady Harbury, who seems to me to be living entirely for pleasure now.'

There was a moment, only a moment, when Ruby didn't know whether she wanted to go into the theatre or not. Fuck that guy. She'd never had a qualm before. Many times she'd been the first to walk into the dark theatre, found her way to the switchboard, no worries.

'Wait,' said Oscar.

'It's fine,' she said, and walked on. She wouldn't give in to it. In any case someone had already switched on the lights. The passageway was its usual dim self, the smell of greasepaint and perspiration lingered in the walls and as always there was that heady mix of drama, despair and delight. Shadows changed shape as Ruby, Rissa and Oscar made their way towards the dressing rooms.

'They could do with more light along here.'

'On the list in the twenty-year plan,' Ruby said.

There was a light in the women's dressing room. Ruby pushed the door open. Daisy sat there, reading. The heater was on and there were fresh glasses of water by each place. She smiled and stood up.

Ruby went straight over and hugged her.

'Still looking out for me?' she said.

'Hard to break old habits. Coffee?'

'Oh yes. Lovely.'

Daisy winked at Oscar.

'I'll give you a hand,' he said, 'Rissa, coffee for you?'

'Yes please.'

Ruby went to the wardrobe. Her costume was all there. All in one piece. Her relief was out of all proportion.

There was a knock on the open door. Auden. As always his rather severe features changed when he smiled. 'Kia ora, Ruby. All okay? Kia ora, Rissa.'

Ruby smiled. 'Yes. Thanks.'

'Kia ora, Mr Porohiwi,' said Rissa.

'Auden's fine,' he said, smiling. 'Now for the rest of the run, someone will be in the dressing room when you're on stage. I've spoken to DI James and he's okay with what I've done. He's coming in to talk to you, Ruby. Jojo's been alerted. Not that she can be expected to do anything while she's managing the lighting, but as a cop she needs to be aware. I'll be making a report to the committee once the run is over. I'm not saying that what happened has got anything to do with the Players. I can't say that because I don't know. But neither Hester nor I wanted you to have any worries at all. Kei te pai?'

'Kei te pai,' she said, 'and thank you.'

He left. Ruby felt the tension that she didn't know she was holding ebb a little.

'Dad said Mr Porohiwi was a great cop,' said Rissa, 'but he left because they wanted him to move up the ranks, which meant moving away. So he got out.'

'Mmn,' said Ruby. She wasn't sure that was all it was but the main facts were right.

Oscar came back with the coffees, gave them to Rissa and Ruby, left them to it. Jane entered the room, followed by Bethany. Jane didn't look any happier than last night, thought Ruby, so maybe Bradley was not the distraction she'd hoped for. Ra must still be out in the cold.

Ruby regarded her face in the mirror. Her eyes looked tired, but given last night was the first night and today had been busy, that wasn't surprising. Never mind, she could sleep in tomorrow. The bed at Meg's had seen better days but tonight it wouldn't matter. She was tired enough to sleep on the floor if she had to. No, wait, she couldn't sleep in. She had to do the interviews for the history.

Bethany was unusually silent. She checked her costume, fiddled with greasepaints, opened a card or two, found the one she wanted, ripped it up and threw it in the wastepaper basket with a grand gesture.

'You might as well *know*,' said Bethany, 'that Colin and I are no longer *together*. I don't want to talk about it.'

Jane said nothing. Rissa and Ruby exchanged a look.

'Naturally I'm very *upset*,' said Bethany, 'but I'm a trouper – the show must go *on*. I assure you I'll be fine. I don't want anyone to worry.'

'Would you like some coffee?' said Ruby.

'Heavens no,' said Bethany, and shuddered as though she'd been offered a cup of boiling bat's blood.

Ruby thought this night was par for the course for every second night of every play she'd ever performed in. Something seemed to happen between the first and second nights of a show. It was like everyone put their heart and soul, their reservoir of high energy, into the first night, lifting the play and themselves out of rehearsal mode and into the real world in front of an audience. Second nights were sometimes, not a relapse exactly, but a fallback from the high of the opening. She felt edgily expectant.

Don't let it drop.

Look on the bright side. At least Rissa's on time.

Another tap on the door. Reilly.

Ruby went quickly over and hugged him.

'Hey,' he said, hugging her back, 'you okay?'

She nodded. 'You?'

'Same,' he said, then gave Ruby a big a smile, 'and we're both good liars huh?' and left.

After the show and the standing ovation for Ruby because all Kristina's whānau were there, she went looking for Bax.

'You were great,' he said, 'again. Everything okay?'

'No scissors tonight.'

'Knowing Auden's interested would be a bit of a deterrent.'

Ruby thought about that. Bax and Ronald Hugh were stuck in their places for the entire show except for the scene changes and

Ronald Hugh's entrances as Canon Chasuble. Bradley had a little more leeway to roam but seemed to like to stick close to that side of the stage. Whoever plunged the scissors into the bench had to have been backstage when the show started. No way could anyone come through the auditorium and up to the back while a show was on, and once everyone was in Bax locked the side door.

When Hester had asked the cast and the crew if they'd seen anyone backstage who shouldn't be there, everyone appeared genuinely puzzled and as far as Ruby could tell were telling the truth. They hadn't seen or heard anyone. But if you were the guilty one that's exactly what you would say, thought Ruby.

When Auden asked if anyone had any idea who it could be, Bethany was the only one with something to say.

'It's the *ghost*,' she fluttered. 'The woman in a blue dress. It's a … *warning*.'

'Thank you, Bethany.' Auden got in smoothly before Hester could utter any of the words they could all see were about to be said. She grinned at her husband and put a finger tick in the air.

'Auden one,' she said.

Ruby smiled, and the smile turned into a yawn. It reminded her of something. 'Bax,' she said. 'I'm on the cadge. Do you have any time Monday to pick up some stuff from Furniture for You for me?'

'Sorry, no. Tuesday morning? Not great conditions where you are?' he said.

'Just old,' she said.

'See you Tuesday,' said Bax.

♠

Ruby took Meg and Spider in a cup of tea. The sitting-room curtains were open and the afternoon sun made the old dark furniture look even more worn. A good clean and some polish, thought Ruby.

'Not bad,' said Spider, after he'd sipped the tea.

'How did the interviews go?' Meg took a piece of the sponge cake Ruby had stolen while no one was looking.

'Juno made that sponge.'

'She can bake,' said Meg.

'Interviews were good. Plenty of recorders, lots of people, buzzy talk. Some good stuff for the history. Which reminds me,' said Ruby, 'can I interview you?'

'It was a long time ago,' said Meg.

'Even better,' said Ruby. 'Won't take long. You were in some earlier productions?'

'She was,' said Spider.

'Only a couple,' said Meg.

'But you did props for ages,' he said.

'Even better,' said Ruby, 'means you'll have heard a lot of gossip.'

'I'll see,' said Meg, taking another slice of sponge. 'What's this about new beds?'

'They're old and the mattresses smell musty. A new one'd be good for your back. You need new pillows too and sheets. Sales are on. I'll go online and have a look. If you're short, I can pay.' Neither Kate nor Marlon would mind if she used some of their money on new beds.

'Okay,' said Spider, 'I'll pay for my half, you pay yours.'

◆

Ruby peered at the mirror on the kitchen wall. A ghostly witch's face with big dark eyes and tangled black hair stared back at her. Oh hell, she thought for the zillionth time, must do something about my hair. You keep *saying* that, she told herself, but you don't *do* it. Maybe buy a better mirror?

She went through to the bedroom. The mirror was no better there. Maybe she should put mirrors on the list? She wrestled a comb through her hair but as soon as she took it away it sprang back into the blackberry bush that was its normal condition. She swept it up on top and held it. Fuck no. Made her look ten feet tall. This could really make you depressed.

Ruby had inherited this mess from someone, maybe she should start looking for people who had this kind of hair? Yeah right. That cut out most of the people on the planet. Had she ever actually seen *anyone* with hair like hers?

There were four bedrooms at Meg's, two of them down this end. As well as the large sitting room in the front there was a small one down the back. It was probably called the breakfast room back in the day. It had French doors opening out onto a rickety wooden porch. Through the windows you got a good view of the green metre-high mess that was once a lawn. It got slashed off about twice a year by someone who wanted it for compost. The grey shed looked like only willpower was holding it up.

Down one end of the room was a small fireplace flanked by a two-seater couch and two wooden-armed and padded (a loose term seeing most of the springs had gone) chairs. There was a bookshelf stuffed with books that had probably never been opened in fifty years, if ever. Worth investigating though. There was an oblong table which looked strong enough to support a laptop and some books.

Across the hall from the small sitting room was a poky room with two tubs, a copper and a very ancient washing machine, probably passed on by Noah's wife when it had served its time in the ark. Pushed under the tubs was a pile of sacks. They looked like the coal sacks she remembered from Kate's woodshed. She'd slept between a couple that first long cold night. Ruby didn't disturb them now. The odds on them sheltering spiders was high.

There was a small window which had ripple glass in it to make absolutely sure that even if it was clean no real light would ever mar the dimness of the room. It had a handle but wouldn't open.

She didn't check but would bet there was a basin of wooden pegs, slightly mouldy, somewhere under the tubs. No clothes basket.

What did Meg use to lug the washing out to the line?

The *bucket?*

Don't go there.

There were probably some more big spiders lurking in the corners, which was why Ruby gave it only a cursory inspection. She considered herself fairly brave but when faced with a member of the arachnid family, she became a gibbering wreck.

'They mean you no harm,' Kristina had said years ago. 'They are sentient beings.'

'So am I and I'm bigger. So why don't they steer clear?'

'When they're frightened or surprised they either attack or run. Just like us.'

There was no access to the outside except through the kitchen or the little sitting room. The clothes line was two long lengths of wire strung between the shed and the house. What the hell? Circular lines had been around before the 1950s. This line was held up by a couple of grey-verging-on-white wooden props.

Ruby's phone pinged. *Bit late but still want to go for a walk?*

Grey sky, chilly. Did she? Oh go on, she told herself. Get it over. A bit of damp and cold won't hurt you, and then you can tick it off the list. Kristina was probably doing what Kate called a 'redeem' for forcing Ruby into agreeing to play cards with Oscar and Juno, so maybe she should let her? Not that anything more had been said on the subject. There hadn't been time.

'Streets or redeem?' Kate had said fourteen years ago when Oscar walked out on Ruby. She'd looked around the flat which was filthy – dirty dishes, rubbish everywhere, empty bottles, more rubbish sweltering in the black rubbish bag. Ruby badly needed a shower.

'What?'

'You heard me. *Streets or redeem?*'

Ruby didn't answer.

'You're six weeks behind with the rent, the landlord wants you out, you're drinking yourself into the ground, been selling furniture and kitchen stuff for money to buy booze, and all because *he* walked *out*. There are six million children starving in Rwanda so one idiot with an oh-so-broken heart simply doesn't rate. Now make up your mind. Streets or redeem?'

Some lingering strand of common sense made Ruby mutter, 'Redeem.'

'Didn't hear you,' said Kate.

Ruby raised her voice. 'Redeem.'

'Right,' said Kate. 'Have a shower. You got some clean clothes?' Ruby frowned. Did she? She nodded.

'Okay, pack the others. Marlon will pay the back rent and get someone to clean up the mess. Although why he should or would is a mystery. I'll be back in thirty minutes. Be ready.'

'Where am I going?' In a way it was a relief to have someone else make a decision.

'Somewhere people have got more to think about than their own tiny problems.'

The women at the Haven had paid absolutely no attention to Ruby's oh-so-broken heart or that her body was in bad physical shape. They wanted toilets cleaned? Ruby cleaned them. They wanted bedrooms cleaned out, food prepped, the vege garden dug? Ruby did it. They wanted to call her to help in the middle of the night and still be up at six the next morning? She did it. She hated their amused eyes, their hard eyes, the way they summed up this stupid little cow who thought the world had ended because some guy had walked out on her. She hated the poky little bedroom and horrible bed with its lumpy mattress and she loathed the fact that when the house was full, which was nearly always, she had to share a mattress on the floor because someone else needed the bed. And the someone else always came first because the someone else had been raped or beaten up or both, her kids terrified, mishandled by unsympathetic cops.

So your poor little heart has been broken? Well, come into the real world, Ruby.

She'd stayed on for an extra six months and then did a journalism course and landed a job that lasted six years before it folded. She and two others lost their jobs. She got a call from the tutor who ran the journalism course, who said she'd heard about the job losses and she had something Ruby might be interested in as a temporary filler. So Ruby signed her first ghost-writer contract. A book about the life of a successful business man. Interesting man when he talked about his business but dull as a fading torch battery on any other subject. She even had to prompt him to write a dedication.

He'd frowned. *Dedication?*

'Your wife,' she suggested, 'you could thank her.'

He looked a bit puzzled.

'She's looked after the house, after you, your four children. She's tolerated the long hours, the boring dinner parties, spent half her life on her own. Did she get a salary?'

That really surprised him. 'A salary? What would she want with a salary? She's my wife.'

'Work it out,' said Ruby. 'It would have cost you at least a million if you'd had to pay someone else to do what she's done. For little thanks from what I can see.'

'But she's got everything she needs.' He saw Ruby's expression and said, 'What shall I write?'

Ruby felt like hitting him. But she'd written the dedication already.

Dedicated with love and thanks to my wife, Leila, without whom I'd never have achieved anything.

He'd read it and then read it again. He still looked a bit puzzled. Then his face cleared. 'Good, for sales,' he said.

She didn't go to the launch but heard it was crowded and the book sold a respectable number. He paid the contract fee immediately and, what was more to the point, recommended her to a couple of friends. Word got around. And here she was.

Thanks, she texted Kristina, *a walk would be good.*

The state of Meg's house puzzled her. It was more than the result of an old woman who couldn't be bothered with housework. Meg might have given up actual cleaning when she was eighty or whatever, but this deliberate neglect had been going on long before that.

The floors of the bedrooms had old cracked lino on them with rugs placed carefully so you could break a limb quite easily if you stepped the wrong way. The reason Meg hadn't broken a leg was because she only came down this end of the house if she wanted to wash sheets or towels. The rest, Ruby suspected, got done in the bathroom basin that was big enough to bathe a four-year-old child very comfortably.

There was no covering on the hall floor, so your steps echoed and moaned if you got up in the night to use the toilet, and if that didn't wake the rest of the household there was the thunderous crash of the flushing toilet.

It was true that Meg was a short-tempered old woman who had, for whatever reason, simply let a house moulder around her but when had this slow disintegration begun?

Ruby's phone pinged again. *Okay if Juno comes on walk?*

No worries.

Good, she thought, good. It was a long time since Kristina had some fun. Sure Juno was a Segar, but nobody's perfect.

20

'To be born, or at any rate bred, in a hand-bag, whether it had handles or not, seems to me to display a contempt for the ordinary decencies of family life ...'

Juno, well rugged-up in a blue rainproof jacket and a blue-and-mauve striped hat with a huge pom-pom, waited in her car outside Meg's until Kristina arrived. When Kristina introduced Juno to Meg, she said, 'Know your twin. Nice boy.'

Juno smiled. 'I like him too.'

'Well if you're going, you'd better go,' said Meg.

It wasn't too bad walking along the path beside the stream. The day was cool and the sky a mixture of drab blue interspersed with clouds that looked like they needed a wash, but the rain was hanging off and the water in the stream was reasonably clear. You could see the hundred and fifty shades of grey in the stones lying on the bottom.

Kristina and Juno were discussing cream sponges with careful casualness. They weren't really talking about sponges, thought Ruby, but sounding each other out. The two women were clearly attracted to one another but there were the usual kind of dance steps to go through before they took it any further. Human beings – we're all mad. But what is the alternative? Cave women hauling and grunting?

Kate reckoned that queers of either gender, or trans for that matter, had been around forever, and takatāpui of both gender had definitely been around and accepted before the missionaries came and said it was against God's law to accept any sexual union but that of a man and a woman.

Ruby's thoughts turned back to the book she was writing. Cross fingers there'd be some stuff from the interviews she could use. Unlikely there'd be anyone who remembered the 1951 production of *Earnest* but there would be something in the Segar collection. Might be good to link the productions over the generations? In 1951 New Zealand would still have been recovering from the war, then there was the wharfie's lockout, emergency regulations, and the family benefit could be cashed in and used as a deposit on a house.

How did the Porohiwi Players keep going? Somehow they managed to buy the building in 1965 or at least put down a deposit and pay it off. The deposit had been an anonymous donation although surely someone would know? A secret was only a secret when one person knew it and there'd have been more than one person involved in that financial transaction. Plus the bank.

Maybe when Oscar went through the treasurers' reports there might be a clue? It would not be right to divulge the name of someone who had been so generous and wanted anonymity, but it would be good to know. And maybe after all this time, if the person were still alive, they would agree that the knowledge be let loose?

The Players had, with great determination, managed the money for rates and insurance, and finally paid off the loan in 1985, which made life easier for future committees.

Upkeep was an ongoing matter that members could be conned or leaned on to do. It was always one step behind but generally got done at some stage. You had to wonder why they did it. She needed to think about this.

And Ruby couldn't just focus the book on one play at a time because they were often repeated every generation. *Earnest* was not the only one. There'd been at least two productions of *Hamlet* including the famous-in-Porohiwi one where Patsy had changed Gertrude's lines. Noel Coward's *Private Lives* had been done at least twice. Thornton Wilder's *Our Town* and Lillian Hellman's *The Little Foxes* were only produced once each. Ruby wondered how they managed the black servants and their *yessum ma'ams*? The casual racism, the taking for granted that whites were a step above blacks, made this play an almost copybook example for students if you wanted to show the degree of racism and classism that was rife at the time and in a lot of minds still. It was a platitude to say that plays reflected their times, and that if you wanted to do, say, an all-male cast of a Shakespearean play it would be a truly authentic production.

Misogynistic crap, thought Ruby. She'd have been more convinced by this argument if the male casts had been *completely* authentic and gone back in time to no toilets, no showers, in fact no personal hygiene at all, except throw on some more perfume to hide the stink. Rotting teeth too.

Ruby suddenly realised that Kristina and Juno were well ahead of her, the pom-pom on Juno's hat bobbing as they picked up the pace. They didn't seem to notice Ruby was trailing behind. She quickened her step.

The plays that made the front page of the Porohiwi Mail were in a class of their own. *HAIR Nudity Shocks Porohiwi Audience. Is this what we expect from our ratepayer-funded theatre group?* Always good for audiences though. That production had got a grant from a community fund on the basis that it was anti-war and had songs. Who would have been in the cast? Nudity was probably easier when your body was young and beautiful – so they were probably solid retired citizens now. Maybe there was a photo somewhere? Might not be kind to use it? Although as long as their faces weren't showing …

There had been no grant from the community fund for another ten years until the unexceptionable and very dull 1995 *A Midsummer Night's Dream* production, in which Ruby had been one of the fairies. A grumpy and reluctant one. She hadn't liked the play or the director. While Kate had agreed that the director was a bit of a featherweight, she said solidarity was the name of the game and the play needed their support.

'And,' Kate added, 'we've all been there. You should have seen my production of *All's Well That Ends Well.*'

At least the Porohiwi Players had done a few New Zealand plays too. Ruby understood the initial reluctance. They had to do plays which audiences wanted to come to see. The fact was that most audiences came out to have a laugh or at least not be made to think, and Kiwi plays were often an unknown quantity and could be demanding. Who could blame people? Ruby didn't, that's for sure.

She understood only too well how after a hard day's work all you really wanted to do was be soothed, entertained, have a good laugh and not spend too much. The Players kept their ticket prices as low as they could but even so it was beyond some household budgets to afford two tickets.

Choosing a theatre programme was such a lottery. What about the changes in British theatre after the Second World War? John Osborne and Arnold Wesker, the 'angry young men' Noel Coward railed about. But whether Coward liked it or not, British theatre changed forever and where they led New Zealand followed. When did *Look Back in Anger* reach Porohiwi? Maybe it didn't.

How old would Meg have been in the fifties? If she was turning ninety in a few weeks she must have been born in 1929. So in 1951 she'd have been twenty-two. Plenty old enough to know what was going on. Hard to believe the sacked writer had ignored the possibility that Meg might have information that would make the story live. Surely no writer worth their salt would do that? Or was Ruby's predecessor enjoying sex on the red couch so much that time just floated by? Anything was possible.

Whatever.

No harm in asking Meg to take part.

'Ruby. *Ruby.* Hello in there?' It was Kristina.

'Sorry,' she said, 'I was thinking.'

'Juno's interested in the Home. Talk to her.'

Ruby only just stopped herself from saying fuck off. Juno had been there when DI James grilled her. Enough, enough. No Segar would know anything but a life where she was always treated well, knew she was loved, had enough food and more than enough money to see her through the science and medical degree fees, and no need to work part-time if she didn't want to.

Whoa, Ruby told herself, the chip on your shoulder just became a log. It's not Juno's fault. You can't help the family you're born into.

'What do you want to know?' she said.

'You were there for seven years?'

'Yes.'

'Talk, Ruby, *talk*,' said Kristina. 'You never know. It might loosen up some memories if you talk about it.'

'So we're doing fucking Psychology 101 are we?' said Ruby.

'Fucking hori,' said Kristina, shaking her head.

Juno looked from one to the other, aghast.

'Aroha mai,' said Ruby. 'Aroha mai.'

'Just try it,' said Kristina, 'that's all I'm saying.'

Juno looked even more mystified. She took off her glasses and rubbed them with a tissue. Always a good move when you need a little time to think. It's hard walking into one side of a friendship that's been going on for years and years, stepping warily around the minefield of old in-jokes and asides, the jargon that comes after a long time of two people being friends.

Ruby faced Juno. 'Yes. I ran away when I was seven.'

'Why?'

'Like I said to DI James, because a man dressed in black wearing a balaclava chased me. And because something had happened to Betty to make her drown herself. I was terrified of a life at the Home without Betty.'

'I'm surprised he didn't catch you.'

'Only because Matron called. I didn't realise he'd stopped. I was so scared I just kept running, and then I got really lost, and I got tired, and I ran down Kate's drive and hid in her woodshed.

'In the morning, I saw her putting out some bread for the birds, so when she went back inside I crept out and grabbed it and started eating. She saw me and,' Ruby's tone softened, 'came out and said, "Hello, I'm Kate, who are you?" I said, "Ruby," and she said, "You like eggs, Ruby? Toast?" and I said yes. "Okay," she said, "follow me." And I did. When I got inside she and Daisy saw the bruises.'

'Who made the bruises?'

Ruby shrugged. 'Staff.'

'Why?'

'I asked for some more bread? Looked at them the wrong way? They didn't need a reason.'

Juno didn't ask any more questions until they got to the back door and Ruby slid a steel card between the tongue of the lock and the wall.

'Breaking and entering?' said Juno.

'That a worry?' said Kristina.

Juno thought for a second. 'Only if we get caught. I could have asked Door or Oscar for the key.'

'This is just between us,' Ruby said. 'No one else, okay?'

'All for one, one for all?'

'Exactly.'

The door creaked as Ruby opened it and the three of them froze. They all heard the running footsteps on the wooden floor. Only for a moment though. They'd stopped.

Kristina and Ruby took off up the passage and into the main corridor.

'The front room,' yelled Ruby.

A window screeched, thrust up by frantic fingers. Two lots of scrambles. But when they got to the big room all they saw was the window pushed up, no sign of people. No sign of anyone outside either but who knew?

Ruby and Kristina were just as fast out the window. Ruby took the side that led up to the house and Kristina took the one that led away. Stupid having this kind of circular arrangement, thought Ruby. Running around in circles got you nowhere.

The bushes closest to the window still shivered as if someone had pushed through them in a hurry, but whoever it was would be well away by now. In any case the shrubby bushes and trees were massed so close you could hardly see daylight between them.

Ruby barged into the bushes. Nothing. She stopped and listened. The pounding of Kristina's footsteps, the silence when she stopped, no other sound.

No car taking off down the bottom. No running feet. Must have a bike or still hiding?

Maybe they went around the back of the stream? Through that old paddock?

She stopped by the path over the large culvert, ignored the stream, and the shallow ground under the stream that suddenly sloped into a deeper channel that the water silently went about filling. She knew the deep part lasted until just past where the Home section ended and the stream bed sloped up to become shallow again.

'Like a bath set in a bench,' Kate had told the young Ruby, 'water fills it then flows back to shallow. Water seeks gravity.'

The banks at the back of the Home side were covered with gorse but there was a narrow curving track up to the other side, a mess of shrubby ferns and weeds. Along the top was a scraggy piece of land set in shade by hills, a few miserable macrocarpas struggling alongside rabbits and rabbit holes. No walking for pleasure there. No one running through it.

Back when Ruby was living at the Home, if you walked over that rough paddock area, underneath the macrocarpas, stepped carefully around the rabbit holes, you came to a plum tree. It was old, gaunt and ungainly, but in the spring it blossomed and after a few weeks had a crop of plums. Just ordinary red-skinned, yellow-fleshed, big-stone plums, but in the eyes of the kids, a feast of god-like proportions. The one time of the year when even kids who hated everyone would fill a pocket and slide one or two into the hand of someone who'd been in the punishment room all day.

Ruby had never seen the tree but Betty told her about it. She'd never seen it because she was too young. If there was trouble you needed to be able to run and hide. You didn't need to have to worry about a small kid dragging along behind. Far better to make the kid wait and then say, 'Hold out your hand.'

She went back inside and down into the large room that had been used as a dining room back then. Juno had looked upstairs. Ruby didn't think the intruders had been upstairs or they'd have heard them come down, but who knows where they'd been before Ruby forced the door?

'Two?'

'Yep.'

'Okay,' said Kristina, 'we need to tell Door because one of them must have a key.'

'Why?' said Juno. She frowned. Thought. 'Yeah. Has to be. So there's another key out there.' She got on her phone.

'Um,' said Ruby, 'we tell him we were breaking in and someone was here before us?'

Kristina shrugged. 'All for one, one for all.'

'Yep, but while I'm here I'm going to do what I came here for.'

Juno put her phone away. 'No answer. He might be helping Hortense. I'll text Os. He's in Paraparaumu.'

'So we've got twenty-five, thirty minutes? Better be quick.'

Ruby walked back to the main corridor and went up the stairs. Waste of time. Absolute waste of time. Thirty years, for god's sake. But. Has to be crossed off.

In the middle dormitory she stood and stared around. The room was large with long sash windows. Her bunk had been opposite the window. Betty slept in the top one. All that was left of the bunks, the hard knobbly mattresses, the shelves where clothes were piled, luck of the draw whether they fitted or not, was dust. The other two large upstairs rooms were the same. The little rooms downstairs, the punishment rooms, were dusty too.

The lounge was empty of kids playing snap – *if you get 'snap' don't shout, just stand up* – there was no one knitting, no one staring out the window, no one waiting for the bell that said food was on the table. Betty taught her not to run. To walk quietly. Look straight ahead. Wait for a prayer to be said. Not to grab. Not to shove. However hungry they were, though, they waited until a member of the staff said, 'Eat.' Sometimes it took ages to say it. Some of the staff liked to lengthen the wait. Always a chance a hungry kid would grab. Make their day.

There was nothing in any of the lower rooms. Nothing in the toilets or the showers. Nothing in the kitchen.

'Well,' said Ruby, 'that's that.'

'Ceiling?' Kristina was looking up at the oblong-framed sliding panel that let you get up into the space under the roof.

'Hardly,' said Ruby.

'We've got about ten more minutes, might as well.'

Ruby shrugged. Went outside. Two wooden extension ladders leaned against the shed. Bugger. One of them looked like it might stay in one piece. It would have to do. Kristina wouldn't give up until they'd looked up in the roof.

'I'll do it,' said Juno, 'I'm good at ladders.'

Kristina smiled at her, put the ladder in place, pushed up the extension, propped it against the frame of the hole.

'Be careful,' she said to Juno. Patted her shoulder.

'My middle name,' said Juno and went swiftly up the ladder that shuddered at every step. She wrestled with the cover then said, 'Stupid

Juno,' found the wedge on the side, pushed it back and the cover slid along the grooves.

They heard her crawling, knee-clumping around the ceiling. Then there was silence. And just when Kristina opened her mouth to yell, a blonde head appeared in the hole.

'Nothing,' said Juno, 'only this old thing.' And she held up a large flax kete. Soft and faded with age.

'Oh *Jesus*,' said Ruby.

'What the …' said Kristina.

Juno chucked the kete down to Ruby. Dust sprayed out into the kitchen. Ruby caught it and shook it, more dust went everywhere.

'Oh hell,' she said, 'oh bloody hell.' She clutched the kete tightly to her chest.

Juno came down the ladder very fast. Kristina put her arms around Ruby. Juno took a wrist and felt her pulse.

'Can't be the one,' said Ruby, 'can't be.'

'Of course it is,' said Kristina. 'They were the plastic bags before we had plastic bags. Everyone had them. You collected shellfish, carried kūmara, cabbage, pūhā. Nothing flash. Plenty big enough for a baby.'

Ruby shook her head. 'In the ceiling?'

'It's the one thing it's got going for it.' Kristina sounded certain. 'Someone put it there. Who knows why? You okay?'

Ruby held the kete against her chest.

Juno was climbing back up the ladder. 'There might be something else up there,' she called back over her shoulder. 'Wait there.'

Kristina made a soft sad sound like one of Karl's. Touched the kete Ruby was holding.

'Funny isn't it,' she said, 'how for some women this is the solution to an unwanted pregnancy – put the baby in a bag and leave it on a door-step like you leave old clothes and other crap at the Sallies. While the rest of us choose not to create a mess for everyone else to clean up …' Kristina stayed absolutely still for a moment her finger on the kete.

Ruby reached out one arm and hugged her friend to her, the old kete between them. 'Thanks for calling me a mess,' she said.

'Oh shit, I didn't think,' said Kristina and started laughing. 'That sounded awful, didn't it? Just that all that shit at the clinic … maybe there was another way …'

Footsteps. Kristina stopped talking. Ruby put the kete behind her. Juno came down the ladder and shrugged.

Oscar.

Karl padded across to Ruby and nuzzled her hand. Then he sniffed, nuzzled the new smell.

'Find anything?' said Oscar.

'Yes,' said Juno.

'No,' said Ruby.

'If you're going to lead a life of crime you'd better get your stories sorted,' said Oscar.

Ruby brought the kete around to the front of her so he could see it.

Oscar walked straight over to her. 'The kete? *That* kete? The one you were dropped off in?'

Karl sniffed. Whined softly.

She nodded. 'Can't prove it. But maybe?'

'It's the one,' he said. 'I'm sure it's the one.' He was smiling. Genuinely pleased.

'It's the only explanation,' said Kristina. 'Someone put it up in the ceiling. Don't know who, don't know why but I bet it was someone who worked in the kitchen and I bet they were Māori.'

She hugged Ruby. 'The first real clue,' she said. 'I'm onto it, okay?'

Ruby nodded, breathed out.

'Okay,' she said.

Juno told Oscar about the two intruders they'd surprised. 'One of them had to have a key,' she said.

'Okay. I'll check with Door and organise someone to put a bolt and padlock on the door.'

Karl leaned into Ruby's hand and she stroked his head. 'It's a kete,' she said, 'harakeke.' He stretched up and tentatively, carefully put out a tongue and touched it. His tongue went back instantly. Nothing there for him.

21

'I am glad to say that I have never seen a spade. It is obvious that our social spheres have been widely different.'

The ducks were sublime. The potatoes crisp. Thank god for Jake. He had taken her to the supermarket and helped her lug the bags inside. He was Kristina's uncle but Ruby hadn't met him through her. She'd met him through Marlon when Jake came back from England in 1990. He'd heard about Marlon and Kate getting married so Kate could adopt Ruby, and wanted to see what it was all about. Jake had always shared a joke with Ruby, and when she and Kristina got to thirteen and started driving every adult in their vicinity crazy, he was one adult who just laughed at their antics.

'Nowhere near my carry-on when I was thirteen,' he said.

When she asked Jake what he was doing in 1981 he said, 'Trying to decide whether I was gay or not. Hoping I wasn't. Flitted around both sides a bit. Randy little bugger. Finally told Mum and she was fine. Big relief. I cried. Marched against the Tour. That was 1981. Did I notice anyone pregnant who didn't have a baby? You're joking. I was sixteen. My attention was all on me. Then I went overseas. Wanted to have a look before the bomb blew it all up. Came back, got in tow with Marlon on a couple of "actions", met Kate, you, went back to my trade and that's me.'

Jake had located a commode. And a pot. So Meg had had a more comfortable night.

The carrots from the supermarket were okay with a bit of orange juice and butter over them. The steamed silver beet was young and delicious. It had been growing in the back garden next to two healthy-looking cannabis plants that should have been harvested four weeks ago. Such close proximity to an illegal drug didn't seem to have affected the legal greens. Interesting though. So Meg didn't believe in drugs, eh?

'Well, you can cook,' said Meg. Her tone implied Ruby was a disaster in every other respect but she had to be fair.

Ruby was tired. Finding the kete had been a shock, then after that she'd gone to the Segar house to look at their Players' archive – spent two hours there amongst the old scrapbooks and dusty bits of memorabilia. She'd let herself in and crept through the house, sat down at the desk in the collection room. Nearly passed out when a voice said, 'Cup of tea, Ruby?'

Olga. She knew the voice, but this woman who looked so tired and worn – was this Olga? Had to be. Pain, thought Ruby, pain and grief have changed her.

She stood up, heard herself say, 'Thanks, I'll get it.'

When the woman in front of her smiled tentatively then let go the breath she'd been holding, Ruby knew she'd done the right thing.

How her face had changed. Fourteen years ago, screaming at Ruby from outside the abortion clinic, Olga still had some of the beauty she was known for, and the suppleness and strength of a much younger woman. But her face was ruined by the hate in it, the words that came from her mouth – outside the clinic and later to Oscar. Hateful words meant to shaft Ruby and wreck a marriage. Nothing altered what Olga had done, and Ruby would never forgive her for it, but this wasn't that Olga. This was an old woman in pain unable to say sorry because that would be too hard.

So Ruby had made tea and they'd talked about roses, then just as she began to say she had to go as she had to cook dinner, Door appeared. He smiled at his mother, then Ruby, and said, 'Research going okay?'

She let the question hang for a second or two. 'Why did you vote against me using the collection, Door?'

For a moment Ruby thought he wasn't going to answer. Then he spoke to her as though she was the only one in the room. Was Olga listening? Did she even care? 'Josie,' he said. 'I thought of my beautiful wife, and how lucky we'd been and then how unlucky. I thought of you and Oscar. Thought if I said no then it might make you talk to him even if it was just to tell him off.'

'Oh for heaven's sake – reverse psychology – such a cliché.'

'Worked,' said Door.

Now back at Meg's all Ruby could think about was an early night. Too many shocks in one day. She started to leave the room. There was a knock at the door. Spider got up, went to the drawer. 'Ask who it is,' he said quietly.

Oscar. It appeared Spider had asked him to pop round. Spider shut the drawer, said, 'You eaten?'

'Not yet. Wanted to finish the hedge before the rain. Cook something when I get home.'

Spider looked at Ruby.

Bloody hell, she thought, but I'm not having a stand-up with Spider.

'Like some roast duck?' she said.

Oscar looked surprised, as well he might. 'You okay if I bring Karl inside?' He looked at Meg.

'What sort of dog?'

'Old,' said Oscar.

'Fit right in,' said Meg.

Karl might be old but he wasn't stupid. He saw the fire with the mat in front, made straight for it, flopped then sighed and closed his eyes.

'I need to wash my hands,' said Oscar.

Ruby directed him to the bathroom. An educational experience for a Segar. At least there was soap and a clean towel there now.

Afterwards while Oscar ate, he and Spider started talking about a couple of kids they supervised weeding pensioners' gardens for community service.

Well, well, well, thought Ruby.

'Didn't turn up,' said Oscar.

'They need to learn how to do that,' said Spider. 'Or don't they teach you that sort of thing on the Other Side?'

Oscar grinned. 'Nope,' he said, 'sadder and wiser. Won't miss another one.'

Meg was listening with some amusement. Go for it, Ruby told herself.

'Maybe the two no-shows should be doing your garden, Meg. Give them something to get their teeth into. Why did you let the rose garden go so wild?'

Without missing a beat Meg spoke. 'There's a dead body buried I don't want anyone to find.'

Ruby felt an inward jolt like an earthquake, as if things inside her brain were moving sharply to accommodate this new information. Oscar paused for a moment then continued eating. Nerves of steel apparently.

'Who?' said Ruby.

'The Arse,' said Meg.

'Your husband?'

'Don't call him that.'

Ruby took another good swig of wine. 'How did it happen? An accident?'

'Hit him with the spade,' said Meg. 'If you call that an accident.'

'Another port, Meg?' said Spider.

'Why not?' said Meg. She pushed her glass towards Spider. 'I'd had enough.'

'So you hit him with the spade?' Ruby needed to get this clear. Her life was now officially out of control. It's the port, she thought, she's nearly ninety. She doesn't know what she's saying. 'You killed him *with the spade?*'

Meg looked straight across the table at Ruby. 'He gave me gonorrhoea, wouldn't let me go to the doctor because he didn't want people to know. When I finally managed to get to a doctor in Wellington – a woman doctor, thank god – I was pretty crook. Had to have an operation, everything taken out. Meant I had ongoing problems. Meant I could never have another baby. Meant there'd been other women. Meant they had to be told. He wouldn't name them. Wouldn't go to the doctor. Refused to tell the women. I knew he wouldn't stop rooting around. Knew by then he only married me because of the money and land. Only decent thing he ever did was help to make Kate. Thankfully before he got gonorrhoea.'

Meg took another good sip of port. 'Love,' she said, almost as if she was thinking aloud, 'is such a bloody wild card.' Spider's hand moved quietly and covered Meg's as it rested on the table. She smiled at him. 'But sometimes that card trumps all.'

Oscar stopped eating again. Looked up.

And sometimes it doesn't, thought Ruby. Sometimes it fucking doesn't.

'Didn't know what hit him,' said Meg. 'Won't be much left anyway. Nearly sixty years ago so I suppose you can do what you like. Surprised Kate didn't tell you.'

'No you're not,' said Ruby. 'If Kate said she wouldn't tell anyone, then she wouldn't.'

Spider sipped his port. Oscar continued chewing on his duck. Karl slept on. As if someone had pressed a button the damn tears rushed out and ran down Ruby's face.

'Shit,' she said.

She grabbed a tissue from her pocket. I'm sick of this, she thought, took another tissue, blew her nose. Swigged another gulp of wine. Stared at the fire.

'You're right,' said Meg, into the silence, 'but wouldn't have been worried if she'd told you. Family.'

Ruby nearly cried again. *Family*. So Meg had got over *this is the stupidest thing you've ever done?* As for the murder, because that's what it was, what could she say? No good going on about it being wrong to kill someone. If anyone had reason, Meg had. Sixty years ago Meg would have been coming up to thirty and facing a life of constant doctor's visits, pills and no more children. Had she wanted more kids? Maybe she had. She'd made a good job of the one she had that's for sure. She and Kate argued a lot but that was just two people who both wanted to be the director.

In any case it was a bit late to worry about ethics. Or was it morals? Probably both. Ruby lifted her glass.

'So,' she looked across at Spider, then at Oscar, 'we're accessories after the fact? Cheers, comrades.'

Spider grinned and Oscar raised his glass.

She drained her glass, stood up. Dishwasher, she thought. Shower, new fridge, freezer. Shower first. No. First check properly with Meg, who probably didn't mean Ruby could do anything she liked simply because she'd offered her the back half of the house. A new stove would be good too.

'Dessert?' she said.

Meg nudged Spider. 'Dessert? Now that's not a word you hear a lot around here.'

'Does it involve cream?' said Spider.

'Yes,' said Ruby, 'but on the side. You can choose.'

'Cream,' said Spider.

'Oscar?'

'Take me to the river,' said Oscar.

Ruby smiled when she placed the lemon meringue tart on the table. Making the meringue with a hand-beater well past its prime had been a sweating, swearing, very slow exercise, but she knew Meg liked this pie and she had lemons on her tree. Ruby would have preferred Meyer but Lisbon was what was there, and she knew the lemon pudding part of the dish tasted wonderful because she'd tried a bit. She added an electric beater to the list in her head.

'A thank you,' Ruby said to Meg, 'for letting me stay.'

Nobody said anything except 'mmm' for five minutes.

When she began to clear the table, Oscar said, 'You cooked, I'll clean up.' He stacked the plates. Karl lifted his head, looked at Oscar, slumped back.

'No dishwasher?'

'Except for the two-handed variety, no.'

'I'll help after Spider's told me what he wants, leave them till then, okay?'

Now, she told herself, *now*. The question that had nagged her for fourteen years. She put the plug in the sink, turned the tap on, squirted a little dishwashing detergent into the water, kept her back to him.

'Why didn't you answer my letter?'

She felt him staring at her.

'What letter?' he said. Then, 'When?'

Ruby sighed her irritation, didn't answer as she filled the kettle, plugged it in, got the tray, set out cups and saucers for later.

'Do you mean fourteen years ago?'

She didn't answer.

'I never got any letter,' he said.

'Okay,' she said, plainly disbelieving and still not looking at him.

She heard Oscar walk out of the kitchen and along the hallway.

The wind started growling outside. Through the side windows she could see the long trails of the rose branches moving like waves of supporters at a rugby match. The sooner she borrowed a chainsaw and got stuck into them the better.

Forty-watt light bulbs cast a dim light but at least the dust wasn't too obvious. LED bulbs tomorrow. Or maybe get an electrician to check the wiring first? She could write a memoir on her experiences with electric wiring in old villas. The first time Oscar stayed the night in that villa in Wellington, he'd blown all the fuses because he'd plugged the cord into a socket that had a notice saying 'Do Not Use' above it. His excuses, which Kristina accepted, were: one – the hall was so dark you needed a miner's lamp or a canary to see a foot in front of you; two – it had taken half an hour to find the bloody socket by feel; and three – he was only wearing jockeys and was fucking freezing.

Outside the wind upped its wails around the house. Sounded like all the ghostly voices had moved from the Circle to outside Meg's place. Rain on the way.

Ruby put some more wood on the fire. Karl lifted his head for a pat. She smiled at him and he smiled back, tongue panting. 'Good boy,' she said. He put his head down again and was asleep instantly.

There was a little silence while they all sipped their tea, then Spider said, 'I need you to do something for me.'

Oh bloody hell, thought Ruby.

Oscar took a larger sip, swallowed, said, 'Okay.'

Spider put his thumb up. 'Here's a thing …' he said.

Then he stopped because a hard whooshing sound like ten steel cans crashing onto the ground reverberated around the room. They all stood up. Only one thing made a sound like that.

Karl struggled up too, gave a little growl.

'*Shit.*' Ruby and Oscar and Spider took one look at each other then they all ran like hell: Spider through the front door, Oscar to the kitchen and out that side door, and Ruby down the hall and into the little sitting room.

She took a look, grabbed her phone, rang 111, got Fire, the woman listened, said, 'On the way.'

Across from the French doors flames rushed up the side of the shed. A dark figure, carrying a flaming branch, ran around from behind it. Ruby shot outside just as the arm holding the branch threw it at the house, didn't have enough thrust, so although it slammed against the wall it immediately veered away, slid onto the wooden steps, spitting sparks. Whoever it was turned and ran back behind the shed.

Ruby kicked at the branch and managed to send it onto the ground. She stamped on sparks, kicked the smouldering branch further away from the house.

There was a growl behind her.

Karl stood in the doorway, sniffing the air. Barked.

'All right, boy,' she went back up the steps, called. 'It's all right.'

And I'm a liar.

The same dark-faced figure barged round from the back of the shed. Karl growled, barked his outrage, ran to the top step and launched himself. The man raised the spade, belted it at the dog like sending a ball to the boundary.

Karl's growl stopped abruptly. He fell. Lay still.

'No,' yelled Ruby. '*No.*'

The figure, still holding the spade, ran straight into the briar patch and forged its way through. In a second it had vanished.

Ruby ran to Karl. She knew it was too late, had to be too late, but she gently touched his chest. No heartbeat. Blood was congealing wet on her hand, one eye was closed, the other had been bashed into his skull. No more blood trickled.

Dead dogs, like dead humans, don't bleed.

She didn't cry, no tears left. She put her head on the dog's shoulder, put her arm around him, whispered, 'Good boy, brave boy, I'll get him. Don't you worry, boy. I'll get him.'

The crackle of flames was very loud. There were no sparks on the house, not even a hint of smoke. She heard her breath go out in a sigh of relief.

Spider and Meg.

Where was Oscar?

There was a hard slam of sound like someone had belted a soccer ball against the shed roof, sparks flew into the air and flames began eating up the shed. The wind swept up some of the sparks and sent them straight at the old wooden house.

She ran into the laundry. Buckets. Ran back, ran down the shaky steps and along to the outside tap.

Spider had vanished into the briar patch. She hoped his sleeves were proof against the thorns. She didn't know if there was any water pressure or whether the ancient hose was capable of carrying water, but she had to try. New hose tomorrow, she decided. She remembered Meg. *Christ.* Then saw her face looking out through the French doors. Felt a rush of relief. Spider would murder both Ruby and Oscar if anything happened to Meg.

She felt around the top of the hose attachment. It seemed to be holding. Ruby turned on the tap, there were two or three farts, some deep grumbling belches, then the water started flowing. She directed it straight at the remains of the shed.

The flames were filtered by water, and the patchy dark and grey cloudy sky looked like it was trying to get away from the flames. Please not the house, she thought. By the time she heard the siren she was sweating but it was with relief.

She heard the fire truck, a sound trail of siren and engine sounds. Must've just turned into Duggan. The flames on the shed roared into new life. Here's a challenge, they seemed to be saying.

No noise or shouting from the briar patch. Surely Spider couldn't get too far into that prickly mess? And what about that figure who set fire to the shed? That fucking dog murderer, where was he or she?

Maybe made for the river? More prickles to get through but possibly safer than trying to get away over Devanny. Wouldn't be the first ones to seek refuge in the river. Rogues or heroes, all had used the river as a hiding place, sanctuary, a way out of trouble.

The siren sounded like a call to arms. Lights flashed and someone shouted from the fence on the other side.

'You okay?'

What do you think? She wanted to scream back. *I'm doing this for fun?*

A couple of seconds later and two men came running around with a larger hose and after a few more long minutes the flames were under control. One of them stopped beside Karl, saw there was nothing he could do, said, 'Can you move him?'

She slid her arms under the dog and, holding him up like a sacrificial offering, moved on her knees towards the steps. She sat on the second step holding the dog.

The shed was beyond help.

As she watched the corner posts crumbled, sent up sprays of sparks that hissed and spat like cats when water was directed on them.

She became aware of other figures standing at the side, watching like witnesses. Neighbours. She wanted to shout at them but it would be a waste of breath.

Then, like it had just remembered its cue, rain started. She felt the wet drops on her face and could have shouted with relief. The shed was a write-off but the house would be okay. She saw the gleam of the fireman's teeth as he smiled, called out to his colleague. Except for Karl, everything was okay. Jeez. Sure he was old and the vet had said any time, but did it have to be so violent? She hoped he'd only known an instant of terror before he blacked out. You'd only need an instant, she thought, a second would be enough. He shouldn't have had to die like that.

Meg opened the French doors. Saw Ruby and the dog.

'Oh shit,' she said. Then she peered into the briar patch. 'Spider?'
Jesus.

Ruby knew, without doubt, that whatever she called this love, friendship, deep affection, that existed between Meg and Spider, she was envious.

She picked Karl up. He still felt warm. *Hell.* She walked over and laid him down near the French doors, ran inside, conscious that drops of rain were falling off her clothes onto the floor. She'd wipe them up later. Ruby grabbed two of the old coal sacks from the washhouse, then ran into her bedroom, took a blanket, tiptoed out onto the now slippery porch, carefully put the blanket over the dog, tucked the sides underneath him, then went on down the shaky steps.

Oscar came round from the side of the house, saw Karl, ran, fell to his knees beside the dog, leaned his face against the furry shoulder.

Ruby felt her face twisting. Remembered Meg's words.
Love is such a bloody wild card.

Oscar patted Karl, eyes wet, then he stood up, took a sack and stood beside Ruby. Then both of them, holding the sacks like shields, ran straight at the overgrown prickly mess like knights of old charging at the enemy. They pushed against the hard resistance of the whippy, stabbing branches and forced their way in. The rain got heavier, drops falling off the torch like stars.

Spider was lying on his side, one arm reaching out, holding a spade, the other clutched against his chest. He was drenched, his grey hair moulded to his head like a bathing cap. He looked like he was asleep. There was blood on his shoulder and chest.

Oh fuck, no.

He opened his eyes. 'Took you long enough,' he said.

22

'I think that whenever one has anything unpleasant to say, one should always be quite candid.'

'So you're the one who's been making eyes at my niece,' said Spider to Juno as she came into the bedroom with Kristina. Juno's eyes were pink-rimmed behind her glasses. She'd stood outside at the open door of Oscar's car, stared at Karl and shaken her head as if to thrust the sight away. 'I'm so sorry, Os,' she said.

Now she looked across at Ruby, who was sitting on the bed. 'You okay?'

'Mmn.' What else could she say?

No, I'm not all right, I'm a mess. But at least I wasn't swiped with a fucking spade.

Ruby had got some towels, wrapped them around Karl's body and watched while Oscar carefully laid him on the backseat of his car.

'This has become personal,' he said. 'If you won't tell Mark about the notebook, I will.'

Bloody hell. He thinks Karl's death is my fault.

She'd walked quickly inside before Oscar saw those stupid tears again.

Spider was lying on his bed looking tired and in pain, but his eyes were dark and indomitable. 'No hospital,' he said.

Juno got on her phone.

'Look, Uncle,' said Kristina, 'it's only Palmy. Twenty minutes to get there, twenty or so minutes inside, twenty minutes back, piece of cake.'

Spider didn't like hospitals. Hospitals were places where people died. Kristina's optimistic view, not only of the hour-long run from Porohiwi to Palmerston North and the hour-long run back but also the hours of waiting in the Emergency Department, was unconvincing.

Juno looked up, eyebrows raised, then went back to her phone. 'Suspect broken shoulder,' she said into it. 'Blow with a spade,' she added.

'Can't find your medical records,' she said after a few more minutes of staring at her phone. 'When was the last time you went to a doctor, Mr Porohiwi?'

'Spider. The name's Spider. Must've been ten,' he said, 'fell over down at the river. Knocked out.' He sighed. 'Interfering passer-by took me to the doctor. Left to me I'd have legged it. I don't like doctors.'

'Careful, Uncle, you'll hurt Juno's feelings.'

'And your birth date?'

Spider ignored Juno and Kristina, looked over at Ruby. Held her eyes. Sent the message. *When is enough, enough?*

She was overflowing. She didn't even sigh as she went across to Oscar, put her arms around him, felt the wetness of his clothes, realised her own were just as bad, said out loud, 'Thanks for everything you did. I'm sorry about Karl.' She felt his shock but almost immediately his understanding. He knew she wouldn't be hugging him unless there was something wrong. He'd have seen Spider's stare. She whispered, 'Guns. Drawer. Sitting room.'

'Jesus, Mary and Joseph,' he muttered. He looked across at Spider, nodded and Ruby could almost see Spider's muscles relax. He knew the police would come. They would have been alerted by the firefighters about the suspicious fire. Probably wouldn't search the house, but who knew?

Maybe they should have left Karl lying where he was for the cops to see? thought Ruby. Did Oscar really think she was responsible for Karl's death? That if she'd told Mark James this wouldn't have happened? Too late now. *Oh hell, maybe it was my fault?*

Oscar left the room and was back almost immediately. 'Meg wants you,' he said.

♣

167

Connor Kelly was wearing a grey windbreaker which looked a little less fashionable than the red jacket he'd worn at the theatre, but he still had that great smile. Another man stood in the sitting room with him.

Oh for god's sake, thought Ruby. When will this end?

Meg indicated Ruby. 'You know my granddaughter,' she said to Connor, and for one terrible moment Ruby thought she'd give way to another gush of tears. *Granddaughter.*

She took a deep breath. 'Hi, Connor.'

Connor's smile got warmer. 'Ruby.'

It's funny, thought Ruby, how every damn stupid thing you've ever done always comes back and spits in your face. Good deeds never do that. Good deeds are invisible, wiped from the memory. Bad deeds are bells that keep on tolling.

He *was* good-looking though. And seemed a lot of fun.

For fuck's sake, get a grip.

'Ruby, this is Murray Hill. The new manager of the Circle. We saw the smoke, heard the engine.'

Of course, thought Ruby, Connor was here as chair of the board of the retirement village. A finger in every pie. She held out her hand to Murray, who took it. He had keen brown eyes and his hand was bandaged.

'Had an argument with a rose,' he said.

'We saw the fire engine,' said Connor, 'came to see if there's anything we can do. Ramona says anything you want, just say. If you want to sleep at the Circle we've got the spare rooms we keep for relatives.'

'Thanks,' said Ruby. 'I think we're okay. If you'll excuse me, I just need to get out of these wet things.'

'Terrible,' said Connor, 'terrible thing. I'm so sorry.' His smile grew a bit more intimate. 'You need cheering up. Dinner tomorrow?'

'No.' Rude, but nothing else seemed to work with Connor.

'Don't be like that,' he said softly. 'Whatever I've done I'm sure we can talk it out.'

I'll kill him, thought Ruby, then told herself not to think those things even in a joke. *Herself* took no notice, wished he'd take a flight to hell and crash the plane on the way for good measure.

'Tell your board this property's not for sale. Okay?'

'We just thought, sorry Mrs Palmer, the place looked a bit unkempt and maybe that was a solution. I'll tell Pete and Corrine.'

'Do,' said Ruby. 'And no more dinner invitations.' To Murray Hill she said, 'Thanks for your kind thought.'

'I'll text you with dates,' said Connor. 'You can't be busy every night.'

I'll have to kill him, Ruby decided. One more body in the briar patch, who's counting? There were footsteps across the hall and Oscar came in. He looked like someone in a hurry.

Connor's eyes sharpened. Bugger. Shit.

'Meg,' said Oscar, 'Spider wants you.'

Ruby went across to Meg and helped her up. They started walking slowly to the door.

'See you soon, darling Ruby,' said Connor and, doing a dramatic ignore of Oscar, let himself and Murray out.

Oscar slid open the right-side drawer, picked up its contents and put them inside his jacket, which he then zipped up.

There was a knock at the front door. Oscar opened it.

Detective Inspector Mark James and Constable Joanna Jones.

Ruby stopped breathing. This was getting more like a French farce every second.

'Hi, Mark,' said Oscar. He held up his phone. 'Just off to see if Mum's okay. She's not answering. Go into the sitting room. I'll be back soon.' And he walked off.

Ruby and Meg went into the bedroom. Spider looked at Meg. Meg looked at Spider.

'Okay?' said Spider.

Meg nodded. 'You?'

'Won't be long,' said Spider.

Ruby turned to Meg. 'I'll get changed and then I'll make some tea.' She walked across the hall to her bedroom, grabbing a towel from the cupboard on the way. Thank god for Stace, she thought, as she struggled out of the wet and blood-stained clothes, and into the ease and cleanliness of dry ones. The kete was lying on the bed. She picked it up, felt around inside. Plenty big enough for a baby a few hours old. Maybe she should ask Mark James about trace evidence?

'Be with you in a minute,' she called to DI James, putting the kete back on the bed. 'I'll get Meg.'

Kristina and Spider were halfway through the kitchen on their way to Kristina's car. Meg stood in the doorway and watched them go. Spider turned back, winked at Meg.

'Won't be long,' he said.

Meg nodded.

Did Connor want the land so much that he'd go as far as sending someone to set fire to Meg's shed? Wouldn't he have known Spider would have him on? And Karl. Only doing his job. An innocent bystander really. If it hadn't been Karl it would have been her because she'd have had to have a go at stopping the guy.

Were the fire, Karl, Spider, down to Connor? Or was it the work of the apartment trasher? What about the cut-up jacket and the scissors? The guy with the spade had been ready to take on anyone who got in his way. So not your ordinary crim? If Connor wanted the land badly enough he might just think setting fire to the shed would change Meg's mind but she couldn't really see him bashing a dog.

Who would burn down a shed, belt an old dog and then an old man just to get their hands on a property? One of Kristina's Porohiwi ancestors had been shot by some of his rellies because they wanted to sell some land and he didn't. History has plenty of evidence showing how a desire for land drives people to commit violence.

So Karl was dead and Spider was injured.

Maybe the hope was that sparks from the shed would set fire to the old house? If that was the case they didn't know Meg very well. This was just the sort of thing that would make her dig her heels in. Especially as whoever set fire to the shed had hurt Spider. In any case Meg would never leave the place while that body was in the rose garden.

And there was Spider. Not to be underestimated. He had a network of people he could call on, a network that included his large whānau, his nephew, people like Oscar, probably half of the population along the Coast. He'd lived his eighty years without applying for any welfare or superannuation and successfully ignoring the health system. He'd made a hurt and physically damaged woman happy in a way she hadn't been before. He'll be all right, she thought, he has to be.

23

'What seem to us bitter trials are often blessings in disguise.'

The cops would cut the branches back around the area where Spider had been hit and where broken branches showed the trail through which the two men had barged their way.

Ruby hoped they wouldn't cut away too much. If someone was to come across old bones in Meg's briar patch it had better be Ruby. She had no idea what she would do if or when that happened but she'd think of something.

Did that man have a car waiting? Or did he run down to the river where he had a boat? Or just nip across Devanny Road to the Circle Retirement Village? Was he connected to the apartment trasher? Or was *he* the trasher having another go?

Did the new manager at the Circle have anything to do with it? He looked respectable enough, thought Ruby. But people do. That's how they get away with things. Everyone feels uneasy when they see a gang member in full regalia walking up the street but no one worries about a man in a good suit and tie walking into a bank, because they can't see the gun in his pocket.

Ruby wondered how deep the Arse was buried and if Meg remembered the spot? Probably not the sort of thing you forget, burying the man you whacked over the head with a spade. Legally your husband. No, Meg wouldn't have forgotten the spot.

Do bones ever rise to the surface? She'd read a Donna Leon novel where bones were seen sticking up from the ground when someone was ploughing. So presumably they did.

'Mind if I have a word?' said DI James from the doorway.

Ruby nearly dropped the tray.

'I'll just pour Meg's tea,' she said. 'You want a cup?'

Why had she said that? Who offered cops tea?

In the sitting room, Detective Inspector James looked at Meg thoughtfully.

Just try it, thought Ruby, just fucking try it. My language – I'm going to have to do something. Gone from bad to disastrous in forty-eight hours. Language and hair. Note to self: *Do something.*

He said, 'I'm sorry, Mrs Palmer, but I have to have a word – just a few questions. We can do it while you drink your tea.'

'Go ahead, Mark,' said Meg.

Ruby blinked.

He nodded. 'My mother was desperate,' he said to Ruby. 'Sister said I'd have to stay in the primers for the rest of my life if I continued refusing to learn to read. Mrs Palmer was well known for teaching reading to unwilling kids. So Mum asked, and I came to Mrs Palmer after school for a term.'

'He put up a good fight,' said Meg, 'but I won.'

James gave a slight smile. 'All this,' he said, indicating himself. 'Down to you, Mrs Palmer.'

'How are you managing? The boys must be fifteen, sixteen now?'

'Yes. Last year at St Joseph's. One wants to go to uni and the other wants to play guitar in a band.'

Meg smiled. 'Following in his father's footsteps.'

'That's what my sister says.' The tone of his voice changed. 'Now, tonight. What happened, Mrs Palmer?'

'Spider heard something – we all heard something. Must have been the shed going up. So he went out to have a look. That's all he did.'

There was a little pause.

'He just went to have a look,' repeated Meg. 'This is my property, why would someone attack Spider on my property?'

'Number of possibilities,' said DI James. 'Spider might have recognised them. They might have wanted to stop him following them. Then again, seeing his aim in life is to upset as many people as possible, maybe he upset someone?'

Meg sipped her tea. She looked very worn and old. Ruby hadn't looked in the mirror recently but thought she probably did too. She put some more wood on the fire.

'We'll find out,' said DI James more gently. 'I promise.' He turned to Ruby. 'So, you and Oscar Segar were here?'

'Yes. Eating dinner. Talking.'

'Must have been a very interesting conversation. Couple of people march in and set fire to the shed and none of you notices?'

'They had to have come through from the briar patch,' said Ruby. 'If they'd come round the house we'd have seen them.'

Something outside began roaring. A chainsaw.

'My team,' said DI James. 'Just clearing a little. They'll be very careful. What's this about a dog?'

Ruby sighed. 'Oscar's dog, old, tried to help, got bashed by a man with a spade. Dead.'

'Where's the dog?'

'Oscar took him home.'

James looked annoyed. 'The dog is evidence. Oscar would know that.'

'He was worried about his mother. Not thinking straight.'

James took a deep breath. Got his phone and wrote a text. Sent it off. No doubt Oscar's phone was pinging irritatingly.

'Any more thoughts on the trashing?'

'None,' said Ruby.

'Mark,' said Meg.

'Mrs Palmer?'

'See anything of Neville?'

Neville aka Moose, patched by the time he was fifteen, had been the leader of Heavy Traffic for some years now.

'Meet occasionally,' said James. 'More in the line of business.'

'I taught Neville to read too,' said Meg. She smiled her rare smile. 'And he taught two boys to put lemon juice in the teacher's milk. He's very fond of his uncle. Won't take kindly to someone belting Spider.'

'No harm in him calling round to see his uncle,' he said.

'I'm planning on restoring the rose garden,' said Ruby, 'any idea how long you'll be?'

DI James looked at her. A look that said, *Don't tell me your problems, I've got enough of my own.*

When he left, Ruby went back to the kitchen. It seemed to be her main place of residence lately. Doing the dishes in Meg's kitchen was like the proverbial hero's journey. The end of the journey, the holy grail, was the achievement of clean plates, cutlery, pots and pans, and a wiped bench and sink.

There were all sorts of setbacks – the bench was wooden and age had rippled the wood, the enamel sink was chipped, the tea towels were threadbare and sodden after just one wipe. It was a triumph worthy of a gold medal just to get the dishes from the evening meal properly clean and dry. She'd put a pile of tea towels on the table and as one got too wet to use, she chucked it in the bucket she'd put on the floor for that purpose. Organising the washing up was not exactly on a par with planning the moon landings but it was a triumph against insurmountable odds. She wondered how Oscar was getting on with hiding the guns.

We were so young, she thought. Too young. At twenty-one you don't care about the future, you're so happy in the present you simply assume it means forever. She and Oscar had lived together from their eighteenth birthdays, married when they were twenty-one, twenty-two when they broke up.

Pathetic.

She admitted, but only to herself, that she still wanted him. A bugger, but that's the way life was. You couldn't always have what you wanted. He'd called her a liar, still believed it. Believed his mother. In spite of his good manners that much was obvious.

Fucking Fate … she could just see her lolling on her black throne, saying, *What's the name?*

Ruby Ruth Palmer.

Okay. Let's see. Oh that's right. Unhappy life choices. Never get over them. Okay. That's her done. Next please?

When Oscar came in she was putting out yet more cups and saucers on the tray.

'Ruby,' he said, 'I didn't get your letter. New Zealand Post must have lost it.'

'What the fuck has New Zealand Post got to do with it?'

'Unless you used a carrier pigeon.'

She didn't smile. She'd reached the end of something. She didn't care whether Meg heard her, didn't care if the whole world heard her. She grabbed the boiling kettle, poured some in the teapot, shook the teapot, rinsed it out, added three teaspoons of leaves plus one for the pot, more hot water and very carefully put the lid on it. Then she faced him.

'I wrote the letter,' she said, 'it took me hours because I kept making mistakes. Then I got on the bus to Porohiwi. I walked the three K from the bus stop to your parents' place, yes, right to the top of that bloody hill, put the letter in the letterbox, walked the three K back to the bus stop, went back to Wellington. Waited. And waited. If you didn't get it, believe me it has nothing to do with NZ-fucking-Post.'

She got the milk out of the fridge, poured some into a little jug, put the bottle back in the fridge. Don't cry, she told herself, don't cry, but she knew those bloody tears were just waiting their moment. She felt the first slosh of them and breathed. Maybe if she just kept quietly breathing it would be okay this time.

'Here,' said Oscar, and handed her some scrunched-up tissues. She grabbed them and went through the routine again. Breathed.

'What was in the letter?'

'Why don't you ask Olga?'

'I did,' he said. 'She doesn't know anything about a letter.'

Ruby looked into his face. 'You believe her?'

'Yes,' he said, 'she'd have said if she had.'

Ruby thought he had more faith in his mother's honesty than she did.

'What was in it?' said Oscar.

'You're deliberately being annoying,' she said.

'Oh no,' he said, 'I can achieve annoying without any deliberation at all.' He took a deep breath. 'I'm sorry, Ruby. I think I gave the wrong impression. I don't blame you for Karl's death. I blame the guy who belted him. But I think Mark should be told about the notebook.'

The relief made her feel light-headed.

'I'll sleep on it,' she said.

She turned back, picked up the tray. 'You want a cup of tea?'

'Before or after?'

She nearly dropped the lot. That had been one of their catchphrases. They had both thought it was funny. Used it all the time.

'Here,' she said, 'carry that into Meg. That last bit of pie is hers.'

He was looking at her, his blue eyes intent.

She smiled. Thought yeah right, probably end in tears, but what the hell.

'Before,' she said.

In bed their bodies remembered each other with great joy.

He kissed her. She kissed him.

He said, 'There've been others.'

'Same.'

'But none ever …'

'Same. Same.'

'Darling …'

24

His phone buzzed.

'What's up?'

'Marcy's dead.'

'Oh fuck. I thought she had a few more months? That's what Spade said. How's Spade?'

'Not good.'

'Well, he was very fond of her.'

'Not that. He says he's out. He doesn't care about being named any more. He was only worried about her finding out. Says nothing matters now.'

'Probably in shock.'

'We've got Diamond running around like a loose cracker looking for someone to scare, now Spade is saying he wants out and if we don't stay away from him he'll talk to Auden.'

'He's in shock. He'll calm down.'

'You don't seem to get it. We need to do something.'

'What I get is that you think you're in charge here.'

'Crap. We're all in this together. Will you talk to Spade?'

'I'll go and see him.'

'And we need to do something about Diamond.'

'I told you, I told Spade, Diamond is trouble. Would you listen? He was trouble in 1988 and he's trouble now.'

'We had to tell him. He was involved. He's in the same shit we are.'

'You went ahead and let him know what was happening so of course he came back. And what does he do? Exactly the opposite of what we said. We all agreed to let Heart do the trash, that was supposed to be our first move. Then Diamond decides to attack her, no consultation, just goes off

half cocked. Then he gets going with the scissors. Then the fire, killing the dog, belting Spider Porohiwi. He's fucking unhinged. You gonna wait till he kills someone?'

'We agreed about setting fire to the shed. Have to expect some collateral damage.'

'He's out of control. Something has to be done.'

'We need to get that notebook and we need to keep searching for the other ones. I'll see to Diamond.'

'You do that.'

'And you'll go and see Spade?'

'This afternoon.'

25

'I have the gravest doubts upon the subject. But I intend to crush them.'

'Six names,' said Stace, 'email attachment. Okay?'

'How much do I owe you?'

'I'll send an invoice.'

'Thanks, Stace.'

'No sweat.'

Ruby ended the call and scrolled through the names on her laptop. In spite of everything she felt a surge of hope. Surely one of them would have been working at the Home when she arrived in the kete? Might know or have heard gossip about whoever dropped it off?

Would they know the names of the card players? Even if they did, would they be likely to say so and incriminate their colleagues? If they were colleagues.

Maybe it was one or two of these names?

What kind of human being would play cards knowing that such a prize had to be about coercion? Surely they knew any arrangement Betty had agreed to would be based on duress. On unequal amounts of power. As in all versus none.

Playing cards in one of the sheds at the Home – surely they'd have been on the staff? The sheds would have been in better condition back then. That little old stove would have been glowing on a winter's night, all very cozy. Lino on the floor but it would have been clean. A wooden table. Chairs. Hardly Koru Lounge but not bad conditions. If one of these names was one of the card players, would they say?

Unlikely. Four card players. Probably solid citizens. Pillars of whatever organisations they belonged to. Late fifties, sixties now. All their past forgotten, safely tucked away because Betty was dead.

Were they members of the Porohiwi Euchre Club? Bridge Club? Both? Those kind of clubs would have been well supported then, not so well now. Robert Segar had been a member. Marlon had joined after he and Kate came to their agreement, but Kate said she didn't have time and anyway she couldn't leave Ruby. Instead she and Daisy taught Ruby to play. Ruby was ten when she learned that playing cards with a partner had unwritten expectations.

'Why didn't you play the joker?' Kate had demanded. 'You know that when the opposition wins the bidding and plays the lead and you're the second player you play high? You had the joker. If you'd played it you'd have altered the course of play and we'd have taken the lead and probably won the game. Playing it at the end to take a few raggy trumps is simply throwing that chance away. Why didn't you play the joker up front?'

'I wanted it to be a surprise,' said Ruby.

'Well that worked,' said Kate.

If Ruby turned up on one of the ex-staff doorsteps and asked about a baby in a kete or some card players in the shed, they'd probably call the cops. Long shot whether they'd know anything about her mother and father anyway, but she had to try.

She turned her attention to what she was being paid to do.

She needed a lead for the book. An idea to base a storyline on, something to give this history a point of view. A green light that said yes, you have a story to tell about this group of community theatricals and it needs to be told.

Once upon a time there were only amateur theatre companies, thought Ruby, no professional companies at all. At that stage the British Drama League competitions, fiercely contested and bitterly lost, ensured standards were kept. Almost every town had a theatre group. No TV then of course. Was the history of one such theatre worth telling, or was it an anachronism better left to quietly fade away – leave drama to the big guys in the cities?

A lead. Her mind was blank. It was always blank at this stage of writing. Terror, she supposed, but terror had a point. Maybe it said that this time the light wouldn't turn green? There'd be pages and pages of blah blah blah, paragraphs of beautifully balanced sentences about plays and costumes, about the exciting time the theatre was painted and – shit, this was enough to make anyone's mind shut down. Coffee. Coffee would help her think.

Right. Ruby looked at the cover of her script. *The Importance of Being Earnest*. Surely this was a play about more than the importance of names? A drawing-room comedy of manners certainly – a play that was set in its time but also a play that had appealed to audiences all over the world ever since, including the three films that had drawn massive audiences. It poked fun at social pretensions and shams. The main character Jack was Ernest in town, Jack in the country. But the title was 'Earnest' not 'Ernest'. Why was that?

She grabbed her *Concise Oxford* from the shelf. Stupid old habit, but Google was never quite the same as the real book.

> **Earnest**. *Adj.* intensely serious. *Noun.* A sign or promise of what is to come. Earnest (money) chiefly US. Money paid to honour a contract.

Roget's Thesaurus, thought Ruby, what would he have to say?

> *Adj.* Ardent, busy, devoted, diligent, eager, fervent. Purposeful. Intent. Resolute.

When Oscar knocked on her open door she was staring into space trying to make sense of what was in front of her. She had no idea why but somehow she knew this was the trail to follow.

'Morning,' he said. Smiled.

'Mmn,' she said.

'How's Spider?'

'*Sorry?*' She frowned at him like he was an interruption that she wasn't prepared to allow. Couldn't he see she was trying to find a solution?

He looked at her. Said nothing. Grabbed her mug.

So this collection of words revealed the meanings of 'earnest'. Had Oscar Wilde pondered them when he was looking for a title? And what did these words have in common with the Players? Other than they'd done the play three or four times before the current production.

Oscar came back, put a mug of coffee on the table.

'How many times have the Players done *Earnest* before this one?' she said.

'No idea.' He waved a hand and left her to it. She frowned over the words she'd scribbled on the paper. *Ardent. Busy. Devoted. Purposeful. Resolute. Earnest.*

Well of course these words could be used to describe the Players over their hundred years, but what about the times when they got lazy, didn't learn lines, argued with the director, balked at going on because someone had poured coffee on their shirt? Or simply because they'd decided they couldn't wear that awful dress? How often had actors arrived at the theatre drunk? Vomited on the floor outside the dressing room because there wasn't time to get to the audience toilets, and the girl playing the junior lead was inside the dressing room fucking the guy playing the adult lead so access to the toilet there was barred. All these things had happened in Kate's productions. There had been rows, rages and reconciliations.

There were times when they were not ardent or devoted, times when they were definitely not purposeful or resolute, but one thing Ruby could be sure of – when rehearsals time was over, however well or badly they'd gone, whatever dramas had happened off and on stage, inevitably they got to opening night. Whether you'd just discovered your lover in bed with someone else, had a furious exchange with your best friend, lost your job, taken one of your kids to hospital, heard your mother had just been told she had cancer and the prognosis wasn't good, *whatever*, you knew that when the stage manager said, 'Five,' there would be five more minutes – then you'd walk out on the stage and be someone else.

So, thought Ruby, what makes me do it? Because people pay money to see the play? Because when I audition and get the part that's the deal? Because Hester bails me up on Main Street and says, 'You're auditioning,' and I'm too tired to argue?

What makes me do it?

What makes anyone do it? Surely one of the most dangerous and terrifying moments in anyone's life is stepping out on a stage as someone else? Especially when the someone else is Lady Bracknell or Ophelia or Shylock, who've all been played many, many times and probably better by professionals like Dench or Pacino?

And we don't just do it once. We do it over and over. For what? So what? And what the hell did all that have to do with finding a driving story for the book? Nothing. Absolutely bloody nothing.

She had not written a word. She hadn't counted how many days she had to write this thing but she had now wasted at least half of one staring into space.

The door opened. Jake. 'Want a pie?'

She rubbed her forehead. 'Hell yes.'

He handed her a steaming paper bag. She grabbed it and pulled the pie out a little and bit into it. Meat, gravy, hint of cheese, pity about the pastry, but delicious anyway.

'It's two-thirty,' said Jake.

'*What?*'

'Two-thirty.'

'Bugger.' She knew there was an answer and she knew it was staring her in the face. Maybe if she went for a walk? She switched off the laptop and went outside, walked up to Main Street, bought another pie. Sat on one of the seats provided outside the shop and ate it. Watched the people passing without actually seeing them. Oh. Was that Pete having coffee with someone in the Mimosa? She knew the guy with him. From where? Short, glasses, bald, nice teeth and smile. Yes of course. Elliot Montague. No doubt Pete was telling him how to run a lawyer's office using time and motion. He didn't look interested anyway. She knew the feeling.

She finished the pie. Walked back to the Swan. Sat down at her desk. She had wasted six hours on this conundrum. She knocked on Oscar's door and opened it.

'Oscar,' she said, 'why does anyone step out on stage?'

'Because if they're part of a play that's where it leads?'

'Mmn.' She was unconvinced.

'They like showing off?'

'Or they're crazy?' she said. 'Why do we *keep on* doing it?'

'Because you said you would?'

'Must be something more. I mean some of us do it over and over. Look at Kate. She got as high as a kite when it went well, moaned and grizzled when it didn't, she had successes and she had failures – why did she keep on doing it? Why does Hester? Why does anyone? Why do I?'

'Love?' he said.

'*Love?*'

'Well,' said Oscar, 'you have a choice. You could read plays, talk about plays, discuss their plots, their characters, the storyline, but you make a more involved and perilous choice. You choose to go *in* them. So you do the first one and you fall in love with the experience. So you keep doing it, maybe looking to duplicate that first feeling?'

'Such a scary enterprise. The only thing worse is writing them.'

'Hell yes,' said Oscar, 'that's why I've never volunteered. For either. I just don't have the guts.' He hesitated. 'Mum said you had a cup of tea together.'

'Yes,' said Ruby.

She went back to her office, thought about the wider theatre story. If the Porohiwi Players came into existence in the early 1950s, they were in good company. The New Zealand Players, Richard and Edith Campion's travelling players, were also early 1950s, weren't they? People were settling down after the effects of war, housing boom, plenty of work available. The Globe? Patric and Rosalie Carey in Dunedin, 1950s too.

Was it surprising that the Porohiwi Players formed a theatre company rather than a play-reading group? Almost seemed like there was something in the air. Then came the professional companies. Downstage in Wellington in 1964, the Court in Christchurch, 1971. And matching this were the smaller groups, professional but not confined to one theatre. Red Mole, Pacific Underground, BATS – who got their own theatre eventually; Tawata, which presented works by Māori and Pasifika playwrights. The Fortune in Dunedin. Wasn't there one in Whanganui? Four Seasons? Check that.

Then Circa, which became a stayer along with the Court in Christchurch, and the Auckland Theatre Company out of the ruins of the Mercury.

Ruby had no doubt there were many smaller groups she'd forgotten or never knew about but looking at the ones she'd hastily called to mind, and all the community groups like the Players, it seemed as though plays and musicals in local theatres, where local people entertained local people, remained a constant in people's lives whatever side of the footlights you were on.

What did she have? The *Oxford*:

> **Earnest**. *Adj.* intensely serious. *Noun.* A sign or promise of what is to come. Earnest (money) chiefly US. Money paid to honour a contract.

Roget:

> *Adj.* Ardent, busy, devoted, diligent, eager, fervent. Purposeful. Intent. Resolute.

She stared at them. She didn't see herself in any of these words. They looked too *meant* for the kind of journey she made into a part. She didn't have an end point she wanted to reach. She learned the words, the moves, the character, learned about her fellow travellers, their strengths, their weaknesses, they learned hers. If anything went wrong she knew which ones she could rely on, which she couldn't. But these things didn't explain why she kept on doing it.

Why *do* I do it? Why did the Porohiwi Players keep on doing it? For one hundred years, for no pay? There was never enough money, and there were never enough theatregoers, or people to do all the jobs that needed to be done. There were wars, financial crashes, illnesses, a fire that started in the men's dressing room, even – for god's sake – a ghost.

And leaving the plays and the actors in any one production aside, you had front of house, cleaning, making cups of tea, doing the bookings, sewing the cossies, setting up the lights, stage managing, building the sets, finding the props, staffing the bar.

Just take one thing, she told herself. One thing. Otherwise the question got too crammed to think. Why would any theatre group do *The Importance of Being Earnest* four or five times?

Ruby realised she was looking at the mirror on the opposite wall. Wondered how long it had been hanging in this office. Old wooden frame. If she stood in front of it she got a face, shoulders and chest. How many faces had it reflected over the years? How many people had looked in and seen the face they took care not to show to the rest of the world?

She needed to change this room around, she decided. Make it hers. Doing that would certainly be more constructive that anything else in this day so far. She stared at the room. A table, a chair, a couch, another chair. She needed to use the laptop, so the placing of the table had to be near a power point. She hated running it on battery when she was working.

Might as well do it. Not getting anywhere staring into space. Ruby unplugged the laptop. Felt the table. Not light. Not too heavy. She closed the laptop, pushed everything on the table into the middle of it, then began edging it towards the far wall which meant she would have the mirror on her right and the window on her left. The red couch could go under the window, one chair for her at the table, the other under the mirror. She sat down at the table. Now she wasn't looking at the mirror, she was looking at the shelves. A completely different view of the room. A completely different view …

And oh shit, oh hallelujah, at that moment the light turned green.

And she got it. She really got it. Yes. *Yes.* She jumped up, ran across the foyer and into Oscar's office. 'Oscar,' she said, 'I've got it. I've got it.'

'What?' he said, his eyes and brain on the screen in front of him. It was his turn to frown and stare in a bemused kind of way. Okay, she knew that look. He was somewhere else.

'Jake,' she called, 'want to go for a drink?'

Jake appeared on the ramp leading to backstage.

'A drink? It's only Monday.'

And on cue a loud crash sounded somewhere up in the dress circle.

'*Shit.*' She ran through the auditorium – avoiding two ladders and a drop sheet – to the stairs, switching on lights as she went. She ran up past the lower seats and on to the circle and right on up to the large dark space at the back where the costumes were kept. *Light? Where's the light? How did someone get in? Hadn't Stace organised a bolt on the door?*

Fritter came running down the stairs towards Ruby. He was panting and looking over her shoulder. He seemed as worried as she was. He saw her and stopped.

'No one,' he said. 'Must've knocked over the cossie rack on his way.' He ran back through the auditorium and outside.

Jake went to the right. Ruby to the left. Nothing. Not a soul. The theatre had that quiet waiting silence it always had between performances.

Boxes had been wrenched off the pile on shelves labelled 'Costume Jewellery' and their contents scattered across the floor. Earrings, strings of beads, brooches, bracelets. All lay scattered or in little heaps on the floor and under the costume racks.

'Be careful,' said Ruby, feeling her foot slip against something. A plastic yellow daisy earring. She picked it up. Glanced around for the other one. She had a weakness for large garish earrings. If she could find its mate, perfect.

'No one,' said Jake, getting down from the long window up on the back wall, 'but there has been. Scarpered out the window and down the fire escape.'

Fritter ran back into the auditorium. 'No one in the car park.'

Oscar appeared at the bottom of the stairs.

'Well, someone's been up here,' said Jake. 'Bloody quick whoever they are.'

'While you're looking, keep an eye out for another one like this.' Ruby held up the yellow daisy earring.

They all had a look around the cossie area to find a trace of the intruder. Peered down the iron fire escape. Nothing. A fine day. Probably wore track shoes. Gloves. Or maybe just walked across the car park, then up the ladder, in through the window. Why was the window open? Had someone opened it? Why the hell would anyone want to muck around in the cossie area? And, when Jake called out, instead of appearing and identifying him or herself, why would they take off?

Nothing appeared to have been harmed. The rack of men's suits that had been knocked over wasn't damaged. It didn't appear anything had been taken.

'A kid?' said Ruby.

'Unlikely. Whoever opened the window knew what they were doing,' said Jake.

'Got it,' said Fritter and held up the other daisy earring.

Ruby grabbed it, stuck both in her pocket.

'You and Fritter are working in the auditorium, if anyone walked across and up the dress circle stairs, you'd know wouldn't you?'

Jake shook his head. 'Been times when I've seen you coming back with a coffee and no memory of you walking through to the kitchen.'

'Don't always look,' said Fritter. 'Get caught up in what I'm doing. Got to take care stripping back the paint. Don't want the place to go up –'

'So anyone could walk through and you'd never know?' said Ruby.

'Jake could you fix a bar across the window?' said Oscar. Then answered himself. 'No, of course not. Fire regulations. Has to be access and egress in an emergency.'

'So any stranger can waltz in, and as long as Fritter and Jake take no notice because they think it's one of us, they're free to do whatever they like?'

'We have to concentrate on what we're doing,' said Jake.

'Not our job anyway,' said Fritter, 'not employed as guards. And,' he added, 'footsteps across the auditorium become normal. Don't take any notice. Did when I first started but now,' he shook his head, 'I suppose I expect it to be you or Oscar. But …' he looked puzzled.

'What?'

'Well that's just it,' he said, 'I'm sure I'd notice if it wasn't you or Oscar. I mean your footsteps, the sound of them are "normal", what I expect to hear, but if it was someone different, I think my subconscious would know and I'd look.'

Ruby knew what he meant. The usual is normal, so why turn your head? Surely our subconscious would alert us to the unusual. Although … she thought of herself and Oscar both getting lost into the work they were doing. When she was totally engrossed, King Kong could pop his head in and say, 'The Martians have landed,' and she'd probably just stare blankly, or maybe not even lift her head.

Or, as Fritter said, would the unusual make her pay attention?

Whoever had caused the crash had not come in through the auditorium. They'd been lucky the costume rack had been knocked over, or they'd never have known that anyone had been up there. Which brought up another question. How many times had it happened and whoever it was *hadn't* knocked over a cossie rack?

And what was the point? A few racks of costumes, maybe a cupboard or two of shelves with dress props and jewellery on them? A couple of shelves of shoes? Hats? Bags? A lot of junk as well. The stuff you see in a box or an op shop with a ticket saying, 'Two dollars the lot.' If someone was looking for something, what the hell could they expect to find up here? No scissors anyway. Stace had taken those.

Then Ruby's heart lurched. She looked across at Oscar. Saw he'd had the same thought.

Fuck.

She tore back down the stairs, across the auditorium, out to the foyer, into her office.

Her bag was gone.

She called out, ran across the foyer and down the front steps. Looked left and right, then down. The bag was lying on the bottom step. She grabbed it, looked inside. Her wallet and a packet of tissues were still there. The notebook had gone.

'Ruby?'

'Oscar,' she said. '*Oh, Oscar.* The oldest trick in the world and I fell for it.'

'It's all right,' he said. 'We'll sort it.'

'My own fault,' she said. 'My own fucking fault.

'Whoever wants that notebook is desperate. There has to have been two people. One in the costume area and one ready to run into your office when his offsider made the noise and you took off. Whoever was in the costume area took a real chance of being caught. Makes me think they meant to knock over the rack? If there were two of them they could have been waiting for their moment. Jake and Fritter leave at four-thirty. I often leave earlier. You'd have been on your own.'

'Whatever,' she said, 'planned or spur of the moment, it doesn't matter. They got the notebook.'

'And we've got a photo,' said Oscar, 'so no worries.'

'They won't know what the symbols really mean.'

'Neither do I but I know there's something. When they realise that, they'll come after you.'

'They might just read the obvious and think they're safe. Might think Betty was just keeping records of the games and the winners.'

'Ruby, I don't know what the backstory is but I know there is one. When I asked you what the prize was, you took the notebook back. So that tells me there was one and that means I can guess and be pretty sure I'm right. These people can do that too. They're not stupid.'

Ruby looked unconvinced.

'And what happens if this guy attacks you next time? I'm supposed to tell Mark I knew all this stuff and never said a word?'

Oscar didn't care that Jake and Fritter were there, both looking uncomfortable. Jake nodded at Fritter and they both moved back to the auditorium.

'Whatever the symbols really mean,' said Oscar, 'and don't bother to tell me there's not something else behind the obvious meaning, whatever it is you need to talk it over with someone you trust.'

'Ah,' she said, 'well, there's the rub.'

Oscar looked at her for a long minute. Then he walked across the foyer, into his office and shut the door.

'*Fuck you,*' she yelled.

Jake came out again into the foyer.

All the world's a fucking stage.

She ignored him, walked across to her office, went inside and slammed the door.

The Swan seemed to shudder.

There was a short silence.

Ruby came out of her office, locked the door, looked across at Jake. Walked over, knocked on Oscar's door, opened it and left it open.

'I behaved like a jerk,' she said. 'I trust you absolutely. Meg's place after dinner?'

'Okay.'

Jake was watching her. 'Fancy another pie?' he said. 'My shout.'

Ruby considered for a moment and then shook her head slowly. 'Two's okay, three means I'm a pig.'

26

'The truth is rarely pure and never simple.'

Oscar laid the photo on the table.

Spider and Meg looked at it.

'Waste of time discussing how they knew you had the notebook. No doubt we'll find out at some stage but the fact is they knew and now they've got it.'

'If only I hadn't rushed off when I heard the noise,' said Ruby.

'No sense worrying about that either,' said Meg. 'It's done.'

They all stared at the enlarged photos of the notebook. Oscar had printed out four copies. Hearts, clubs, diamonds, spades. The suits of playing cards. Different order in each line. At the end of each line was the equal sign and then one of the symbols. Underneath some of the symbols was a little line.

Ruby knew what those little lines meant. She wished she didn't.

'So each symbol represents one of the four people who played?'

'Five hundred. In the shed,' said Ruby.

'And the one after the equal sign is the winner for that week.'

'And this charts three months.' Meg was thinking aloud.

'Why did Betty keep records?' asked Oscar.

'The first lot of notebooks were records of my life.'

'First lot?' Spider this time.

'Seven. Each one recording a year of my life. Notes about my weight and height. Birthdays. When I learned to wash myself. Feed myself. When I walked. Talked. When I learned to read, when I went to school, the books I read, the first time I said a poem from memory.

Betty taught me to read by printing out words and then she wrote stories. When she was satisfied I could read a story from scratch, she got me to read the notebooks to her. She had very clear writing, easy to read. I don't know where she hid them. She said it was better. If I didn't know I couldn't be made to tell.'

She thought of those times by the stream, Betty's finger on the words, her patience, her determination that Ruby would learn. Ruby's determination to learn. To anyone else those little notebooks were simply a record of a child's progress but to Betty they represented survival not only of the subject but of the writer as well. What had happened to the stories Betty had written in the exercise book?

'This one? She say anything else other than not to show it to anyone?' Oscar was being very careful.

Ruby felt a wave of tiredness so palpable she almost swayed on her chair.

'Ruby,' said Oscar, 'it's okay.'

You're not seven now, she told herself, just do it. You can't keep this secret any longer, it's too big, too painful. Without raising her head, she began talking.

'I asked Betty where her story was. She'd written mine, so I wondered. She said it was between the lines.'

Ruby felt sick saying the words out loud. Especially to people who hadn't known Betty.

'No other lines,' said Spider, 'apart from the ones already on the pages of the notebook.'

'How did you get it?' said Oscar. 'The notebook.'

'She put it under my pillow that night. Told me to look after it, not let anyone see it. I asked when she'd be back. She said not to worry, she'd be there.' Ruby's voice trembled. Stop it, she told herself. It's because Kate's just died. Brings everything back. 'So when I woke up that morning and she wasn't there I decided I'd better hide it till she returned, so I found a singlet in the clothes bag and wrapped it round the notebook and shoved it in my knickers. Then I went looking for Betty.' She swallowed. 'I found her.'

'Club seems to have won a few,' said Oscar.

'The thing is,' said Meg, 'I've just thought …'

Oscar took a deep breath.

'Yes,' he said. 'They were the winners but what was the prize?'

They all looked at Ruby.

'Between the lines,' repeated Ruby, 'between the fucking lines, okay?' *Get it over, just say it.* 'Betty didn't mean the little marks under the symbols or the lines already there in the notebook, she meant the ones that form the equal sign. Okay?'

There was no need to say any more. The faces around the table told her they knew exactly what she meant.

The prize the four staff played for was Betty.

'And you know why? If she went along with this they would persuade Matron to let her stay on at the Home. She was nearly fifteen, girls were usually sent away somewhere by then but somehow – and now we know how – Betty stayed. Why? Because she was determined to look after me. She said it a lot. *Don't worry, kid. I'll always be here. I'll look after you.'*

'Why? Why was she so determined to look after you?'

'She'd looked after me since I was a baby? I don't know exactly, but I do know that from the time they were little, scores of kids were sexually or physically assaulted. Or beaten. Whipped. Caned. By the people who were supposed to look after them. Betty arrived at the home when she was eight. I don't know what happened to her, but I'm certain it was why she was determined that it wouldn't happen to me. She agreed to do what the card players wanted because she knew that if she was around I'd be safe.'

Ruby tasted that unmistakable sour wash in her mouth again. This time she really was going to be sick. She pushed her chair back, put her hands over her mouth and ran for the bathroom. There she vomited until there was nothing left. She washed her face, rinsed out her mouth, brushed her teeth. Then she went and sat on her bed and stared at nothing.

She heard footsteps. A knock on the door and it was opened.

'Ruby?' said Oscar.

'Fuck off,' she said.

'Tell Mark or Auden, or I will.'

'Two days,' she said.

'What difference will two days make?'

'I'll have my car back.'

Which was no reason and she knew it.

She could tell he wanted to argue and then made a decision to go with it.

'See you tomorrow,' he said, closed the door, then opened it again.

'You said something to me once about the man in the balaclava. That he was bending over Betty?'

'He was taking the brick out.'

'How do you know he was taking the brick out? Maybe he was putting it in her pocket.'

She stared at Oscar. 'Oh hell. Of course. Of *course*.'

It was like a curtain had been pulled back. Of course Betty would never have drowned herself and left Ruby to face the terrors alone. How could she ever have thought otherwise?

'When did Betty draw in it?'

'I don't know. I'd never seen it before she gave it to me and that was the night before she died.'

'So is that when she told you about her story being between the lines?' Oscar's voice was gentle but he wasn't going to stop.

Ruby shut her eyes, rubbed her forehead. 'One day we were talking and I asked her why the staff were so nasty to us and she said because we didn't matter to them. We didn't matter to anyone. And I said yes we did. She mattered to me and I mattered to her. I said she'd written my story because I mattered to her. And now I could write her story because she mattered to me. And she said she was writing her story herself, and I said where was it and she said, "Between the lines, kid, between the lines." She always called me kid.'

'The guy who trashed your apartment knew about the book,' said Oscar. 'The attacker did too.'

'How?'

'Doesn't matter, does it? You read Conan Doyle? When you've excluded the impossible, whatever remains, however improbable, is the truth.'

'It's been sitting in an envelope in Kate's box or whatever, her files anyway, at the lawyer's and I only got it a couple of weeks ago.'

'It's an office,' said Oscar. 'Other people work in offices. And there are clients, cleaners, couriers. Most of us are curious and most offices are a bit like railway stations – could have been anyone.'

'It was locked away.'

'You're sure you were the only one? Betty only told you?'

'Absolutely.'

'And we know Kate didn't tell anyone. So it has to be the other end.'

'Those card players knew they could get away with doing what they did,' said Ruby. 'Why? Because people make judgements. How could someone in the here and now understand? A nearly fifteen-year-old Māori girl? You know what they'll say. She asked for it. That's what they'll say.'

Ruby shook her head. 'Years and years for any government, left or right, to even agree to hold an inquiry into the treatment of state wards, to even admit that an inquiry was necessary. Up until a few years ago all the blame was heaped on the kids. In any case, whatever they did, none of the staff will ever be charged. Why? Because they were state employees and the state protects its own. Same with the churches. Priests and nuns, devout Christians of any denomination, Anglican or Plymouth Brethren. Captains or majors if they were Sallies. This inquiry they're holding will go nowhere. None of them will be brought to justice for what they did to kids in their care. *Care*? Now there's a word. And some of those same people say we shouldn't have abortion on demand because it's not fair to the unborn child? Hello?'

'What is it about us adult human beings and kids? What the hell do we think we're doing? For a lot of kids, being born into this world opens up a big dangerous cauldron of horrors. You know Hortense? Until I hugged her once as we said goodbye, she'd never been hugged. She was sixteen, seventeen at the time. I saw her surprise and her instinctive pull-back, so I asked her, and she told me. If it hadn't been for Betty and Kate and then Kristina, I'd have been another Hortense. I just hope Door is patient.'

Oscar came in, sat on the bed beside her, put an arm around her shoulders. 'It's okay.'

'The thing I'd like more than anything is to find out Betty's real name. She was eight in 1981. Arrived at the home in April of that year. Means she was born in 1973. She must have had parents, someone must know.'

'You'll tell either Mark or Auden about all this?'

She sighed.

'Two days?'

'Two days,' she said.

27

'But where did you deposit the hand-bag?'

Ruby opened her laptop, looked at her emails. Reilly had moved, *temporarily*, he emphasised, to his mother's place. Around six months, the nurse said. He'd seen the doctor who'd said it was more likely four, and that Nona could be kept at home until it was time for the hospice. There was nothing Reilly could do except make his mother's last months as comfortable as possible.

Ruby rang him. 'You okay?'

'Nona just told me that my father didn't die. He ran off with a woman from the law office where they both worked.'

'Shit. You going to contact him?'

'You *crazy*? He left me too.' Reilly sounded really tired and really fed up. 'It's over twenty years ago and he's made no attempt to approach me. I don't even know his address.'

'What about the play?'

'Go mad without it. The one thing in my life where I forget everything else and focus on being someone else in a totally different world. Couldn't be better.'

'Another reason why we do it,' she said.

'Do what?'

'Does Nona have a lot of friends?'

'None who've called round while I've been there. Maybe they leave it until I'm not there? In case they catch something?'

'Has she said anything about the time when she kicked you out?'

'No need,' said Reilly, 'she'd just say I had a choice.'

'Hobson's,' said Ruby. 'See you tonight.'

Now to work.

Text from Kristina. *Found the woman who put kete in ceiling. Pick you up in ten.*

♣

Hana Porohiwi had trained as a nurse and now worked part-time at the Circle Retirement Village. When she was fifteen and still at school, she'd taken a job at the Home as a kitchenhand. She wasn't the only college girl employed over summer, but then she and another girl were offered more work in winter. It was Hana's last year at school and her application into nursing training had been accepted, so her mother said it was okay to take the job and earn a bit of money for clothes. Which was why Hana was there in the kitchen of the Home when a kete was found at the back door with a baby in it.

Hana was in her fifties, short and lean. Her kitchen was almost spartan in its neatness, the cloth on the table the old-fashioned kind, edges crocheted, embroidered flowers on the corners, and the chocolate cake on the plate was home-made.

'It was a Saturday morning,' said Hana, handing Ruby a mug of black coffee, 'breakfast was on the go in the kitchen. We heard a baby crying and one of the women opened the door, and there was this kete with a baby screaming its head off. Can't say I blamed it.'

'Were they surprised?' said Kristina.

'The kitchen staff were. Matron didn't seem to be but she was like that. Never showed much. She said to find the old pram and get a blanket, cut up two flannelette sheets for nappies. There were no clothes small enough so she said she'd send a message to the church ladies the next day. In the meantime she said the baby could be wrapped in a towel or a sheet.'

'Bottle?' Hana had said over the baby's screams, 'Teat?' She was the oldest of five and knew all about babies. Someone knew someone and a bottle arrived. There was nothing like formula at the Home so one of the women thinned down the cow's milk with water and put a little sugar in it, and the baby sucked it up like it was starving.

So, thought Ruby, I knew even then that if someone offered food you grabbed it before they changed their mind. That determination to survive, even in a small baby, is amazing … terrifying. That baby was me.

'Matron sent for a girl called Betty,' said Hana, 'and told her to push the pram around until the baby went to sleep. And then everyone started making up for lost time and the kitchen was flat out. It was a real nuisance because it was the day the guy arrived to stick rat poison in the ceiling. Not very nice while we were doing food but it was his only free time. He was in a hurry and waltzed off and left the ladder propped in the hole, so I grabbed the kete and whizzed up the ladder and shoved it in the ceiling.'

'Why?' said Ruby.

'I don't know. I really don't know. I just – like I was the only Māori in the kitchen that day and the baby definitely looked like half anyway, so I thought we'd better stick together. I thought they'd throw the kete out – and it was all the baby had. Then I shut the hole cover and took the ladder away. I was glad to leave that place.'

'Bad working conditions?' said Kristina.

'Hard. But I was used to that – Mum was pretty strict about jobs around the house. It was the place. The atmosphere.'

'Did the staff live in?'

'Half and half I think. I didn't. Mum and Dad wouldn't have it. The only reason they let me go pre-nurse training was that the Matron at the staff hostel kept a strict eye on the younger girls. I was turning sixteen at Christmas so started proper training the next February.' Hana grinned. 'Those were the days. Never held hands with a boy till I was nineteen. *Sheesh*. So you're the baby?'

'Yes,' said Ruby, 'I'm the baby. I can't thank you enough for saving the kete.'

'No sweat,' said Hana. 'Kristina says you ran away when you were seven?'

'There was a man wearing a balaclava. Chased me.'

'So they were still doing it,' said Hana.

'*What?*'

'Pack of idiots,' said Hana. 'I mean I like playing cards but I don't have to get dressed up in a balaclava to do it.'

Ruby and Kristina stared at her.

No one spoke. Kristina reached for Ruby's hand, held it.

'What do you mean,' said Kristina finally, '*they?*'

'Bits of folded paper left on one of the benches under a glass. Apparently the card players would come in and take one. Four of them had card symbols on. You know: clubs, hearts, diamonds, spades. If you got one of those it meant you could play on the Saturday. The rest were blank and that meant better luck next time. I didn't see anyone take one, but I knocked off at five. One of the girls told me they dressed up, wore a balaclava so not even the other card players knew who they were playing with. Pākehā. *Crazee.* I mean my dad played cards at the marae a lot at that time and no one got dressed up there. But you know Pākehā ... yeah. Thought of it again when I read about the girl drowning, but I was expecting by then and my partner had taken off so I had other things to think about. Sometimes ... you have to wonder about people, don't you?'

Kristina and Ruby finished their tea, had another slice of Hana's chocolate cake.

'Kristina says you're old Mrs Palmer's moko?' Hana smiled. 'She taught me at primary. Taught me to read. She and Uncle Spider are good mates. See him occasionally.'

'Good working at the Circle?' Ruby asked.

Hana shrugged. 'Work's hard to find round here.'

'I'd better get on,' said Kristina.

'You know where I am,' said Hana, 'come again. You going to the Circle Market?"

Ruby nodded.

All questions answered. Here I come.

28

'I am sick to death of cleverness.
Everybody is clever nowadays.'

The sun shone on an unexpectedly beautiful Saturday in June. People were carrying their jackets and scarves, talking in groups or twos, taking advantage of the warm temperature. Maybe, thought Ruby, the spirits had decided that winter could take a backseat for the day? Dark clouds and cold winds to the back please? Make way for blue sky and sunshine.

'One out of the box,' old Mrs O'Rourke called out to Ruby. She lowered her voice. 'If you want some decent lettuce, get to the vege stall now. Only two left. Picked fresh this morning.'

'Already done,' said Ruby, tapping the bag she was carrying.

Mrs O'Rourke smiled approvingly, caught sight of someone and called out, 'How's your broad beans?' and moved on.

The Circle Market was crowded. Lots of Porohiwi Players, thought Ruby. Kristina would be pleased. There were tents selling baking, clothing, books. A refreshment tent and Look Into Your Future tents, with signs that said 'Tarot', 'Hands', 'Crystal Ball'.

The college jazz band played 'When the Saints Go Marching In', and anyone over sixty nudged their friends. The Combined Church Choir sang 'How Great Thou Art'. Everyone it seemed was either performing, buying, having their fortune told or jostling friends as they made their way around. There was a sign which invited you to go for a row on the river. Ruby wondered who was doing the rowing. Last year there had been an unfortunate incident when the mayor overbalanced, fell out of the rowboat and took a header into the water. Served him right, was the general consensus, might stop him thinking he knows everything.

Large red umbrellas covered tables, and college kids ran around wearing rubber gloves and picking up rubbish.

'Look what I got,' said Bradley, holding up a frypan for Jane to admire, 'three dollars, can you believe it?'

'Any more?' said Jane, her dark hair glossy in the sun.

'A smaller one,' said Bradley.

'Be back in a minute,' she said, and vanished.

Sam Markis waved at Ruby. There was a younger man with him. Tall, skinny, fair. He said, 'Hello, Ruby, long time no see. Coffee?'

Who the hell is that? she thought. 'No thanks,' she said.

'Good call,' said Sam. 'It's instant. But the sandwiches are great.'

It was nice, she decided, to be in a crowd and not actually with anyone. She only had to smile vaguely at people and was free to think. Not for long. Pete was coming rowards her in his red mohair jersey, eyes working the crowd. Ruby told herself not to be a cow.

'Afternoon, Ruby,' said Pete. 'Did you know the first-aid course is nearly full?'

'Fabulous.' She even managed a smile.

He looked gratified for a moment.

'*Pete?*'

It was Corrine, smiling her shark smile. She must be having a good day.

'You know he left?' Ruby heard a woman she didn't know say to another woman.

'*No,*' said her friend.

'Good riddance,' said the first woman, 'that's what my sister says.'

A child clutching a large white bear broke through a knot of people and made a dash for freedom, but too late. An older boy grabbed him and took the bear and said, 'No, Jonathan, it's not your bear, it's Justin's.'

The little boy screamed and his mother ran up. 'Never mind,' she said. 'We'll find another one.'

'Good morning, Ms Palmer.' Detective Inspector Mark James, casual in jeans, black T-shirt, smiled at her. 'Enjoying the market?'

'Yes thanks,' she said, then added, because she had to say something, 'you on duty?'

He smiled. It transformed his face, thought Ruby, made him look years younger. 'Sort of. My sons play in the college band, one on sax, one on drums, so I'm on Dad duty.'

'They're good,' she said, 'did you teach them?'

'Just the basics,' he said, 'sent them to a teacher for the real stuff.'

Two women walked past.

'I said to him he could either have sex on the right date or not at all,' shouted the short pretty blonde, 'I've got my ovulation dates all marked up on the wall, there's no excuse.'

DI James took a deep breath. It looked like he wanted to laugh but was restraining himself.

Ovulation chart on the wall?

Well, works for some, Ruby supposed. Maybe she'd been trying to get pregnant for a while? She hoped the woman got lucky.

'Ruby?' It was Bax, looking like he didn't have a care in the world. 'You know Mum?'

'Yes of course.' Ruby hugged the short woman with the big blue eyes her son had inherited, and Bax's mum hugged her the same way Bax did, with her whole body.

'Want a coffee?'

'No thanks,' said Ruby. She'd always wondered how such a small woman came to have such a large son. His father's genes no doubt.

In the distance she saw Jen and Patsy in earnest conversation and hoped it wasn't about Patsy's play. Patsy had been trying to get *Down by the River* staged for the last ten years. So far the committee had held out. And there were Hester and Auden. Both looked happy. He was carrying a bag of vegetables.

'Mrs O'Rourke's garden?' asked Ruby.

Auden nodded. 'So she tells me. How she knows a particular cabbage is from her garden, she didn't say.'

Ruby hugged both of them and they moved off. Good one, she thought. I've contributed to their happiness by helping Hester out.

'Kia ora, Ruby.' Oscar. Smiling at her. 'You want a coffee?'

'Thought you were supposed to be supervising your charges on Saturdays.'

'Time off for good behaviour,' he said, 'Spider says it doesn't hurt to be flexible. And one of mine is helping with the rowing.'

'Should we cross fingers?'

'He's been on the river since he was small,' said Oscar. 'Knows every twist and turn, just has to learn the police launch is quicker.'

This is ridiculous, she thought, standing here talking about nothing. She put out a finger and tapped his arm. 'Okay?' she said.

He put a hand over hers. 'Very,' he said. 'You?'

Someone was calling her.

Ramona was standing outside her tent, beckoning. The same old man's shirt, untidy grey plait.

'Damn,' said Ruby, 'that's my crystal-ball reading.'

She hurried off to Ramona's tent as someone started calling, 'Ruby, Ruby.' It was Bethany. Ruby waved but kept going. She wasn't in the mood for Bethany or the ghost in the blue dress.

The tent was just a small space with a table and a chair each side. Ruby sat down and waited. It wasn't a bit eerie, there was no hint of mystery, just that kind of dusty smell that hangs around tents. Ramona peered into the crystal ball, which looked like an upturned lamp on a stand. No misty shapes, no smoky trails, no mysterious lights, just an upside-down lamp glowing dimly.

Ramona stared at it. Ruby stared at it. Ramona frowned. Shook her head.

'I don't know why they decided I should do the crystal ball,' she said, 'I'm not good at it. Much better with tarot. More reliable. Sorry. I mean that wisp could be an "E" or a reflection from the tent flap.' She looked a bit irritated. Ruby supposed it was quite annoying when the spirits didn't co-operate.

Ramona frowned again, peered. 'The letter E mean anything to you?'

Ruby shook her head. 'No,' she said. One of her previous clients had been Eloise but she hadn't seen her for years and that guy, what was his name? Edward? Edric? No, Eric … liked to be called Ric. Long gone. Hadn't seen him for years. Big mistake anyway.

Then she thought, said, '*Earnest*? The play? That's the only "E" I can think of. But all's going well for me there.'

'Your Bracknell's brilliant,' said Ramona. She sighed. 'Come and see me again and I'll do the cards. Much more reliable.'

Ruby said she would, but on her way back to Meg's she knew she wouldn't. This world was hard enough without adding the other world in as well.

29

'Well, my name is Ernest in town and Jack in the country ...'

On Monday Ruby got to the Swan just after nine. She was heading for her office but stopped when she saw the group in the foyer.

'You stole my house,' Delia in a blue coat and high heels was shouting at Hester and Ronald Hugh.

'Let's just go through to the kitchen,' suggested Auden.

'It wasn't your house,' said Hester. 'It was Ronald Hugh's.'

'I had a *moral* right,' said Delia, 'I was the *oldest.*'

Jake, entering the foyer, seemed to sum up the situation in a second, did a large curve around the group and headed for the auditorium to start back on the renos.

'Delia, Ronald Hugh owned half the house, all legally assured, and had actually paid it all off, both his half and Joan's – I mean Marissa's.'

Auden looked like he'd said this a few times already.

'Oh *legal*,' said Delia, waving her arms around. 'What has *legal* got to do with it?'

'Everything, you hopeless cow,' said Hester. She saw Auden's face and said, 'Okay, okay.'

Auden looked like he'd decided they were not going to make the kitchen so he might as well say it in the foyer.

'You made the threat to sue the theatre because you're upset with Hester?'

'And that interloper,' said Delia, pointing at Ronald Hugh.

'Are you aware that the Porohiwi Players could sue you for mischief?' asked Auden.

'Me?' said Delia, in throbbing tones, '*Me?*'

'You made a threat to the previous writer and you made the same threat to the current one. You owe Ruby an apology and you owe the theatre an apology.'

'Oh I know,' said Delia, 'I know when the cards are stacked against me. I know who is at the bottom of this. Very well, I withdraw my words, but just let me say that you see before you a broken woman. I have been betrayed by the very person who should be my shield and defender.'

Hester stared at Delia, took a deep breath.

'Hester,' said Auden quickly, 'don't say it.'

'But –' Hester glared at her husband.

'Darling,' said Auden, 'darling.'

For a moment Hester paused, then decided. 'Thought you said we were going to have coffee?'

'Delia,' said Auden, 'coffee?'

'Is there sugar?' said Delia. She paused. 'Oh god, don't tell me there's no sugar.'

'Jake?' called Auden, heading off to the kitchen.

'Two minutes,' said Jake, and ran through the foyer and away.

'Kettle's on,' called Daisy, 'fresh scones,' and she disappeared too.

There was just Oscar left. He winked at Ruby and vanished into his office.

She went into hers. The recorders were on her desk. She'd already made an electronic copy of all the interviews, filed them, sent a copy to Kristina.

She sat in her chair, decided she had to stop thinking about what Hana had said, those men, their collusion, the way they kept their identity secret from Betty, who would – Ruby was convinced – have known who they were anyway. Betty's sole purpose had been to keep Ruby safe. Oh stop it, she told her brain, you don't have time to run over this again.

The Saturday night performance had gone well. Bethany had totally shone as Miss Prism. They all seemed to be staying on top of their lines. Good audience. Hester was pleased. Ruby was pleased too. Only three more performances to go. Roll on Thursday, Friday and Saturday. She would miss it the following week but Meg's birthday was coming up. Had to organise something.

Reilly had looked tired. He'd hugged her. 'See you next Thursday.'

'Got anyone to do the nights with your mum yet?'

'No,' he said. 'Still looking.'

Ruby had gone over to the bar to get a drink. She knew what she had to do but a sip of wine would be good first. Ra was serving.

'Kia ora, Ruby,' he said.

The crowd around the bar got heavier so there was no chance for a conversation even if Ruby had wanted one. She smiled at Sam and Rissa. 'Red?' she asked.

'I'll get it,' said Sam.

Ra got glasses, poured the wine.

Do it, Ruby told herself, just do it. She walked across to Bax then beckoned to Sam, who hesitated before deciding he'd better co-operate.

'Reilly's mother is dying,' she said to them both. 'She's ignored him for fifteen years but … anyway, he's doing his own work, very busy time of the year for accountants, and he's looking after her as best he can. He's got Serena from Clean Rooms helping with housework two mornings a week and a neighbour coming in two mornings just to be there, but he's doing everything else — making sure there's someone there in the day, doing the nights himself. I know he's a flirt but he's a friend. Friends help each other.'

'I'm sure Reilly will sort it.' Bax aimed for indifference.

'I haven't finished, Bax,' she said. He blinked at her tone. 'You can't blame Reilly for what Sam said. So just get over it. As for you, Sam, you knew he was a flirt. You're a flirt too. So you got a taste of your own medicine? Tough shit.'

There was a tight, charged silence. Sam's face went that burned grape colour again. This time it looked like contrition.

'Sorry, Ruby,' he said. 'Sorry. I tried to apologise to Reilly but … I apologised to Hester.'

Ruby almost laughed. She wouldn't have minded being a fly on the wall during that conversation.

'Either of you know anyone, an ex-nurse perhaps, who could do some part-time work helping with Nona? Or someone who could do a few hours in Reilly's office so he can help his mother without worrying? I mean you're either a friend or you're not.'

Sam looked like he might burst into tears. Don't tell me you're sorry, you little madam, she thought.

'Sorry, Ruby, sorry,' said Sam. 'Have you got his mother's address? I'll have to go in person because he's blocked my calls. He'll probably throw me off the property but ...' Sam sighed. 'Sorry again, Bax.'

Bax looked at Sam, shrugged, which was better than his previous reaction. Sam looked just a little happier when he walked away.

Ruby remembered. 'Sam,' she said. He turned. 'The Samuel Markis who gave the first Players the copy of *Earnest*, was he a relation?'

'Yes,' said Sam. 'Bad-tempered old coot from all I've heard.'

'Any letters that might mention the Players, or some diaries?'

'I'll ask Mum,' said Sam. 'She's keen on that sort of thing.' And this time he smiled properly.

Ruby turned back to Bax.

'Sorry,' he said. 'Sorry. I'll talk to Mum. She was a nurse. She might know someone.'

'Thanks. What were you doing in 1981? You were four? Five?'

'I was four,' Bax said, 'and very keen on riding my new trike to Wellington. My dad found me pedalling flat out along River Road.' He grinned. 'He told me just last year he didn't know whether to slap my bum or hug me, so he did both. Why?'

'Asking everyone. Trying to fix a context. Year of my birth.'

'Well,' said Bax, '1981. I was happy. Life was very simple. All those roads waiting for me to pedal down.'

She leaned forward and hugged him. 'Lots of roads still waiting, Bax.'

There was a knock at the office door and Oscar put his head round.

'You still want the programmes for the three *Earnest* shows?'

'Yes please.'

She didn't need them particularly now that she'd worked out a line, but she'd have to look through the programmes anyway. In any case she'd learned very early on that you took any information you were given. Might not be exactly what you were looking for right now but there could be something there.

He handed over the three printed pages folded in half to make programmes. She said thanks and put them on the desk.

He didn't mention James. Or Auden.

She was mulling over that. She had an idea.

Ruby smiled. Two strikes. She'd worked out the line to follow with the book and had some good interviews. She felt much happier. She decided to get a cup of coffee and plough on. Whoops, had to do without coffee, she thought. No one in their right mind would go into the kitchen right now with Delia holding court. She picked up the three programmes Oscar had brought in.

The first was the reading in 1919 at a Mrs Carmichael's home. Ruby looked at the list of readers. Samuel Markis wasn't among them. None of the names meant anything but that didn't matter.

It was 1953. The second *Earnest* was a full production. The photograph showed a beautifully dressed cast with Lady Bracknell in the middle. The cast list was full of names Ruby didn't know but Meg might remember.

The third, 1980, had more detail. Good wardrobe too. She looked at the faces. Gwendolen and Cecily looked so young. Didn't someone say Stace had played Gwendolen? Yes, she could see it was a young Stace although her hair was long back then. She was beautiful. Ruby's eyes travelled down the list of actors' names and when she read the name she nearly passed out.

E, she thought, fucking *E?* I don't believe it. But there it was.

She sat for a while staring at the page while a thousand dominoes fell into place.

Then very carefully Ruby put the programme on the table, got up, walked across the foyer.

She knocked on Oscar's door, opened it. He looked up. 'Ruby?' He stood up quickly. 'Darling?'

'Need to go to Wellington,' she said. 'Just letting you know. Be away a few hours.'

'What's wrong?'

She shook her head.

'I'll take you.'

'You don't …'

'I'll take you.'

She was silent on the way in. Once in the city, he drove where she directed. He stopped outside a large well-kept house in Kelburn.

'Shouldn't be too long,' she said.

The door was open so she walked in. Stace was sitting in front of a laptop, looking at the screen. 'Won't be a minute,' she called. Then she turned and saw Ruby.

'Hi,' she said, 'what's up?'

'It was you, wasn't it?' said Ruby. 'You put me in the kete and dropped me at the back door of the Home.'

'Oh *Christ*,' said Stace, whose real name was Eustacie. The 'E' that was all Ramona could get from the crystal ball. The 'E' Ruby almost dismissed. To hell with whether she believed in spirits or not, she supposed they had to be right sometimes.

'Ruby –' said Stace.

'No,' said Ruby. 'Don't say anything. There's nothing to say. I never want to see you again. Clear?'

'Clear.'

'Who is my father?'

'He doesn't know,' said Stace, 'I never told him.'

'Who the *fuck* is it?'

'Jake.'

Jake? *Jake?*

'He doesn't know,' Stace repeated.

Ruby took a deep breath. It was too much. Way too much. She walked out to the car. Climbed inside.

'Can we go home now please?'

Oscar turned the key in the ignition and they slid into the city traffic.

'Well,' said Ruby, 'surprise, surprise. I've found my parents. Stace and Jake. Only Stace says Jake doesn't know. So it'll be a rude awakening for him when he gets her call which will probably be about now.'

She supposed Stace had thought she was safe from the past, from having to ever face the daughter she'd so determinedly cut out of her life.

'Is that why you wanted the programmes?'

'No, that was just an idea I had. When I needed a line for the history. Thought they might help. It was Ramona. All she could get was the letter E and that was vague. At first I thought of *Earnest*. I had no idea. No idea her name started with "E". Wouldn't have taken any notice except Ramona said it was that letter. Bit of a joke really because I don't believe in crystal balls and tarot cards. Funny, isn't it? I run away from the Home and Kate decides to adopt me, and Stace turns up at Kate's and, along with Daisy and Jake and Marlon, takes a hand in looking after me.'

They were turning onto the new expressway. Oscar's hands on the wheel looked sure and confident. Lucky Oscar. Always knowing who he was, who his parents were, surrounded by photos and memories of family. No idea what it was like to live half your life ignorant of who you were.

'Must have known who I was … yet … all these years, not a word. To Kate or me. I suppose she thought she'd got away with it. And she had. Even Ramona wasn't absolutely sure the "E" meant anything. Sorry,' said Ruby, 'I keep repeating myself. It's such a fucking mess. I'm in the same play she was in, she did the wardrobe for this one, she loaned me clothes after the trashing. I'm working at a theatre where my father is also working, although he's only just learning that now.

'Jake was around a lot once he came back from England. He thought the world of Marlon, and was very good to me. Put up with me learning to play cards. Kristina's uncle, for god's sake. It's such a *fucking* mess. I really like Jake, *liked* Jake. Now I don't want to see either of them ever again.'

She stopped. She'd said enough.

Kate said it was better to know but it wasn't. It was much, much worse.

Oscar drove through Waikanae the old way. Maybe he thought it'd be more peaceful or maybe he preferred the old road. The trees were certainly more beautiful. There was much more green and the hills were closer. Oscar pulled over by a coffee cart.

'Coffee?' He put his hand over hers for a moment. 'Pie?'

'Hell yes.' She was starving. The emotionally-upset-unable-to-eat response was not her. Whatever happened she seemed to still want food.

She watched Oscar walk over the coffee cart, stretching his arms as he went. He came back with two potato-top pies and two small coffees. Drove to Porohiwi and down to the river. They ate while staring at the river. What did the river care? Already seen it all. The pie tasted like it had more gravy than meat and there was some unidentifiable taste in the potato topping but Ruby ate it anyway.

After a while of looking at the water, she said, 'Not seeing them won't work, will it?'

'No,' said Oscar.

'It'd only cause more talk and it would all last longer. So scrap that idea.'

She would only tell Daisy, Kristina, Meg and Spider. But it would still get out. Porohiwi was good at that. So the less worried she appeared to be the better. Just another role to play. Only this time the stage was larger and she didn't know the lines.

'We'd better get back,' she said finally. 'I'll just concentrate on other things for now – finishing *Earnest*, writing the history, finding twelve kids who can walk, dance and sing on stilts.'

'Jesus wept,' said Oscar.

'He won't be the only one,' said Ruby. 'I must have been crazy when I wrote it.'

'What's it called?'

'*Revenge of the Moa*.' It sounded so ridiculous she wanted to laugh but controlled herself. Whoever heard of such a stupid title?

'You spoken to Mark or Auden yet?' said Oscar.

'Tomorrow,' she said.

30

'Well, I won't argue about the matter. You always want to argue about things.'

The next day was remarkable. No one attacked her, no one trashed anything, no one stole anything from her bag. Ruby worked on the history of the Players in perfect peace with the world.

In the afternoon she went back to Meg's, and Jojo arrived – the only cop Ruby could bear to talk to right now – and they sat in the small sitting room at the table opposite the French doors and talked about Betty.

Jojo was kind but detached. A trained police officer, a listening ear, who kept asking question after question. She'd requested permission to record their meeting and Ruby'd agreed. She thought Jojo understood her reluctance to reveal Betty's story. But whether she did or not, or whether she was patient and kind or not, she went through every detail until Ruby could have screamed.

'I'll type it up,' said Jojo at the end, 'and be in touch. Okay to come to the office? Once it's signed I'll pass it on.'

Ruby had heard and seen nothing of Stace, and Jake was keeping out of her way. Old Lady Fate had really got it in for Ruby Ruth Palmer so there was no use whining, she just had to suck it up. And there were some good things. Joseph, Auden's cousin, said he'd do the plumbing at Meg's and put in a shower; Bax would fix the doors and anything else. All she needed was an electrician.

Bax's mum was doing three nights a week at Nona's and Reilly was looking a little less strained. Sam had gone off and found a university student who could do some part-time work for him.

She'd told Kristina about Stace and Jake, and her friend had looked a bit shaken.

'Uncle *Jake?*' Then she sighed. 'Well at least you know,' she said, 'and not all bad.'

She hugged Ruby – her dark eyes wet with tears. 'Fucking hori, always said we were whānau and I was right.' Kristina wiped her eyes, said, 'Wouldn't like to be in Jake's shoes when Mum gets onto him.'

Ruby frowned. 'He said he was a randy little bugger.'

'Nothing wrong with randy, but he obviously didn't use condoms. Lot wrong with that. If he gets an ear-bashing from Mum, serve him right. However,' Kristina hugged Ruby again, 'she'll probably forgive him eventually.'

Spider and Meg took the news with hardly a flicker. Spider said, 'Far out, this means you and me are whānau.' Nothing much surprised Spider.

Meg said, 'Best to know.'

Daisy said, 'Well, that takes care of that.'

'Did Kate know?' said Ruby.

Daisy shook her head. 'We knew there was some mystery about Stace, something she never talked about, but assumed it was a love affair gone wrong or something. She and her mother argued a lot.'

'So did Meg and Kate.'

'There was no malice in Kate and Meg's disagreements though. Stace and Liz had terrible fights. Liz was a fervent Presbyterian, conscious of what people might be saying. If she knew or suspected her only daughter was playing around, and with a Māori, she'd have gone up in smoke. Stace was young, good-looking and had a mind of her own.'

'Now we know one of their fights was over me,' said Ruby.

She remembered Stace saying 1981 had been spent arguing with her mother and that she'd moved out. Now Ruby knew why.

'And even if Liz didn't know what, she'd know *something* was up,' said Daisy. 'Might have suspected but she didn't know. And I only know what I've picked up since I came here, nothing about you. Mary O'Rourke would know if Liz knew.'

'As if,' said Ruby.

'Mary's okay,' said Daisy, echoing Meg. 'If she says she won't tell anyone she'll keep her word. And in this case, she'd be quite right to tell you.'

'So Liz was my grandmother.'

'One of them,' said Daisy. 'Don't worry, we're all made up of bits and pieces, ragbags the lot of us.'

♠

Compared to what it had been before, the briar patch now looked like someone was taking an interest. The chainsawing wasn't finished and didn't make a perfect job anyway, but once it was done, you could see a vague shape appear. Ruby would do a hard prune next year.

She hadn't asked Meg to tell her where the Arse was, and so far so good. She'd dug a swathe around a relatively large area of rose bushes and the next thing would be planting. The weather had not been great but she couldn't let it matter. She asked Meg what she'd like and said they'd better be quick. Spring seedlings would be at the garden centre in a couple of weeks.

'You want to come?'

Meg looked at her. 'Be a bit slow.'

'Not as slow as me.' said Ruby. 'I'm going to look for things that smell good. You can shout afternoon tea.'

'I'll pay for the plants,' Meg said.

'The plants are on me,' said Ruby.

Meg looked as if she might argue. 'You're paying for the electrician,' Ruby said, 'and you're paying Bax and Joseph to move things. You're paying for a new washing machine, a new stove, a new fridge, new shower, and I'm paying for new carpet. I'll shout myself a couple of new chairs for the little sitting room and when it's all done I'll get some new curtains for the windows and maybe some blinds for the door. We're sharing the cost of the cleaners but I'm still on the winning side so I'll pay for the seedlings, okay?'

'Huh,' said Meg.

'And we're going shopping,' said Ruby. 'New clothes. Gotta wear something flash for your birthday.'

'Haven't bought new clothes for over fifty years,' said Meg.

'Then it's time you did.'

Meg tried and failed to stop a grin on her face, and that was enough to stop Ruby thinking about the mess with Stace and Jake, the notebook and the balaclava man, and so she smiled back.

Ruby supposed that everyone felt cheated when someone they loved died unexpectedly and left them behind. Like reading a book and loving it and then discovering someone had ripped out the last chapters. In this case, it was more important than pages from a book. Ruby had missed all the rest of Betty's life. Betty had missed the rest of Ruby's.

Betty had been her teacher, reader, singer, bulwark, defender, yet Ruby didn't even know her real name. She felt disgusted that she'd waited so long simply because the idea of walking up that drive, or looking seriously for the notebook, scared her stupid. She wasn't like that about other things. If there was pain or trouble coming she wanted to know so she could meet it full on.

When Kate got her diagnosis Ruby had immediately organised her life to be with her as much as possible, do anything she wanted done and deal with the idea of a world without her. She didn't know how other women felt about their mothers but Kate was more than that to Ruby. She not only saved her from the Home but she changed a little girl's life, made it good. She didn't do this by changing herself. She was impatient and set high standards in terms of manners, work and life. Being kind was something she prized, and if being kind meant getting onto Ruby about her behaviour, like she did when Ruby went to pieces after Oscar left, then she would do it.

Ruby remembered Kate in all sorts of ways but for some reason Betty was different. Every time she thought of her it was like Betty was frozen in time. The only clear memory was the one of her lying on the path, water trickling off her face. The rest of it was that feeling of being safe, of being protected, of being loved.

Hey, she told herself, you were only seven. And after Kate took you in, you tried very hard to forget everything about the Home and to only remember Betty. But that didn't really work. Or not completely. And it didn't take away the feeling that in some way, for some goddamn reason, you were responsible.

There was a knock. Oscar opened her door. His face was set hard.

'You haven't told Mark or Auden,' he said.

'No,' she said, 'I had a better idea.'

'You *promised*,' he said, and for the first time in a long time looked totally pissed off with her.

'What I did was –'

'I should have known,' he said. The words were expressionless but his eyes said *once a liar always a liar.*

He turned and moved back across the foyer towards his office.

'You idiot,' she yelled, 'I told Jojo.'

Oscar stopped like he'd been hit, turned. 'Oh *Jesus* …' he said. 'Ruby, I'm sorry.'

'No,' she shook her head and one of the daisy earrings fell off. 'No, you're not. I'm over it. I'm not a liar, I never have been a liar, I never will be a liar. I despise you and your willingness to believe I am one. Just stay out of my way.'

She bent down and picked up the earring, went back into her office and closed the door.

When Kristina knocked and came in, Ruby was staring into space. She knew her face must look like the Porohiwi bar moments before a storm.

'Oh hell,' said Kristina, 'what now? What's happened?'

Oscar and Juno were staring at his screen when Kristina knocked on his office door and opened it.

'See you for a minute?' she said.

'I'm pretty busy. Trying to sort out this page. Juno's helping.' Oscar looked tired.

'Won't take long.'

'If you've come to tell me I behaved like a shit to Ruby, forget it. I already know.'

Then he saw Ruby. Beside Kristina, gripping her friend's arm as if she was keeping her upright. Or Kristina was keeping her upright. It was hard to tell.

They walked into the room.

'There's something I need to tell you.' Kristina took a deep breath.

Oscar stood up. 'What's happened? Are you hurt? Ruby?'

He looked from one to the other.

'I'll go,' said Juno.

'No,' said Kristina, 'stay. Ko koe ko au, ko au ko koe. All for one and one for all. It was me,' she said, 'I was the reason Ruby was at the clinic that day.'

Then she told Oscar and Juno the whole sorry story. The three men, the rape. *One good fuck and you'll forget all this lesbian stuff.* The pregnancy. The abortion clinic. Ruby at her side, sworn to secrecy. The tears running down Ruby's cheeks. The screaming women outside. And Olga as they left. That look on her face. Full of what she was going to tell Oscar the minute she saw him.

31

*'Something tells me that we are going to be great friends ...
My first impressions of people are never wrong.'*

At four-thirty, the day got worse.

Meg came into the kitchen. 'You've got a visitor,' she said.

Stace looked terrible. Obviously hadn't been sleeping.

'A minute?' she said.

Ruby couldn't raise the energy to refuse. She took her down to the little sitting room.

'Well?' It sounded mean but she was over this day. In fact she was over a lot of things.

'I was sixteen. Mum had kicked me out. I didn't have a job. I had a bed in a friend's flat that was already overcrowded. One day Mum came and said she'd spoken to the Matron. The arrangement was that she would look after you on the condition that I paid a weekly sum and kept out of the picture. She said it wouldn't be fair on you or the other kids.

'It was only when you landed at Kate's that I realised what had been happening and that the money I'd been paying into a bank account every week for seven years had been going into Matron's pocket.

'I thought of you every day of my life and wished things could be different. I was so tempted to go to the Home and ask to see you, but then I'd think about what she'd stipulated and made myself stay away. I truly didn't know about the conditions until Kate called me to come and meet this kid she was adopting. As soon as the kete was mentioned I knew it was you. Had to be. I thought about telling

Kate but there was all that business and worry over whether the guy would barge in and try and stop you talking about what you knew. I told myself I didn't want to add to it, but the truth is I was terrified. I knew you would hate me. I thought I might risk that but in the end I decided I'd be of more use helping out than being right out of the picture, which is what would have happened once Kate and Daisy knew. So I said nothing.'

Stace stood up.

'That's it. That's all I wanted to say.'

'I'm sorry, Ruby,' she said, 'so sorry. You'll never know. Thanks for listening.' She moved to the door.

Oh for Christ's sake. She was sixteen, no job, terrified, she did the best she could.

'Just a minute,' said Ruby.

Stace stopped, her shoulders looked as if they were braced for another blow.

'The kettle's on. Would you like a cup of tea?'

There was a small silence then Stace nodded.

Next morning there were ten missed calls from Oscar. Thank god she'd remembered to block the sound last night. She blocked his number then put the sound back on.

She was tired. Everything was an effort. She washed, got dressed, had a quick coffee, decided not to think about Oscar or about Stace. She'd call into the Loop after work and see Kristina. She made two slices of toast, buttered and jammed them both liberally, went through to Meg and Spider's bedroom and asked if they wanted another cup.

'Nah,' said Spider, looking up from the crossword, 'thanks, but time I got up.'

'New bed still good?'

'Don't nag,' said Meg.

'How's the shoulder?'

'Been better,' said Spider. 'Moose drop the chainsaw off?'

'By the step, so really handy for me to trip over.'

Spider grinned.

'Meg,' said Ruby, 'your birthday?'

'No party,' said Meg.

'I was thinking a cards party,' said Ruby. 'Daisy, Kristina, Reilly, Bax. Anyone else you want? Kristina's mother? Spider's sister? Moose maybe? Does he go to parties? You make a list.'

'No party,' said Meg.

'Maybe start with drinks and some nibbles at five, everyone seated by six. I could organise tables. Maybe two in the sitting room, three down the hall. Have something more substantial a couple of hours from then? Kristina and Reilly and Bax will help.'

'*Five* tables?' said Meg. 'That's *twenty* people.'

'I'll organise the food,' said Ruby, 'and we can discuss the drinks.'

'I don't want them roaming all over the house,' said Meg.

'They arrive, say hello, chat for a few minutes, sit down at the tables,' said Ruby, 'Spider and I will see to it.' She smiled at Meg. 'Actually, no. I think we'll ask everyone for four so they can have a standing-up chat, have a look at the briar patch, get all that over, and start cards at five-thirty.'

Meg shook her head, sighed.

'What's your favourite cake?'

For the first time Meg looked interested.

'Know how to make a Napoleon?'

'Puff pastry, raspberry jam, sponge in layers, pastry on top, pink icing? Whipped cream?'

Meg nodded.

'You shall have a Napoleon,' Ruby promised recklessly, 'homemade pastry, sponge. I'll whip the cream, might even make the jam myself if I get some frozen berries, certainly the pink icing. Okay?'

'You're on,' said Meg. 'And ... better ask Stace.'

'Ah,' said Ruby.

'Took real spine for her to come here,' said Meg.

Ruby told Meg that Kristina had arranged two seats in the front row for *Earnest* on Saturday night, so Meg only had the outside steps to climb.

'Ramp next time,' said Ruby. 'Promise.'

Kristina had tried to talk to Ruby but Ruby had held up her hand.

'Is it about Oscar?'

'Yes.'

'Over it,' she said, 'over it. So no more, okay?'

'Fucking hori,' said Kristina and hugged her, 'so we're both on the outer? We'll survive.'

Now Ruby sat in her office reading her notes from the interviews. A text. She looked at it suspiciously. Kristina.

East wind on the way.

What the hell?

There was a knock on the door and she called out, 'Come in.'

The woman opened the door and strode in like she owned the place. So they'd sent in the big gun. Polly was the oldest sister, then there were some boys, then Sophie and Jake.

Oh jeez. Ruby gaped and then she remembered her manners. Stood up.

'Kia ora, Ruby,' said Polly. She had a strong face and a strong-looking body, like she could take the world on and win. She strode over, hugged Ruby and kissed her cheek.

'Kia ora, Polly.'

'*Auntie* Polly,' she said, 'and this is your cousin Aria. Aria?' A younger woman – large, sullen-looking – came through the door. She had her phone out. 'This is your cousin Ruby.'

'Kia ora,' said Ruby.

'Are you going to stand gaping at me like a cartoon fish?' said Polly, 'Or are you going to ask me to sit down?'

Ruby leaped into action. 'Aroha mai, take a seat,' she said. 'There's the couch or the chair.'

'I'm not sitting on that couch.'

'It's been cleaned,' said Ruby.

'Then you can sit on it,' said Polly and sat on the chair. 'Jake rang me. Sophie rang me. Kristina rang me. Jake says you don't want to speak to him. Total rubbish. He's your father. An idiot, I grant you, but we don't get asked, do we. Of course you have to speak with him.'

'Would you like a cup of tea?' said Ruby. *Thank god for the good old New Zealand emergency response.*

'Yes please,' said Polly. 'I bought a cake.'

She fished in her large bag and pulled out a plastic container.

'Chocolate,' she said. 'Bring a knife and some plates.'

'Want to give me a hand, Aria?' asked Ruby.

The girl didn't reply but she followed Ruby across the auditorium into the kitchen. Ruby heard her mutter, 'Yo, Uncle,' as they passed Jake, and although he was apparently so gripped in admiration of his work he hadn't seen them, he managed to mutter, 'Hi, Aria.'

When they got to the kitchen Ruby filled the kettle and Aria got out the mugs. Ruby opened the fridge. No milk. 'You and Polly take milk?'

'Auntie does,' said Aria.

Ruby wanted to swear but didn't. She went to the door of the kitchen. 'Someone go and get some milk?'

There was silence, then Jake said cautiously, 'Full cream?'

Ruby looked at Aria, who nodded.

'Yes please,' said Ruby.

A grin sneaked itself onto her lips. Get over it, she told herself. You've been well and truly trumped. Polly had played the shock-and-take-over tactic very well. She'd not only got a sodding march she'd won the game before it even started.

Ruby and Aria carried the steaming mugs back to the office. Polly was staring out the window.

'You'd think they'd have done something about that car park,' she said. 'I'll speak to Jen.'

Now that would be an interesting conversation.

'I used to be a member of the Players,' said Polly, 'but then I met this Ngāti Porou guy.'

She sat on the chair. Aria put the plates down, got the cake out, stuck it on one of the plates, cut it up into large slices. She picked up her cup, took a slice of cake, looked at the couch, looked at Ruby, who got off her chair and offered it to Aria.

'I'll take the couch,' said Ruby.

Jake tapped on the door and brought the milk in. Kept his eyes down, but that wasn't going to work.

'Kia ora, Jake,' said Polly, 'what the hell were you doing not using condoms?'

Jake could be an entertaining man but not right now.

Ruby felt a bit sorry for him.

'Mmn,' he mumbled.

'How's the fishing?'

Jake thought about that. Would answering make the situation better or worse? 'Got some flounder,' he said finally, 'you want a couple?'

'Is the Pope a Catholic?' said Polly. 'Help yourself to cake.'

Jake nodded but didn't accept the offer. He grabbed the milk and left, carefully shutting the door behind him.

Ruby, Polly and Aria sipped their tea, ate cake. For once in her life Ruby didn't know what to say.

'Well,' said Polly, after she'd finished, 'this is a bit of a surprise.'

The understatement of the century.

'Don't blame you for being angry,' said Polly, 'and my brother needs a good kick up the bum.'

'To be fair,' said Ruby, remembering Stace and the cup of tea, 'I don't think he knew.'

'He knew he'd been playing around,' said Polly, 'should have been more careful. Should have used a condom. *Men.* I've told Aria, N-C-N-S. No condom, no sex.'

Ruby caught Aria's eye and nearly grinned. Nothing worse when you're fourteen than an auntie who talks about *it* in public.

'Aria's mum went to the States,' said Polly, 'so Aria lives with me because her father works in the forestry and only comes home at the weekend. He sold his place and he and Matiu added two bedrooms to the back of our house, which is my good luck because I now have a backup against my husband and our three sons.'

Ruby and Aria looked at each other but said nothing. The looks said they didn't think Polly ever needed backup, that there was every possibility that Polly could have taken on the entire Māori Battalion and made them back off.

'You look like my mother,' said Polly. Then she added, 'Your grandmother. It's the hair. I brought you a photo.'

Bloody hell, thought Ruby.

The woman in the photo was larger than Ruby, but she was tall like her and she had the hair all right. A black wiry mass that looked like it would burst out of the photo if it hadn't been for the black plaited flax ribbon bound around the thick fall of it. Large brown eyes looked steadily at the camera, a slight smile on her full lips. For the first time ever, Ruby thought of her own hair and felt pleased.

'Beautiful woman,' said Polly, 'you take after her. You would have liked her. A bit on the bossy side, but.'

She sipped her tea, ate a piece of cake. Then said, 'You know anyone who'd take Aria as a boarder during college term? She wants to do the next two terms at Porohiwi College. Don't ask me why. There's a perfectly good college in Ruatōria. Even named after Āpirana Ngata. However. If she likes Porohiwi College she can go there for her final year before she goes to uni.'

'Can you walk on stilts?' Ruby asked Aria.

Aria shrugged, 'Course,' she said, and stared out the window.

'Okay, you can stay with me,' said Ruby.

Aria's head snapped round.

Polly sat up straighter.

Good, thought Ruby. So now you know you're not the only one who can steal a march.

'What's this about stilts?' said Polly.

There was a knock on the door and it opened. Oscar.

What the hell? She'd refused to answer any calls that came without a name and stayed in her room when he'd come round to Meg's. Basically they hadn't spoken since she'd yelled at him in the foyer, but she'd sent him three emails about the history that needed a response. A deadline was a deadline. So far there had been no acknowledgement.

Did he know about the ultimatum Juno had given Kristina? Apparently if it was okay for Juno to stay at Kristina's overnight, it was okay for Kristina to occasionally stay with Juno at the Segar house overnight. When Kristina continued refusing, Juno – on her second week as on-call nights doctor, when she'd been called out four out of five nights – blew. There'd been a loud shouting match, Juno had lost her cool, and Kristina hadn't seen her since. For some reason Kristina appeared to hold Ruby responsible.

Now Oscar gave a badly simulated show of surprise and said, 'Kia ora, Polly, sorry, I didn't realise you were here.' Then he went bright red to the roots of his blond hair. He'd always been a bad liar. It was that pale skin of his, showed everything.

'Kia ora, Oscar,' Polly stood up and walked over to him and they hugged. 'Recovered from that cards party yet?'

He grinned. 'It was Matiu's home brew. I think it needed more time.'

'Needed something,' said Polly, 'less of it perhaps? And have to tell you, Oscar, you're not really a singer.'

He laughed. 'Ten points for trying?'

'Very trying.'

'How's Mat?'

'Said to say you were lucky. Next time he'll beat your arse.'

'Hope on, hope ever,' said Oscar. Then he looked over at Ruby. 'See you for a minute?'

Ruby wanted to tell him to fuck off but Polly was looking curious. Aria had been looking at *Roget's Thesaurus* on the shelf like it might bite her if she wasn't careful, but at Oscar's entrance had turned around. This was more interesting.

'Excuse me,' said Ruby, and went out into the foyer.

'I got the letter,' he said. 'And yes, I want to come back. Bring my bags around tonight.'

The world shifted on its axis. She felt the blood leaving her face. Her heart start to beat rapidly.

'Don't be silly,' she said, 'I delivered that letter fourteen years ago.'

'But I only received it late last night,' he said. 'Fair's fair.'

Ruby decided she shouldn't have got up this morning. Having a lie-in would have been a much better option. And what a useless thing to say. *Fair's fair?* What exactly is *fair* about anything that had happened to her recently?

'Door and Juno and I cleaned out Dad's workroom,' said Oscar. 'What a mission. The word "hoarder" doesn't do him justice. Your letter was in with a pile of advertising. Dad must have emptied the letterbox and not seen it. It's been sitting there for fourteen years.'

Jake appeared in the foyer.

'And what do you want?' said Ruby, 'You got a letter too?'

'Um,' said Jake.

Polly appeared in the office doorway. Shook her head. 'Spit it out, bro,' she said. 'You're so deep in the shit with everyone it hardly matters.'

'I was, ah, just, ah, wondering if you'd, ah, like a fresh coffee, Ruby,' said Jake, face as red as a bushfire. 'Because if so, I'm, ah, happy to make it.'

And everyone – Oscar, Polly, Aria and Jake – stared at Ruby waiting for answers to their stupid questions.

32

'I have never met any really wicked person before. I feel rather frightened. I am so afraid he will look just like everyone else.'

The last night of a run. Always a mixed bag of feelings.

She wanted it to be over.

She wanted it to go on forever.

Just like every other last night of every character she'd ever played, she knew she was only just getting Bracknell right, just beginning to feel like she really was Bracknell. Like every role, however small, however large, it wasn't until you got the vulnerability that you got inside. Bracknell was an old dragon but she'd once been a Gwendolen.

Aria was settling in well. She had the room with the wardrobe in it and Bax had secured it to the wall as a temporary measure.

'Needs a built-in,' he said. 'Do it in about a month?'

When Ruby asked him about the stilts, he sighed, gave her a hug.

'Have to measure the kids for the real stuff but for auditions I can do a couple of average size. What age group?'

She stared at him, crossed her eyes. They both laughed.

Ruby hoped Aria would be happy. This afternoon had been mixed, starting with a conversation about bees.

'So,' said Aria, 'the big one latches on to the queen, they have sex and then he falls to the ground dead? And she goes off to the hive and has hundreds of babies?'

'Yes,' said Ruby.

'Fuck,' said Aria, 'it's not *Romeo and Juliet* is it?'

Why had she started talking to Aria about this?

Aria sighed. 'He's dead, she's pregnant – hope they think it's worth it.'

'Bees don't think.'

'So,' said Aria, 'do bees ever do it for fun? Like it's Friday, they meet up by chance, like the look of each other and whoa … and afterwards she zooms off with a smile and not pregnant with millions of babies and he flies off happy and not dead? Do bees do that?'

'No,' said Ruby, 'never.'

'Why?' said Aria.

Ruby, back against the wall, looked around the garden. The chainsawn roses and luxuriant weeds had nothing to contribute.

Desperation time. Then – *bingo.*

'No condoms,' she said, 'bees don't have condoms. If you want to have sex for fun you need condoms.'

Aria rolled her eyes.

'You and Auntie Polly sing in the same choir?'

'From the same page,' said Ruby.

What did Polly mean about Aria's mother going to the States? How could you just leave your husband and your daughter and take off like that? I'll ask Jake what happened, she decided.

'I hate lettuce,' Aria said, when Ruby served dinner.

'I hate carrots,' said Spider.

'I hate broccoli,' said Meg.

Aria tried not to grin but didn't succeed.

Dinner was early because Meg and Spider (and now Aria) were going to the last night. Aria wouldn't be able to sit with them because the house was booked out, but Daisy would put a chair on the side. Aria understood she had to move into the kitchen between acts.

Ruby's phone pinged. What could Hester want? Why couldn't it wait?

She wanted her at the Swan now. Damn nuisance.

Get over it, Ruby told herself. You were going to the theatre anyway. The woman's pregnant and happy, a bit of a triumph these days. Going in a little earlier is not a big deal.

♠

Ruby opened the side door and went into the passage. Lights? Where was Hester?

She groped her way to the side and felt for the switch.

Out of the dark two arms grabbed her, something was pulled over her face and a hand clamped over her mouth. She struggled and got a swift belt on the side of her head and while the stars were still sizzling she was bundled back out the door. She resisted but the grip was strong and the hand over her mouth hard and firm. She tried to hold back but the voice said, 'If you don't want to be hurt, you'd better move.'

A strong arm gripped her shoulder and walked her along. Someone, surely *someone* must see them?

She felt cold. Fear. Ignore it. Think.

My bag. Let it slide. Go on …

But I won't have my phone …

Neither will they, you idiot …

She let the bag slip …

Ruby felt the ice of rain, the disorientation of being unable to see, the hot blast of outrage laced with lightning darts of fear.

They were walking on concrete. Footpath. Then strong hands on her body turned her sharp left. Okay. Car park? He stopped, held her while footsteps approached and someone else opened up a door of a car.

Whose car? Concentrate.

Not all that new by the smell of it. The man shoved her in and got in beside her. Backseat.

'You make a move and I'll open the car door and chuck you out,' he said.

'Can't breathe,' she said.

'Any attempt to attract attention and you're out on the road. You might not be killed but you'll be mashed into a gibbering paralysed idiot because I'll make sure your head hits the ground first.'

He took off the hood.

She breathed, deep breaths, slid her eyes around.

All in black, wearing a balaclava.

Was that face the last thing Betty saw?

Would it be the last thing Ruby saw?

She was cold, heart thumping. Breathe, she told herself, fucking breathe.

He put his mouth against her ear, 'Down on the seat.' His hand pressed the back of her neck.

'Okay, drive,' he said to the man in the front.

His hand remained hard on her neck, holding her face jammed into the seat. Smell of a body, combination of ... what was it? Fish? Maybe. More like – something like – the sea? The river? No, the sea. Mixed with something else though. Something she knew as well as she knew the sea and the river.

Dusty curtains and dry flats mixed with paint, human fear and excitement, the heady wash of laughter and loss, fear and frenzied dread, the love.

The Swan.

And the voice? Low register obviously put on. Even so, there was something. Listen. *Listen.* You *know* that voice.

'See anyone?'

The voice from the front sounded like it was muffled. Probably got a scarf on.

Think, she told herself, think.

Two men. One driving, one in the back with her.

Had a key to the theatre so not strangers.

The one place where she felt totally safe, completely at home. Where she knew every corner and cupboard, every step around the stage. Could find her way all over the auditorium in the darkness, like that night when all the lights went out in the middle of Sarah Delahunty's *Eating the Wolf* and everyone else was, it seemed, either frozen on the stage or in their seat as the window over the bar shattered and wind roared its triumphant way inside. She'd groped her way to the switchboard only to find that Bax was already there. They'd located the emergency torches, and the moment they switched them on the panic stopped.

This secure place had turned its back on her and handed her over to the wolves. Now it was telling her there were no certain places of refuge, she was a hostage to uncertainty just like everyone else.

The car moved out, turned to the left, so they must be going up Main Street, thought Ruby. Black inside the car but even with her head down on the seat there was a difference in the quality of light inside the car as they passed other cars or street lights. The car slowed, stopped, then veered smoothly around to the left, back round to the right and straight ahead. The roundabout?

So must be on Grace Street?

Oh Christ …

She knew where they were going now.

She could scream and shout, but she told herself, shut it, you have a choice.

Fight, flight or freeze.

This is freeze time.

The car turned left. Up a slope. And she was certain. The Home. The drive. Same rough surface. Fear, vivid and numb as a nightmare, stomach clenching with terror. His hand on the back of her neck, face into the seat.

Stop it. You can fight back.

Two against one. Two stronger simply because they were male.

Only one against Betty and Betty had lost.

The car stopped. He got out, opened Ruby's door, hauled her out, pushed her forwards.

It was the Home. That's where he wanted her to go.

Ruby resisted. He hit her shoulders with something and she staggered.

'Walk.'

She was bundled over the rough surface of the yard and inside the door the other one had unlocked. The door was shut, the dark was split by the light from a torch.

The hard arms turned her left, walked her along the wooden floor, that long narrow space that was the passage, then turned right, must be a room. She was shoved and put her arms out to stop falling, felt walls. Match lining. Varnished wood.

Oh Christ. One of the punishment rooms.

She turned to face the dark figures in balaclavas.

They stood in front of the doorway, staring at her.

The little lines under the symbol meant that one had watched while someone else did something.

'So what's the story?'

The voice. Vaguely familiar but the balaclava muffled it so she couldn't be sure.

'About what?' she said.

The man on the right walked over and slapped her on the face with his open hand. Instant fire. She staggered. Felt her cheek swelling. Same side as last time. Her eye stung like it was being pinched with pliers.

'Don't fuck about,' he said. 'Next time it'll be a closed fist.'

She knew that voice.

Hell.

Fritter? Fritter.

'Cut it,' the other man growled, 'we don't have time.'

Fritter grabbed her face and gripped hard.

'Now listen, bitch. We've got the notebooks and we've got the one you had. You want to get out of here alive you'd better talk. What's the story? Has to be one. Obvious what the first seven are and what the symbols mean in this one of yours, but what's the key? What's *underneath*? A code? What did that little bitch tell you? Names?'

'Diamond. Easy.' The other man muttered. 'Don't make it any worse. We need to get it over. Not much time.'

She knew that voice too.

Her whole body felt the chill of recognition. *Colin?* Not Uriah Heep at this moment, more like Bill Sikes.

He wasn't trying to disguise his voice. Meant he didn't care if she recognised him. Meant they weren't planning on her leaving the Home alive.

Ruby didn't know where the other card players were and she didn't care. She knew with cool certainty that she could either die fighting, or just stand still and let one of them kill her. Nothing to lose.

Fritter looked at his watch. 'Time,' he said, 'we've got a bit of time. Time for a bit of fun.'

He reached out and put his hand on her breast.

She twisted as far away as the arm allowed.

'I like a woman who fights,' said Fritter. 'Result's the same but it's more fun.'

'No,' said Colin, 'none of that.'

'You're not in charge,' said Fritter. 'She thinks she's so fucking smart, and I'm going to show her she's not. Now,' he said, looking at Ruby through the holes in the balaclava, 'this can be as easy or as hard as you like. Your call.'

Like fuck, she thought.

'Colin,' she yelled, 'you going to let him get away with this?'

'A step in the shit is a step in the shit,' said Fritter, 'ankle deep or up to your knees doesn't matter. Still shit. If he's shy he can shut his eyes.'

One arm held her arms still and the other one pushed up inside her jersey. She struggled and he laughed. 'Save your strength,' he said. 'You're gonna need it.'

Another sound? The back door?

Running footsteps.

Another one?

The door to the punishment room burst open. Another man stood there.

'What the shit?' said Fritter.

The third man shouted. His voice was panicky, hoarse.

'Garth's dead. Topped himself. Left a note for Auden. We're fucked.'

Garth too?

Fritter and Colin had turned sharply towards this interruption, like they were puppets and someone had pulled the strings.

Ruby wrenched herself away from Fritter, leaped at Colin and pushed. He staggered. She shoved at the third man – she'd guessed from the voice it was Elliot Montague – barged through the door and ran.

Two seconds. I've got two seconds.

She ran down the passage, opened the back door, slammed it and took off. The left side of her face and her eye jerked and twitched like they'd received electric shocks. Tough shit. More things to worry about than a sore face.

Rain lashed her. Felt good as the drops hit and ran down her cheek.

Where was that light coming from?

No doubt she'd find out.

Which way? Ah. Now she saw. The car Elliot had arrived in still had its lights on.

Footsteps pounded behind her.

She took off towards the culvert.

Two men or one?

Who cares? Just run.

She ran into the water, ignored the rain and cold, pushed her feet across, not too deep but her feet slid on the slippery stones. For Christ's sake, she told herself, clench your feet so they don't slip.

Splashes. He was in the water. No shouts. Wouldn't want the neighbours to hear. She didn't care. It was the only weapon she had.

'*Help*,' she shouted, '*help me.*'

She scrambled and lunged up the bank and onto the path, stumbled as she reached the top, forced herself upright and ran some more. Her breath sounded even louder against the opposing roar of the wind and rain.

He wasn't far behind. She could hear his breathy grunts. Not a runner. That, she thought, makes two of us.

Then she realised she was wrong. These weren't the grunts of someone who was physically distressed, they were the sounds of anger and frustration. He could run, no doubt about it.

She heard a car start up. Colin or Elliot?

In the distance a siren. The rain fell steadily. The grass beneath her feet was slippery glass.

Keep to the path.

But if I keep to the path he'll catch me.

For Christ's sake don't fall.

She veered to the right and nearly slipped.

Shout, she told herself. Make a noise. Shout a name, that's what she'd been told. Shout a name. Make it personal. People were more likely to take notice.

'*Kate*,' she shouted, '*Betty*. Help me. Help.'

Her breathing started that grating sound it makes when you're asking too much of your lungs. How much longer?

Footsteps crashed behind her. No light. Oh, of course. Light would reveal her but it would also reveal him.

She felt a wave of that old terror. 'Like fuck,' she muttered. 'You're not going to cry and you're not going to hide …'

Shit it hurt.

Then came a flash of insight so hard it was like Ruby'd slammed into a wall. *You thought Betty drowned herself. Now you know this man killed her.*

If you're going down, she thought, you're going down facing him not running away. He's not a faceless man in a balaclava, you're not a little kid of seven.

She stopped like someone had put on the brakes very suddenly, turned and threw herself towards him.

His shock only lasted a second.

But it was long enough for that moment of startled surprise and then she was on him and her momentum took them both down onto the treacherous ground.

Something like a growl came from his throat. Like he was pleased. Like he'd been waiting for this.

She kicked. He grunted and rolled over trying to get her underneath. Her fist went for his eye, missed and got his nose. He grunted, swore, slapped her again.

She brought her fist up again hard, and this time – *yes* – connected with his balls.

He yelled, a sound of disbelief and shock, and then the wave of agony got him and he arched back, his hands slipping from her, his body racked in an unstoppable arc of pain.

She forced herself away from him, tried to stand up and failed, then tried again. Heavy hard sounds came from her throat as she heaved and panted, her body rebelling against what she was asking of it. She gave another push and this time, staggering with the effort, she stood upright, swaying on her feet.

Step away, move away. He was hurt but his arms still worked.

She moved, the soaked grassy mucus making every movement dangerous. In the distance she saw the blur of car headlights on Grace Street.

Need to get down to the driveway. Even loose gravel is better than this wet grass.

'Jesus,' Fritter grunted, '*Jesus.*'

He rolled, tried a different position, some relief, but there was none. His body was a tight spear sliced with agony.

A car raced up the drive, headlights blazing, then another, this one with a siren screaming.

She forced herself back along the path. Her body was yelling at her to let it drop, just lie down where she was.

Voices. *Friend or foe?*

'Ruby? Ruby?'

Oscar.

Kristina.

She thought she really would fall over with relief.

'Here,' she called, her voice a thin wavery sound like a recorder played by a child.

Her legs were staggery. She was shaky and weak. Great waves racked her whole body.

It's shock, she told herself, but she couldn't stop shaking.

Oh hell.

'I'm going to fall.'

'Hang on.'

Easy to say. She moved sluggishly, shivered, but stayed upright as the two figures came running and slipping along the stream path towards her.

She stopped as another car barrelled up from the other side of the drive, braked, but too late. Elliot's car banged straight into Moose's beautiful new Forest Ranger double-cab ute. Moose was out and shouting and hauling at the driver's door. Elliot scrambled out, saw the patches on the jacket. Ran.

'Come to Mama,' Moose shouted, and, making a sound deep in his throat, he ran straight at Elliot and headbutted him. With a screech of pain Elliot Montague fell. Moose, his face covered with blood, turned towards the approaching car. It braked sharply, stopped, and Jake got out.

Through the blood, Moose grinned. He shook his head and splattered Jake's T-shirt.

'We're gonna have to stop meeting like this.'

Jake caught his cuzzie as he staggered and nearly fell. Just for a moment the two men stood there locked together, then Moose straightened, shook his head again, stood upright.

Ruby decided to sit down. Just for a couple of seconds. She needed to get her breath back.

'Just give me a minute,' she said.

'Darling. You all right?'

Oscar knelt down beside her. He sounded terrified. What on earth was wrong with him?

'You okay? Can you stand? Mark's ringing the ambulance. Won't be long. It can take us to hospital.'

'Like fuck,' said Ruby, 'I need to get to the theatre. I'm on in thirty minutes.'

33

'It is a terrible thing for a man to find out suddenly that all his life he has been speaking nothing but the truth. Can you forgive me?'

'Stand *still*,' said Stace, for the third time. 'Hester and I will do it.'

Like a wax model Ruby stood while they bathed her face and body, patted her dry, dressed her.

'No,' Oscar had said. 'Hell *no*.' But there he was, face pale as death, dressed in Garth's cossie as Lane.

'Don't worry,' Sam told him. 'You can say anything you like, I'll cover.'

Oscar stared at Sam. He looked like he wanted to smash that confident good-looking face. His main fear seemed to be not that he wouldn't say the lines, but that he wouldn't be able to make his body move at all. He'd have to stay in that one place through the entire play.

Jake stood by the piano while Ronald Hugh played his usual bracket of numbers before the show started.

'No,' he'd said to Hester. 'Sorry, I just can't.'

'Just check that jacket,' said Hester to Stace and she patted around Jake's back and under his arms.

'You're not *listening*,' said Jake.

'Okay,' Hester said to Stace.

'Whoever heard of a Māori butler?' He was desperate.

'As Merriman you have three entrances,' said Hester. 'But don't fret, I'll be there to push you on. Reilly will cover for you.'

'You don't understand,' said Jake. 'I actually *can't do it.*'

'Stace, are those trousers a bit long?' said Hester. 'We don't want him to trip.'

'Fucking Caesar's balls,' said Jake. He looked at Ruby. She could tell what he was thinking: So this was payback. Dues had been called in on every stupid witless thing he'd ever done.

'Keep your voice *down*,' hissed Stace. 'The audience is coming in.'

'Don't tell me,' said Jake. 'Just don't fucking tell me.'

Out in the foyer people were cramming in, hustling for tickets. They took no notice of the woman in the pink dress and pearls as she repeated over and over again, 'There are no more tickets.'

Then as they seemed slow to get the message she said, 'There are *no more seats.*'

'I'll sit on the floor.'

'I can stand.'

'But I'm Oscar's *brother.*'

'Come with me,' said a voice behind Door. 'I'll take you to the kitchen and we can watch from there.' Hortense. Door followed like a little lamb.

Despite the fact that Lane remained mainly mute throughout his scenes and that Merriman made up the lines liberally laced with pleas to the Almighty as he went along, Lane and Merriman got a standing ovation. They both froze, transfixed by this new horror for which they were not prepared.

'Move,' hissed Reilly.

When Oscar and Jake remained standing because their feet were stuck to the floor, Reilly and Sam dragged them away from the loud clapping and cheers so finally Gwendolen and Cecily could take their bow, then they stepped back and Miss Prism was able to take her bow. When Lady Bracknell walked out the auditorium erupted. It was like standing in a gale at the Porohiwi River bar, the noise and force of it unstoppable.

Ruby managed to stand and smile for a long minute before she hissed to Kristina and Stace standing at the side.

'Going to drop. Get me off.'

When she got to the dressing room Ruby knew if she sat down she'd never get up again so she stood mute while Stace helped her remove the cossie skirt and jacket, and then painfully, cursing at each move, she pulled on the black trousers, the shirt and the kimono.

'Love this,' she said, indicating the kimono. 'Beautiful.'

Stace nodded, couldn't speak, nodded again, left.

Oscar stood in the doorway still in his cossie.

'Congratulations,' she said. 'Best Lane I've ever seen. *Electrifying*.'

'Promise me you'll never ever refer to it again.'

She tried to grin. 'Dreamer.'

As they came out of the dressing room they nearly bumped into a couple locked in a passionate embrace. Bethany Clark and Connor Kelly?

Well, thought Ruby, well, well.

Oscar and Ruby smiled and nodded at everyone as they made their way slowly to Ruby's office where DI James waited. He smiled, his head-prefect smile.

'Unexpected depths, Segar?' he said.

'Fuck you,' said Oscar.

Supper was laid out on her desk. Among the goodies were Daisy's little meat pies. Ruby was starving. Some things may change, she thought, but pies remain.

'We have the original notebooks,' said DI James, indicating a little pile of seven notebooks on the desk. 'And of course the one with the symbols. Need to have them checked for traces but you will get them back. Now there's just a few things to go over ... and I've got someone searching for Betty's real name. She's the best researcher we have. If she can't find anything it will be because there's nothing to find. But she'll find something. She always does.'

Finally, DI James said his thanks and Oscar took her arm and they went out into the foyer. She stopped and hugged him tight.

'I thought,' she said, 'I thought ...'

She shook her head against the memory knowing it was useless, knowing she would remember that fear forever. Then they walked down the steps and out to the car park where Spider, Meg and Aria waited for them.

Acknowledgements

Huge thanks to Mary (*Nearly there, Renée*) McCallum at The Cuba Press for her magical eye, attention to detail, her editing skills, her poetry and her friendship. Thanks to Sarah Bolland for the cover, and to her and Paul Stewart for all the work they did to make the book beautiful.

Thanks to Sarah Delahunty for being my first reader and giving me my first feedback (*Too many characters, Renée – cut some*). I'm grateful to Ann, Margaret, Rozellia, for being guinea pigs on that first Breaking and Entering: Writing a Crime Novel course, and for your friendship and laughs that continue. Thanks to Kim for listening as I solved writing problems out loud and for pruning my roses.

Finally thank you to Ōtaki and Wairoa, the two country towns I know best – I hope something of your character has surfaced in my imaginary Porohiwi.

About the author

Renée (Ngāti Kahungunu/Scot) turned 90 in 2019, celebrating by publishing her first crime novel – *The Wild Card*. She was awarded the Prime Minister's Award for Literary Achievement in fiction in 2018 and the 2017 Playmarket Award for a significant artistic contribution to New Zealand theatre. She has written nine novels and over twenty plays, with *Wednesday To Come* perhaps her most loved work, and has published her memoir, *These Two Hands*, which she read on RNZ. Renée lives in Ōtaki, where she teaches writing workshops, including one on crime.